# GREY ZONE

*A Selection of Recent Titles by Clea Simon*

# GREY ZONE

*A Dulcie Schwartz mystery*

## Clea Simon

This first world edition published 2010
in Great Britain and in 2011 in the USA by
SEVERN HOUSE PUBLISHERS LTD of
9–15 High Street, Sutton, Surrey, England, SM1 1DF.
Trade paperback edition first published
in Great Britain and the USA 2011 by
SEVERN HOUSE PUBLISHERS LTD.

British Library Cataloguing in Publication Data

Simon, Clea.
    Grey zone. – (Dulcie Schwartz feline mystery)
    1. Women graduate students–Fiction. 2. Animal ghosts–
    Fiction. 3. College teachers–Crimes against–Fiction.
    4. Detective and mystery stories.
    I. Title II. Series
    813.6-dc22


ISBN-13: 978-0-7278-6992-0  (cased)
ISBN-13: 978-1-84751-324-3  (trade paper)

*All Severn House titles are printed on acid-free paper.*

Severn House Publishers support The Forest Stewardship Council [FSC],
the leading international forest certification organisation. All our titles that
are printed on Greenpeace-approved FSC-certified paper carry the FSC logo.

Typeset by Palimpsest Book Production Ltd.,
Falkirk, Stirlingshire, Scotland.
Printed and bound in Great Britain by
MPG Books Ltd., Bodmin, Cornwall.

For Jon

# ACKNOWLEDGMENTS

Books may be written in solitude, but they are best revised in company and Dulcie has had the benefits of a wonderful crew. This is a work of fiction; neither these crimes nor many of these places (including the Poche Building) exist, but lots of kind people have helped me flesh out what is pure fantasy. Forensic specialists and fellow crime novelists Doug P. Lyle MD and Lee Lofland both shared their extensive (and bloody) expertise, as did Detective Charlotte Dana Rowsey of the Charlotte (WV) Crime Scene Unit, police investigator Dan Christman, and several of their colleagues in the Yahoo bloodstains and patterns group. I learned far more than I got to use, but I am most grateful for your time. Dan Riviello, communications specialist for the Cambridge (MA) Police, helped track down answers when he didn't have them immediately to hand – and didn't laugh. My fearless readers – Chris Mesarch, Brett Milano, Naomi Yang, Michelle Jaeger, Lisa Susser, Karen Schlosberg, and Jon S. Garelick – gave me time, feedback, great comments, and tons of support. Wonder editor Rachel Simpson Hutchens' eagle eyes saved me from embarrassment. My agent Colleen Mohyde and editor Amanda Stewart have believed in Dulcie from the start and been just unfailingly wonderful. And Jon, well, without you . . .

# ONE

Writing, writing furiously, she pushes back her long, loose curls, heedless of the ink that smudges her pale cheek. Heedless, too, of the sparks that scatter, each time the fire pops and hisses in response to the storm outside. Rain and wind hurl themselves at the window, dashing against its many panes and finding their way down the old chimney, their mission carried through by smoke and crackle, by tumbling embers. They want her out; they want her gone. Still she scribbles, but time itself runs short, snatched away by the fury outside. The storm that floods o'er all. One line – one phrase to make her case. 'Such noisome beasts as do attack . . .' No, she scratches it out. 'The pernicious spirit . . .' Not that, either. If only she had time. The thunder cracks the night, and the sparks fly. Two hover, glowing an unearthly emerald green and growing into almond-shaped eyes. Cat's eyes, staring . . .

They want her dead.

'You've got murder on the mind.'

The disembodied voice could have been miles away. In front of her, the kitten blinked, and Dulcie, thinking of her dream, found herself drawn into those glowing eyes, unable to decide if they were more yellow or green. Unable, as well, to block out the terror she had felt early that morning when she had woken, gasping, in the dark. Hours later, the horror still lingered, chilling her like a draft. Or the presence of a ghost.

But the voice persisted. 'You do, you know. Murder.'

Chris, Dulcie's boyfriend, was on the phone. It was almost noon, a workaday Monday. The wisps of the dream should have faded as Dulcie sat at her desk with a pile of student papers before her. But while the sun, for now, shone brightly and purposefully through the window, and though her sweetie sounded equally intent, Dulcie couldn't be dissuaded.

'I don't simply have "murder on the mind," Chris.' A doctoral candidate in English literature, Dulcie considered herself an expert with words, and this inability to explain her suspicion was frustrating. 'I just know something happened.'

In the light of day, sitting in the cozy, albeit slightly shabby, apartment she shared with her best friend Suze, it did seem silly. Maybe that's why she hadn't told Chris about her nightmare right away.

It didn't help that he wasn't there. Not that she could blame him. Ever since the spring semester had geared up, her computer geek boyfriend had been hard at work, picking up the overnight shifts that paid the most, even when they conflicted with the Red Sox preseason. With the onset of midterms, two weeks earlier, he'd been stuck in the Science Center basement almost every night, helping clueless undergrads with their programs. He needed the money, she knew that. Living on grants and student loans like most grad students, they were both struggling to pay their bills.

Dulcie had a full schedule, too: wrangling freshmen through English 10 and tutoring several upperclassmen one on one. These days, she barely found time to work on her own thesis, a study of an obscure Gothic novelist – and, if her suspicions were true, possible victim of some kind of crime. Their romance, she realized, was paying the price.

Besides, she would never be able to describe how scary the dream had felt. How real. Chris might love her, but he was a computer guy. A mathematician. He'd taken a lot on faith from Dulcie, but she knew she'd be on more solid ground detailing her suspicions in scholarly terms, without reference to her strange and troubling dream. If only she could do that.

Trouble with her thesis she was used to. But trouble talking to her boyfriend? Dulcie felt uncharacteristically tongue-tied.

'I believe you, honey.' Chris was trying, she could tell. 'But I'm not on your thesis review board. And you do sound kind of obsessed over what is basically a hunch.'

As if on cue, the kitten jumped to the desk, reaching one white paw for Dulcie's red pencil. 'No,' said Dulcie to both members of her audience, clear at last. 'It *is* more than a hunch, Chris.' She could stick with what she could prove and still make her point. She was Dulcie Schwartz, soon-to-be

PhD. 'You don't know the history of this woman like I do. The writing. The work.'

Dulcie looked over at her bookcase: five collections of Gothic literature, their battered black spines as familiar as Chris's face. A library book of essays, soon to be overdue. And her copy of *The Ravages of Umbria*, its fanciful title set off in gold ornate type, with the single credit, *Anonymous,* just a little smaller.

'Nobody knows her name,' Dulcie continued. 'But I know her writing style as well as my own, and there are signs of her all over the canon. Repeated phrases, specific images so distinctive they have to be from the same writer. They show up in essays, letters, as well as the fragments of her novel, all going up until about 1794. And then, nothing. No, Chris, I have my reasons. There must have been a threat or pressure. Something nefarious. People like her do not just disappear because of natural causes.'

'Maybe she didn't disappear.'

Dulcie swallowed what she was about to say. Had he had the same dream?

But, no. True to his discipline, Chris was trying to be rational. 'Maybe your so-called victim simply stopped writing,' he was saying. 'Had kids. Retired to the country. It happens. Maybe—' He paused. 'She died. I mean, health care wasn't the greatest in her day, right?'

'But, Chris, obituaries – at least death notices – were fairly common by then. I've scoured the papers, hoping to see some mention of *The Ravages*. Maybe find out her name. And there's nothing, not even a remembrance, of any "she-author" or "lady of letters."' Dulcie began summarizing her research for Chris. Waving her pencil in the air as she talked, she cited paper after paper, their dates stuck in her mind like cat claws in velvet, until the kitten interrupted, reaching up to bat at the pencil's eraser. Kitten? Esmé, the one-time foster she'd adopted, was looking more and more like a cat every day. But not, she thought with a twinge of sadness, any more like her old cat, Mr Grey. 'She's just gone,' said Dulcie, ceding the pencil to her pet.

'Well, it's not like you can call the police, Dulcie.' Chris sounded tired. He'd never tell her, but she suspected that her call had woken him up. With his hours, that was always a risk.

'I know; it's just preying on me.' She should have told Chris about her nightmare right away. She should have trusted him to have faith in her. Maybe, she realized, she didn't entirely believe in the power of her vision.

'I can't help but think something was going on.' The feeling had begun to fade. Her boyfriend, daylight . . . the kitten. But then the image of a woman, writing for her life, flashed before her. 'Something besides kids, or an early retirement, or— or some sudden illness.'

As Dulcie talked, the certainty grew. 'My author was silenced, Chris, and I'm going to get to the bottom of it. Even if I am two hundred years too late.' With that, she reached for her pencil, ready to get back to work. But the kitten was having none of it and nipped her outstretched hand, before knocking the pencil to the floor and darting away.

# TWO

D ulcie was still thinking about the missing author as she left for campus. She wasn't sure who the woman in her dream had been, she realized as she locked the door, slipping her keys into her pocket. After all, she didn't have a name for the author she was studying, much less a portrait. But even as she made her way down the front steps and on to the sidewalk, she couldn't shake off the sense of dread the nightmare had carried. Dread, but also purpose. Something was amiss; someone had wished the mysterious woman ill, and Dulcie couldn't help tying that strange moody feeling of impending danger to the scholarly mystery before her.

She bent into the wind as she made her way along the busy Cambridge street. The bright midday sun had disappeared into more typical March clouds, but the weather only served to make Dulcie more determined. *Abandon'd there upon her windswept peak, plagued by the vengeful spirits* . . . The writer who could pen that didn't simply stop writing. Someone was plotting trouble – or had been.

Chris was right, of course. If there had been some kind of

malfeasance, it was way beyond the jurisdiction of the authorities. Even beyond the reach of the university. Dulcie paused
in a convenience store doorway. Harvard was only about a
mile from the apartment, but on a blustery day like today, the
easy walk became a trek. What if she had been abandoned
on a windswept peak? A woman alone on a mountainside,
desperate and reliant on her will alone . . .

It was no use. She couldn't distract herself, not even with
one of her usual fantasies. The dream loomed too large in her
mind. Just such a craggy scenario had figured prominently in
*The Ravages of Umbria*, the novel Dulcie was studying – the
one major work her unnamed subject had left behind. Before
she had disappeared. Before . . .

There was nothing she could do. Not from Massachusetts.
The woman Dulcie was worried about had been British. A
writer whose name had been lost to history, and who – foul
play or no – would have been long dead by this century
anyway. But Dulcie felt the impact of the crime as if it were
personal. The missing author was more than an academic foot-
note, or even the subject of her thesis. Ever since she'd read
the remaining fragments of *The Ravages of Umbria*, Dulcie
had been taken with the unknown author's colorful phrases
and smart arguments. A tale of heroism, of a lone woman
who had to fend for herself in a haunted castle, it had won
Dulcie's mind as well as her fancy.

Hermetria had been a woman she could relate to. Strong,
smart. *Alone but for her companion Demetria, a noblewoman
of good family, whose fortunes had fallen prey to evil times,
she would gaze over the majestic peaks, whose summits, veiled
with clouds, revealed at times their jagged teeth . . .*

There were ghosts, of course, but the story had so much
more. And where others had dismissed the little-known Gothic
as supernatural fluff, Dulcie had found wisdom. In the dialogue
between the main characters, she had spied a smart dramati-
zation of ideas – the kind of ideas that got women in trouble
in the eighteenth century. Since that first discovery, she'd
unearthed several essays, too: more blatantly political works.
It was heady stuff for a scholar of Gothic fiction. Whoever
she was, the unknown author had been a groundbreaking
thinker, one of the first proponents of women's rights. And
then she was gone.

It was a problem Dulcie was still wrestling with as she passed by the small, modern building that housed Middle European Studies. Hunched like an orange hillock, the strangely rounded building made Dulcie long for the soaring stone turrets described so well in *The Ravages*. At least they had some kind of grandeur. This orange lump had none and had already been eclipsed for novelty. A few blocks away, just visible over its sherbet-colored roof, stood this year's architectural wonder, the Poche Building: seven stories of developmental psych. New to the skyline, it had already won the sobriquet of 'Porches', for the tiny but decorative balconies that broke up its glass and steel facade. But if the encircling railings – smaller than the average fire escape – were supposed to make the building look more welcoming, they failed. Dulcie had grown up without many modern conveniences, but she could never look at those rails without thinking of braces on so many teeth. The effect was humorous and made her fonder of the building than of most of the university's other modern attempts, and more accepting of it than many of her peers.

As she approached the small clapboard house that served as home to her own department, she was reminded of why not many of her colleagues shared her view. Gray, with white trim, the English and American Literature and Language office might not have Gothic grandeur, but it looked cozy and welcoming. So unlike the newer buildings that towered over much of the rest of the Square. As if on cue, the sun broke through again, lighting up the trim and glossy black shutters. And, just as suddenly, the scene before her darkened. Although Dulcie did not subscribe to the theory that the placement was intentional – another blow in the continuing war between social sciences and humanities – there was no doubt of the effect. After more than a century of enjoying the afternoon sun, the little clapboard house was literally eclipsed as the shadow from the Poche cast its gray sides into a gloom the author of *The Ravages* would have recognized.

With a sigh, Dulcie turned into the little clapboard. She had a meeting with her new thesis adviser, Norm Chelowski. Soon he'd have to file his first report on how his new doctoral candidate was doing, and while Dulcie didn't usually cast herself in the role of beleaguered heroine, she feared he would not be impressed with her progress.

'Hi, Nancy.'

The departmental secretary, a warm, motherly sort, looked up from her keyboard and smiled. 'He's waiting.' She mouthed the words. 'Good luck.'

Swallowing, despite the sudden dryness in her mouth, Dulcie took the old stairs two at a time, skipping over the cracked one second from the top. Maybe the department had been shorted on funding.

'Mr Chelowski?' The door to the second-floor seminar room was open. Peering in, she could see the top of a man's head, a few long strands of hair pasted over a pale scalp. Chelowski was a tall man, but despite his perpetually poor posture, this view was not one to which she could ever become accustomed.

'Ah, Ms Schwartz, Dulcie, come in, come in.' He unfolded himself from his awkward pose and rose to greet her, patting at his hair as if to reassure himself it was still there. 'Please, have a seat. I've been reading.'

As she divested herself of her heavy duffle coat and bag, Dulcie looked over. '*The Ravages of Umbria*,' she read under her breath. 'Tracking an Unknown Author.' While she hadn't begun writing her actual thesis yet, she'd started putting her thoughts on paper in a series of essays. These papers, spread over the stained oak table, were her latest – containing all the speculative ideas she had about the anonymous author's mysterious disappearance.

Norm Chelowski was lower by far on the academic hierarchy than her previous thesis adviser. But while Professor Bullock had been a full university professor, he had not been the most attentive adviser. If Chelowski had an uncanny resemblance to a weasel – something about his mouth and the long lines of his body – at least he seemed to take her work seriously.

'Oh good, you got my pages.' She'd dropped them off the previous Friday – and emailed copies, as well – but hadn't gotten a response. Some things, she figured, never changed.

'Yes, yes, quite interesting. As you can see, I've been reading.' Maybe he was an enchanted weasel, she mused. Minor nobility under a spell. And as he bent over the papers again, Dulcie tried not to stare at the sheen of lamplight on his scalp. Instead, she let her eyes wander around the room.

One window, grimy, opened on a fire escape cast in shadow. Pressed wood bookcases, the veneer peeling. The kind of bookish shabbiness she'd always found so appealing, but which her colleagues increasingly and volubly resented. Another floor lamp hovered in the corner, its bent frame secured with gaffer tape. It was possible, she allowed, that some of her peers had a point. 'Quite interesting,' he said, not looking up.

She waited. She'd been a graduate student for three years. Long enough to know that 'I've been reading' was code for 'I haven't looked at these until now.' At least he was reading them now.

And reading. As the light shifted from gray to grayer, Norm pushed a page aside and muttered. Pulled another toward him and marked something with his pencil. Ten minutes or more had passed, and Dulcie was just beginning to wonder if she could take out some pages of her own when her adviser looked up and she noted the rodent-like dentition again. At the very least, he was a conscientious weasel, she told herself, forcing a smile. He was making the effort to get up to speed on what she was doing, rather than just rubber-stamping her for another semester. Professor Bullock had rarely bothered even to catch up with her work.

'Very interesting.' He was nodding, and Dulcie revised her opinion. He wasn't a weasel; he was one of those bobble-headed toys. 'I see you've made some interesting breakthroughs.'

Didn't he have any other word? 'Thank you.' She made herself smile. 'As you'll see in my opening, I've found evidence that *The Ravages of Umbria* wasn't the disposable fluff that so many critics have thought. Instead, it's brilliant.'

He didn't look that impressed, but as Dulcie went on, the nodding continued. She explained her discovery: that the language in the book not only revealed the true villain, the heroine's lady in waiting, but also made a cunning argument for women's rights, in an era when 'the woman question' was being hotly debated. 'So, you see, by looking at the pages marked, you can find that Hermetria, the heroine, is espousing equality in her mountain castle. While Demetria, her companion, is the real bad guy, even worse than the mad monk and the shifty knight – and the "spirits," the ghosts that are standard for a book like this, are the different philosophical arguments of the day. It's all ingenious, really.'

He stopped nodding and made a note with his pencil. Dulcie strained to see, but couldn't.

'I've read extensively in the non-fiction of the period,' she continued. 'If you want to see more of my notes, I'll bring them in. The author is quite clever in how she picks up phrases from the press.' She waited, watching him, dimly aware that in the window behind him, the weather had started to change.

'Professor Bullock thought that my work was truly original.' A shadow fell over the table, highlighting the nicks in its surface. Her adviser stood to turn on the arthritic floor lamp, using one hand to balance it as it wobbled, and Dulcie was struck by how rundown the office was. 'He thought it was publishable.'

'Yes, yes, I could see that.' He returned to his seat and shifted a few pages. 'The textual analysis is quite – interesting.'

Only an effort of will kept her from rolling her eyes.

'But to be quite honest, Ms Schwartz, I believe you could have started writing more than a month ago. All this new material.' He waved one hand over several of the pages, her more recent work, which he had pushed to his left. 'I'm not sure what you're getting at here.'

'Getting at?' Dulcie found her own head bobbing, and stopped it.

'All this speculation about the author. Is it relevant? I mean the text you're studying, *The Rampages—*'

'*Ravages.*' She couldn't quite keep her correction under her breath.

'—yes, yes, *The Ravages*, has been pretty definitively dated, hasn't it?'

'Yes, from the work I've done –' she couldn't resist – 'it seems likely that the novel was written between 1790 and 1791, and then serialized beginning sometime the following year.'

'Exactly.' He sat back in his chair. 'And why are we concerning ourselves with events that may or may not have happened perhaps four years later?'

This was more or less the same question Chris had raised. 'Because I'm interested.' One eyebrow arched behind the wire-rim glasses. 'Because establishing the identity of the author is a key component of my thesis.' She rephrased her argument in language even Chelowski should understand. 'Not only will my thesis present a new theory of *The Ravages of Umbria*,

but I will also make the case that the author used her novel to
popularize the political and philosophical ideas she wrote about
in her essays.'

He opened his mouth, but she didn't let him continue. 'And
those essays, I have reason to believe, may have resulted in
her being silenced somehow. Threatened, perhaps.'

That shut him up. As Dulcie watched, he blinked once,
twice, three times. She waited. Her reasoning, she felt, had
been flawless.

'Ms Schwartz, Dulcie.' The change of address had to preface
an admission of defeat. 'I don't know how to say it.' She
waited for his apology as he took off his glasses and rubbed
the bridge of his nose. 'But all of this? It has me worried.'

'Worried?'

'All this is so speculative. It's positively off track.' He waved
a hand over her pages, as if he would make them all disappear.
'Now, I understand the pressure of the doctoral candidate. I
was there not that long ago, you know.' He smiled again, wider
this time, and Dulcie fought the urge to recoil. 'Even without
all the . . .' He waved one long, white hand, as if brushing away
the unpleasantness of the world. 'We all experience it, you
know. It's an extremely difficult time.'

Not until stars appeared in front of her eyes did she realize
she was holding her breath.

'None of us ever wants to finish our theses. It's scary out
there, academia being in the state it is. Not everyone is fit for
it.' He sat back, resting those long sweaty hands on the arms
of the black enamel chair. 'That's why the department has
instituted this system of reports every semester. I know some
of you grumble, but it isn't only about resources. It's for the
students' benefit as well as the department's. Not everyone is
cut out for a doctorate.'

'Wait, you think I don't really want to get my degree?' She
heard her voice rising, the tension building in her throat. 'You
think I'm going off on tangents to avoid finishing my thesis?'

Chelowski shrugged. 'You're probably familiar with the
statistics. As a grad student, you can stay enrolled for up to
seven years, as long as the department sees progress. But, as
your thesis adviser, I'd be lax in my duty if I permitted that
kind of malingering.'

\* \* \*

She couldn't believe it. He thought she was off on a tangent. No, worse. *Malingering*. She didn't even know how she managed to be civil, stuttering out a promise to 'get back to work' as she fled the room. Flame-cheeked, she clattered down the stairs and out the front door without even stopping to chat with Nancy. That little clapboard house had once been her shelter. Her safe place. But now it had a bigger shadow on it than any new building could cast. Now it had Norm Chelowski.

What a waste of time. Her shock turned to anger as she stomped down the street. Not writing. Not *wanting* to write. Dulcie found herself digging up her store of Shakespearian insults as she walked, her collar up against an increasingly fierce wind. She couldn't wait to tell Suze. Suze would understand – the next time she saw her. Or Chris. But, no, hadn't Chris said something similar, only a few hours before?

Twice thwarted, and with her academic rigor impugned to boot, Dulcie decided she deserved some comfort. And since she'd already had lunch that meant the library.

Truth was, she probably should have been there already. Reading and rereading in the hope of tracking down one more piece by her mysterious author. One more clue. Instead, she'd wasted it with that useless Norm Chelowski. And, she had to admit, thinking about that strangely disturbing nightmare.

What had that dream meant? What had the woman been writing, and what had those green eyes been trying to tell her? In front of her, a light turned just as bright, and Dulcie crossed. Oblivious to the cab that screeched to a halt, honking furiously, Dulcie found herself thinking of that final luminous vision – and of the kitten's new habit of biting her in play. Esmé didn't really hurt her when she nipped. The rough wool of Dulcie's mittens scratched almost as much against her skin as the kitten's tiny teeth. Still, it bothered her that the kitten was so aggressive. The tiny black and white puffball she'd adopted only a few months before was already looking like a cat, rangy and long. Mr Grey had come into her life as an adult cat, and he'd never been anything but gentle.

Mr Grey. Dulcie paused on the sidewalk, and it wasn't just the delayed effect of that disastrous meeting or the raw March wind that brought tears to her eyes. Mr Grey had been the cat of her heart, her devoted companion for years until his death the previous spring. No wonder the season's slow change, the barely perceptible shift from deep winter freeze to March slush, hadn't brought its usual thrill. This May would be the anniversary. One year would have passed without the large gray longhair she had loved with all her heart. Mr Grey would have listened. He'd have comforted her after a meeting like the one she'd just had. And he would never, *never* have nipped her hand.

'Mr Grey, can you help me?' Dulcie kept her voice low, a little self conscious as she began walking again, slipping past the red-brick gate of Harvard Yard. 'I don't know what's going on any more. Am I totally off track with my thesis? And, well, should I be training the kitten somehow?'

The wind whistled, burning her ears. But no feline voice followed. She wasn't surprised, not really. Maybe because she'd been so busy, what with classes and her thesis, the new kitten and Chris, but she barely heard from Mr Grey any more. Sometimes, she lost faith that she ever had, wondering instead if those times when her late cat had seemed to come to her had been born out of her neediness, her sadness and grief. Sometimes, she knew, she kept herself busy, too afraid to call on her spectral companion for fear he would not respond.

More reason to get to work, she reminded herself, putting her head down as a particularly nasty gust threw dust and gravel in her face. A large man, made larger by an oversized blue parka, powered by.

'Watch it!' Dulcie stumbled off the path. 'Hey!' She called after the large man, but he was nearly to the gate and oblivious to the fact that he'd shoved one short grad student into the semi-frozen mud. 'Ah well, it's almost spring, right?' She stepped back on to the path and held up one boot to see how much mud she'd managed to collect. As she did, a movement caught her eye. A fat gray squirrel, its coat thick for the winter cold, stood frozen. The rude stranger must have disturbed them both.

'Sorry little fellow.' The little nose twitched, and Dulcie felt her mood lifting. Something about those sharp dark eyes, the gray fur . . . '*Mr Grey?*' The squirrel flicked its tail. 'Is that you?' Dulcie's voice sank to a whisper. 'Oh, Mr Grey, there's been so much going on. The kitten, my thesis . . .'

But just then, two more blue parkas jostled by, deep in conversation, and the spell broke. With a leap, the small, fat creature took off, bounding over the patchy snow like his cousin, the rabbit. Dulcie's eyes followed his flicking tail as he raced toward another path and passed just behind another lone walker. A woman, if the long dark curls cascading from beneath the knit cap were any indication. Slight, almost invisible inside her olive wool cape, she was hurrying from the Poche Building. Head bent into the wind, body folded forward, she seemed to be having even more trouble with the weather than Dulcie had.

'At least I'm not the only one,' Dulcie murmured to herself. Beyond the walker, the squirrel had stopped. Visible against the black mud, the little gray beast sat up and flicked his tail again. And then, with one giant leap, he was gone.

# THREE

Three hours later, Dulcie felt like singing – and quickly bit her lip. Widener might seem half empty, but she'd been a tenant of the giant library long enough to know that in its depths other scholars were hard at work. Even though she now had her own reserved carrel, down three levels and tucked into a corner between Elizabethan and Jacobean plays, she sensed the more contemporary drama going on all around in the hushed mutterings, the deep sighs, and the occasional hurried footsteps. March meant midterms for most of the nearly two thousand undergrads at the university – and a flurry of deadlines and postgrad exams for everyone else. But amidst all the craziness, her equilibrium had been restored. Tapping a particularly toothsome passage in the leather-bound volume on her lap, Dulcie knew she was on the right track. This was the stuff: the author of the *Ravages* was a thinker. A strong woman, and an early feminist of the caliber of Mary Wollstonecraft.

*Those critics who, like noisome beasts, would bind us with their fancies. Would drag us down—*

An author this passionate did not simply stop writing.

*—into their lairs, imprison'd and unprepar'd for that which life would grant us.*

Unsigned, unattributed, but so distinctive, this essay had to be from the author of *The Ravages*. But this was the last. Dulcie had searched through all the periodicals, reaching beyond London to the smaller, regional presses, and found nothing. No more essays, no letters or stories. That, to Dulcie, meant the author had disappeared. If anything, her recent experience with what might be deemed supernatural – or, yes, deadly – only made her more convinced that such things happened, even in educated society. If Chelowski – or Chris – didn't buy it, she'd simply have to work harder to find proof. But she would. She was Dulcinea Schwartz, after all. That had to stand for something.

The basement carrel might not be quite the same as a mountain aerie. Might, in fact, be pretty much the opposite, but there were similarities. She could hole up to defend her thesis – if not herself – without fear. Unlike those of poor beleaguered Hermetria, the only spirits left in Dulcie's fortified keep were benign.

Had Hermetria ever gotten lonely? Dulcie looked up from the very large page of very small type to stare at the metal bookshelf above her. One of the basic tenets of her thesis was that Hermetria, an impoverished noblewoman, had been a strong and independent figure, a 'modern woman' stuck in a stereotypical dilemma. Her only companion, the treacherous Demetria, represented all that was hackneyed about the over-the-top tales of the time.

Dulcie was lucky not to have that kind of living arrangement. She and Suze had been room-mates since sophomore year and, with the exception of one bad summer sublet, had always managed to keep a peaceful home. But in the past few months, Suze – a third-year law student – had been around less and less. Both of the roomies had spent the semester break with their boyfriends: Dulcie going down to the Jersey Shore to stay with Chris's mom, and Suze driving cross-country with Ariano. Since then, Chris and Dulcie had sunk back into their old routine – too much so for Dulcie. Computer geeks – applied math majors – tended to be nocturnal, and with Chris grabbing as many help-desk shifts as he could, he probably saw more of his geek buddy Jerry than he did of her. Once the Sox season started in earnest that would certainly be the case. Plus, Chris had started one-on-one tutoring this spring with a handful of undergrads. All of which left more time for Dulcie to work, doing the reading that might help her track down her elusive subject. But it also meant more time alone. And while Esmé, her kitten, was as playful a companion as she could hope for, the little tuxedo cat just wasn't the conversationalist that Suze was. Or Chris. Or, for that matter, Mr Grey.

Mr Grey . . . Thoughts of the elegant cat who had been such a wonderful companion flooded her, and Dulcie let the thick volume sink back to the carrel surface. The resulting thud earned her a nasty look from a pasty undergrad who had been passing, and Dulcie made a face at his back.

It was time for a break. With a sigh, she closed her laptop and shoved it into her bag. The long yellow legal pad that Suze had given her went next, and for a moment Dulcie considered the bound volume. *The Woman Question: 1785–1792, Vol. 1* had other essays besides the one she had just reread. If Chris was working again, she might be able to get back into it tonight. Yes, she'd check the book out. And she'd make some time to play with the kitten. After all, she reasoned, as she threw her bag over her shoulder, a girl deserves some fun.

Especially after a full day's work. March wasn't spring, not in New England, and Dulcie emerged from the library to a chill Cambridge dusk. Blinking to accustom herself to the low light, she stood at the back entrance of Widener, bracing herself for the bone-chilling walk home.

'You OK, miss?' Despite several years of nodding hellos, neither she nor the portly security guard knew each other's names.

'I'm fine, thanks.' She turned and smiled, and then stepped out into the cold. A blast coming in from Mass. Ave. made her cringe. Wrapping her long, multicolored scarf, one of her mother's knitting projects, around the lower part of her face and pulling her wool hat over her brassy curls, she started off along the inside of the Yard. Gates every dozen feet or so pierced the brick enclosure of the college green, but for those blessed few moments between, she'd be shielded from that biting March wind.

'In like a lion, indeed,' Dulcie mused out loud. 'But shouldn't a cat have more grace?'

Some people, she noticed, didn't seem to mind the weather. As she passed one of the prettier openings, an arched brick walkway, she saw a couple leaning together in a romantic moment. He was tall and looked as slim as Chris in profile, despite his winter wear. She was shorter and seemed to be talking intently as he bent toward her. The hanging lantern cast a golden glow over them, and Dulcie paused, just for a moment, to bask in their shared warmth.

'No!' Suddenly, the scene changed. The woman had raised her voice and was gesturing with her hands. The man had stepped back – into the shadow of the arch. 'You can't! I won't let you!'

Dulcie stood frozen. Was this a private argument, or something more serious? Like every other woman on campus, she'd seen the fliers warning about a recent spate of attacks. The crimes had all been minor and relatively odd – several women had entered university cloakrooms to find their coats slashed. Two undergrads had been pelted with mud from an overhead walkway. The most serious had involved some shoving in the dark, during a screening of a historical film. That had resulted in a fall and a sprained ankle. The Harvard Harasser, some wag had named the perpetrator – or perpetrators – and nobody took it too seriously. But if Dulcie was witnessing one of those attacks . . .

'Hey!' She stepped forward, pulling herself up to her full five foot four. She tasted wool and realized her scarf must have muffled her words. 'Hey, you.' She reached up to pull the offending outerwear from her lips. 'Stop it!'

Scarf or no, Dulcie didn't know if her voice even carried over the wind, but the motion must have caught the woman's eyes. Pushing the man back, both hands on his chest, she turned. Dulcie had a clear view of a dark-haired young woman with full arching eyebrows over her wide set and frankly terri-fied eyes. For a moment, Dulcie paused – she knew this woman, although she couldn't quite place her – and then started forward, ready to help. Only, at that moment, the combination of the wind, the unwinding muffler, and the weight of the books inside pulled her bag from her shoulder, and she stumbled, grabbing at the strap. And at that, the young woman turned and ran.

'Wait!' Abandoning her bag, Dulcie started forward, a little less sure. The man, all in shadow, waited. 'Mister—' And then he, too, turned and took off into the night.

# FOUR

'You *what*?'

Dulcie had been thrilled to find Suze at home when she arrived, a little short of breath having trotted most of the way. Her room-mate, however, seemed less than enthusiastic about Dulcie's exploits.

'You went after an armed man?'

'Suze, don't exaggerate.' Now that the slight scare had faded, Dulcie basked in a bit of pride. She *might* have gone after an armed man or broken up a fight. But her essential honesty won out. 'I said they were squabbling, not that he was armed. Besides, I don't really know what was going on. At first, I thought they were just talking, or, you know, cuddling.'

Suze looked up over the pasta sauce she was stirring and made a face. She'd moved from volunteering at the law school clinic to helping out with a women's shelter this semester. It hadn't made her any more sympathetic to Dulcie's heroics. 'You do know about the attacks, don't you?'

'I've seen the fliers. But they're for little things. Crazy things.'

Suze shook her head. 'This kind of violence can escalate, Dulcie. If you heard some of the stories I hear at Safe Place, you wouldn't take this so lightly.'

'I'm not taking it lightly.' Dulcie poked about in the cabinet until she found a box of grissini. 'I mean, I *didn't* go after the guy.'

'I know.' Suze reached to take a breadstick from the box. 'But you are more concerned with a crime from the year 1800.'

'Seventeen ninety-four, really. And, Suze, that's my thesis.'

'But this is your community, Dulcie.' Suze used the breadstick like a pointer. 'You should go to the police tomorrow. Tell them what you saw.'

'Uh huh.' Dulcie finished her breadstick. 'But I didn't see
the guy. I'm not even sure I saw an attack.' Rather than
argue, she started to retreat. As she did, she felt her ankle
encircled and the pinprick of teeth through her wool socks.
'Esmé! No!'

'She's been staring out the window all afternoon.' Suze
checked the other pot, lifting the lid to a cloud of steam.
'Probably desperate for someone to play with her.'

'Guilty as charged.' Dulcie scooped the kitten up and held
her, looking in her eyes. 'Now, what would Mr Grey say about
biting like that, kitty?'

'He'd probably say that some animals are born hunters.'
Suze reached for the box of spaghetti. 'And the rest of us
ought to watch out.'

Once again, the night was stormy. The wind, wicked, whipped
through the trees and slashed its way through the dark mountain gulleys. Dulcie, waking in her upstairs bedroom, wondered
for a moment at the ferocity of that wind – and of the steep
mountain pass, funneling its force upward. A tempest was
brewing: something so big that it threatened to shake her castle
keep.

'*There are forces at work.*' She sensed the voice, rather
than heard it, and imagined herself looking out a window,
down into the stony dark below. '*Forces that buffet us, that
shape us through their pressure. Forces that we respond to –
for better or for ill.*'

'I'm dreaming,' she muttered to herself, before flipping
over.

'*Yes, little one. Yes, you are.*'

'Mr Grey?' Suddenly the wild weather seemed less threatening, and she remembered those glowing eyes, emerging
from the sparks. But when she reached out blindly, hoping to
find the large longhair, all she felt were little paws, grabbing
at her hand as if to play. 'Oh, Esmé.' She pulled her hand
away and faded back to sleep.

'So there are forces at work?' Suze was gone by the time
Dulcie awoke, and so she called Chris as she made her way
into the Square. 'Do you think that means anything?'

He sounded a little loopy, as he often did at this hour. While

Dulcie knew the large travel mug of caffeine she carried would solve most of her mental problems, her nocturnal beau probably needed a good eight hours of sleep before he could do more than just parrot back her words.

'Some kind of malevolent forces.' Dulcie took a sip. 'Though, I don't know. Mr Grey said something about "shaping," and that makes me think of teaching. You know, we shape young minds and all?'

'Mr Grey?'

Damn, she hadn't realized she'd mentioned her dream's feline narrator. It wasn't that Chris didn't believe, exactly. It was more that he thought the enigmatic ghost was some manifestation of Dulcie's consciousness, of her desire for her lost pet. Sometimes, Dulcie thought he might be right. But when she heard his voice so clearly . . .

'You heard his voice again?'

Had she said that aloud? 'Yeah, Chris, I did.' They'd been together for long enough; there was no need to lie to him. If he was going to drop her for being loopy, well, he'd probably have done that already.

'Dulce, you do know that you don't actually know what Mr Grey's voice would sound like.' His voice was soft; he would always be a gentle man – but he couldn't help being rational. 'I mean, beyond "meow" or something.'

'Forget it, Chris.' She did not need to have this conversation now. Not when she was late for a departmental meeting. Martin Thorpe, the acting chair, did not tolerate latecomers, and the quiet little man had a dozen ways of needling the tardy. 'I was just wondering about the message. I mean, am I stirring up trouble?'

'I thought you liked your students this semester?' She could hear him yawn and felt a twinge of guilt. He'd probably only just gotten home when she'd called him.

'I do, but maybe breaking up that fight last night—'

'What?' Her boyfriend was awake now. 'You didn't tell me about a fight.'

Hadn't she? With a sigh, Dulcie gave him a quick recap. 'So, I didn't really get involved. I just yelled, and they both took off.'

'Dulcie, sweetie, you've got to learn to take care of yourself.'

'But I didn't *do* anything.' Neither Chis nor Suze seemed

to be hearing what, to her, was the major point. 'If anything, I wonder if I should have.'

'No.' Chris sounded quite decisive. 'No, you shouldn't have. You should have run back to the library and alerted the guard. Or used one of those blue-light emergency phones. I think they've added more of them, you know, since the attacks.'

'But it might just have been a lovers' spat.' She paused for a moment to think about their recent past. 'And I wasn't sure what was going on, not till it was too late.'

'Sweetie, that's the problem.' He was sounding sleepy again, and Dulcie wondered if he had taken her admission for an apology. 'That's always the case.'

'Suze thinks I ought to tell the university police.' She waited for him to say this wasn't necessary. When he didn't, she offered a prompt. 'I don't even know what I'd tell them, though.'

'You want me to go with you? I should be free by one or so.' That wasn't the answer she wanted. But he was fading, she could tell.

'No, I've got to meet with one of my students. You working tonight?' The question was automatic. Still, for a moment she hoped.

'Yeah, all week.' Dulcie didn't trust herself to say anything more. 'I'm sorry, sweetie. I'll see if I can get away for an hour or two. Leave your phone on?'

'Of course,' she said, working hard to keep the disappointment out of her voice. 'Love you.' But he was already gone.

'Nobody understands me but my cat,' Dulcie said to the uncaring emptiness as she rounded the corner to the departmental headquarters. After yesterday's meeting, it didn't look quite as welcoming. Maybe her colleagues were right, she mused as she walked up the street. Maybe the looming new psych building *had* ruined the little house's appeal. She checked her watch. If the meeting were on time, it would have started. And while that was doubtful, it did mean she didn't have time to touch base with Suze, either. Another gray squirrel, this one halfway up a denuded maple, paused as she spoke. 'Even you are more thoughtful than my kitten. Or my friends,' she said, addressing the bright-eyed creature. It raced up the tree, and with a sigh, Dulcie mounted the steps.

'Conference room,' Nancy stage-whispered, pointing toward the back.

'Just a quick refill.' Dulcie popped the lid of her mug. As she did, she looked over at the bulletin board, where ads for sublets and calls for journal submissions usually held sway. To her surprise, a large flier took precedence today, tacked boldly over something about the undergrad poetry magazine. The flier, dated that morning, asked in bold letters: HAVE YOU SEEN THIS STUDENT? Underneath was a little information: the student being sought was named Carrie Mines. She'd lived off campus and so was affiliated with Dudley House. She was a sophomore. In her distracted state, Dulcie felt a memory tickling. The name was familiar. Had she had her in a section? Dulcie moved closer to examine the face. The photo had clearly come from an ID card, the kind everyone grimaced over and would never willingly share. To make matters worse, it had been blown up almost to the point of graininess, but the face was still distinctive. Striking, rather than pretty, with wild dark hair and wide-set light eyes, maybe gray, maybe blue. Underneath, bold type read: 'Campus police are seeking any information.'

'Dulcie?' The secretary was holding a full pot, ready to pour. But Dulcie wasn't looking at her. Something about the eyes in that photo – a little too open, a little wild – had finally sparked a connection. The picture – the grainy head-shot – was of the woman she had seen last night. The woman who had run from the arch.

# FIVE

'**M**s Schwartz?' Dulcie stumbled into the conference room, oblivious to the particularly pointed look Martin Thorpe was giving her over his glasses. 'So nice of you to join us.'

'Dulce.' A flash of silver caught her eye. Her buddy Trista was nodding her over to an empty seat, the ring in her nose as effective as a lighthouse in her current fog. Trista's specialty was nineteenth-century fiction, her thesis on 'Characterization through Metaphor in the Late Victorian Novel,' but in appearance she was adamantly postmodern. As Dulcie slid into the seat, Trista leaned over to whisper: 'Thorpe's gonna blow.'

Dulcie waited till the acting chair seemed diverted before responding. 'What's up?' It came out louder than she'd meant, and instinctively they both glanced over. Thorpe was bent over a schedule, his fluff of white hair glowing in the fluorescent light. 'Is it about that missing girl?' she continued, her voice softer.

Trista shook her head. 'It's Dimitri. He's a no-show.' Her friend had misunderstood her, Dulcie realized as she glanced around. The handsome transfer, a new addition the previous fall, was not among those seated around the big table. 'So, how'd the meeting with Chelowski go?'

'And do you have the new forms, Ms Wright?' Thorpe's question caught Trista off guard. 'The question was rhetorical,' he continued, as she started to stutter some kind of response, and tossed some sheets of paper on to the table in front of her. Only then did Dulcie realize that nearly everyone else had already taken their copies from the acting chair's three neat piles. 'The problem will be real, however, if you don't learn the Coop's new procedures for taking book orders.'

Dulcie picked up her copies and pretended to peruse them as Thorpe droned on. She didn't really want to talk about her disastrous meeting with her adviser right now. Besides, she kind of liked the acting chair. His specialty, Renaissance English poetry, bored her to tears, but the man himself, little and nervous, had her sympathy. Maybe it was because of her own fashion sense – or lack thereof – but she identified with his rigid uniform of khakis and pullover sweater vests. Growing up on a commune – what her mother called an arts colony – she had found life back East mystifying in so many ways. These days, she had her own uniform: layering the bulky, but colorful sweaters her mother knit, usually out of commune-carded wool, over jeans or, when the occasion merited, a long gypsy-like skirt. Thorpe's argyle fixation was another issue – the socks matching the sweater vests matching his scarf – but, after years of fashion faux pas, she could relate. Or maybe, she realized as he wiped his pale hands together for the third or fourth time, it was that he looked a little like a mouse. A diamondback mouse. But surely these forms weren't as important as a missing girl. A student. There was something else about the girl, something Dulcie couldn't quite place. Maybe she had sat in on a class once.

'Ms Schwartz?' The mouse was addressing her.

'I'm sorry?' She sat up, aware of all the eyes on her.

'Your new student?' That was it. She'd been in one of the sections Dulcie led – the discussion group for one of the big survey courses – but hadn't stayed. 'Ms Schwartz?' Dulcie looked up and realized that Thorpe wasn't the only one waiting. 'A Ms McCorkle?'

'Yes, she's one of mine.' Across the table, Dulcie saw Lloyd, her office mate, wince. So that hadn't been the question. 'I'm sorry, Mr Thorpe. My mind was wandering.' Dulcie had been at the university long enough to know something about politics, and an apology delivered with a big smile was as good as she could do.

To her surprise, Thorpe smiled back, briefly, and then colored and ducked his head. 'That's fine, that's fine.' He cleared his throat and rubbed one pink, paw-like hand over his mouth. 'What I was asking, Ms Schwartz, was how our various honor candidates are doing. I have your report on Ms Hall already.' Raleigh Hall, undergrad wunderkind and Lloyd's not-so-secret girlfriend, was wrapping up her senior thesis with aplomb – and with very little need for Dulcie's help. Even Thorpe probably realized that she was likely to head up the department one of these days.

'Oh, Corkie's doing fine too.' Across the table, Lloyd sank a little lower in his chair. A sharp kick from Trista brought Dulcie back to reality. 'I mean, I have found Ms McCorkle, Philomena McCorkle, to be an engaged and enthusiastic student.' She kept talking, piling on the jargon while quickly looking through her notes. Somewhere she had an actual report on the junior honors candidate, not that the dry departmentalese would do her student justice. Corkie had been assigned to her in January, after returning from a semester's leave. While Dulcie wasn't sure of the details about why the cheery Midwesterner had taken time off, she suspected it had done her student good. The junior, who would be writing a junior paper – a kind of pre-thesis – under Dulcie's guidance, was both smart and directed. 'While she has some notable gaps in her knowledge of the core canon— Ah, here we are.' She paused and looked up. Lloyd had his hand over his face, but she could have sworn he was laughing.

'While Ms McCorkle began the semester slightly deficient in the core canon, she has been both enthusiastic and aggressive in her remedial work and is quickly filling in the gaps in the American side of her reading.' The woman had attacked Henry James and the other Anglophiles like they were toffee pudding, she could have added. Particularly because she had recently discovered that she and her large-framed student shared a sweet tooth. Not that this was any of Martin Thorpe's business.

'And in her own area, the novels of Smollett, Sterne, and Fielding, she's completely on top of the material. In addition, she's taken on some tutoring of the younger students in her house.' Raising a hand for silence before Thorpe could object, Dulcie kept on talking. 'As her tutor, I was suspicious at first, but accepted that this showed her willingness to become involved with the complete university experience. In addition, neither this additional work, nor her other commitments, seem to be holding her back in any way. I'd say that the semester off did Corkie a world of good. Corkie – Ms McCorkle – may not graduate with her class next year, but unless I'm highly mistaken, she's going to graduate with honors, possibly with high honors, in both the department and in her area of concentration.'

'Good save,' Trista whispered as Dulcie pulled her notes together. Thorpe had already moved on to one of their less troublesome colleagues and so missed Dulcie's deep, dramatic sigh.

'Man, with everything else going on, I totally forgot about the midterm reports, Tris.' She leaned toward her friend, hoping not to be observed. 'I don't think I told you what my own research has turned up.'

'Tell!' Trista leaned in, her silver fingernails on Dulcie's forearm. But Thorpe had turned their way again, and, lesson learned, Dulcie kept mum.

'So, no matter what Chelowski says, I'm thinking that lack of material isn't just because papers have gotten lost.' Dulcie had meant to ask about the missing girl, but as soon as the meeting had broken up, Trista had jumped in, demanding to

hear about Dulcie's meeting with her adviser. With one thing
and another – mostly, Trista's righteous anger on her friend's
part – she ended up talking about her thesis topic. Or what
would be her thesis topic if she ever did end up writing it.

Trista had been a friend for long enough to know about
Dulcie's research, including her breakthrough with *The
Ravages*. Walking toward the Yard, Dulcie summed up her
theory about the work's anonymous author. 'And I think that's
a big deal. A huge deal. He says I'm wasting my time, but
think about it. *The Ravages* was pubbed in '91 or '92, latest.
And I've found a score of other essays that I am pretty sure
are hers from the years before and for about two years after:
she's got some very distinctive catchphrases. These appear
pretty steadily going up to 1794, and then – nothing. What,
did she just disappear?'

Trista bit her lip. 'Could have, though. Couldn't she? We
wouldn't know. I mean, she published anonymously, right?'

'She *published* anonymously, and *we* don't know her name.
But nobody writes – or gets a book published – in a vacuum.
People have reasons for not using their names, maybe this
woman especially. But after her death?' Dulcie shook her head.
'People would talk about it. There'd have been a notice of
some kind.'

'If only this had all happened a hundred years later – you'd
have been golden, Dulce.' As a Victorian, Trista had an easier
time with research. 'My people saved everything.'

'But then there might not have been anything left for me
to discover.' No matter what the challenges were, Dulcie
wouldn't trade. 'And, I mean, it's not like we're talking pre-
Revolution. Nobody was burning papers, not usually. Unless,
I don't know, they were seen as a threat for some reason.' She
paused; her train of thought followed the hypothetical pages.
A flick of a tail – silver gray, probably another squirrel –
brought her back. 'Anyway, my author writes these essays,
and then, for some reason, she gives up on them. Maybe
they're not having any effect. So she writes *The Ravages*.
Then a few more essays, but bolder. Like, she's really sick of
people not *getting* it. For a strong woman, the 1790s were not
an easy time.'

'Wollstonecraft.' Trista didn't have to say more.

'Yes, but these days everyone looks at the *Rights of Woman*

like it was some marvelous piece of writing. Which it is,'
Dulcie added quickly. 'But it wasn't entirely original. There
was so much going on then. The Romantics were coming in.
Science. Industrialization. Women's rights were just one more
cause – and not a popular one. I mean, when did women get
the vote?'

Trista started to answer, but Dulcie kept talking.

'What I mean is, we tend to look at that era with feminist
hindsight. To be an actual independent woman back then, a
woman writing about these new ideas, must have been hard.
Dangerous, even. And so here's my author, speaking out –
and suddenly, nothing.' She stopped short, and Trista turned.

'What?' Trista waited.

'Oh, dear Goddess, Chris was right.' Dulcie smiled. 'He
didn't mean to be, but he was.'

Trista looked at her, not even sure what to ask.

'My author? The woman who used her so-called radical
theories to bring *The Ravages of Umbria* to life?' Dulcie posed
the question for her. 'There is one good reason she might have
disappeared without notice. One thing her family would not
have wanted known. She really might have been murdered.'

# SIX

Trista might have been more sympathetic than Chelowski
had been, but not by much. By the time the two reached
Memorial Hall, she'd listed a half dozen reasons why
Dulcie's theory was, at the very least, premature. It was with
some relief, then, that Dulcie waved her friend off toward
Emerson, where Trista had a section to teach. She hadn't even
gotten around to telling Trista about the odd confrontation
outside of Widener. But she knew she'd probably see her
friend later – pub nights at the People's Republik had become
one of the few times the harried grad students got to hang,
though even these congenial evenings were becoming more
sporadic as the term ground on. The week before, Dulcie
recalled, Trista hadn't even made it to the Republik, and Chris
had spent the evening dissecting the Sox pitching prospects

with her boyfriend, Jerry. Well, it wasn't like Tris would have anything to add to what Suze had said, and Dulcie had no time to file a report about something that she might have misunderstood anyway. She had a student waiting, and so she descended into the subterranean warren of offices that she shared with most of the department's grad students, and particularly with Lloyd Pruitt.

'Hey, Lloyd.' She opened the door to the sight of Lloyd's balding pate. Only twenty-four, Lloyd had the face of a teenager – but the scalp of a fifty-year-old. Unlike Chelowski, Lloyd didn't resort to a comb-over. He didn't need to: despite his unprepossessing looks, he had managed to secure the heart of Raleigh Hall, Dulcie's senior tutee. It was a blatant breach of university rules, but it seemed to be working. Perhaps, thought Dulcie, because Lloyd was such a genuinely nice guy.

''Scuse me?' Dulcie said. Lloyd had muttered something, but since he hadn't lifted his face from the blue book in front of him, Dulcie had no idea what it was.

'Your student – big girl? – came by. Philomena?' Lloyd looked up, his pale face drawn. 'She came by. I told her you'd be here in a few, but she said she couldn't wait. Couldn't stay for her tutorial even if you were here, she said. She was going to leave a note.'

'Great.' She didn't mean it, nor did she mean to cause the look of distress that passed over her office-mate's face as she slumped into her desk chair. 'Sorry, I just sort of winged it in a report about her and was hoping to actually catch up. It's just been that kind of morning. You know that poster? The one about the missing girl?'

'Uh huh.' He made a few more marks on the student exam book. 'Carrie Mines? Not one of ours.'

'You knew her?' Dulcie looked over a little surprised. So she had looked familiar.

'So did you. She was supposed to be in your English 10 section, remember? Last fall? We were all taking on extra students, but you lucked out.' That was because she'd been given Raleigh as a senior honors student. A fact that must have hit them both at once. 'I mean, I'm glad you did. And so are your students.' He still avoided saying his girlfriend's name in public. 'But Carrie was sort of a troublemaker. Flighty, at least. I forget the details, but she ended up changing her concentration, I believe. Wanted to spend more time on some extracurricular or something. At any rate, I think she dropped the course.'

'Did any of us talk to her?' Dulcie was afraid to ask. 'I mean, ask her what was wrong?'

'Not unless you did.' Lloyd didn't sound concerned as he reached for a second blue book. Students dropped out, changed majors, all the time, but grading was eternal. 'I mean, she would have been your responsibility.'

'My responsibility.' The words carried a horrible chill. 'And now she's missing.'

'Dulcie, what's wrong?' Something must have carried on her voice. 'We don't know what's going on, and whatever it is, it probably has nothing to do with the department or last year's course. She was a frosh, then. A baby. They cruise concentrations like . . . like . . . mayflies.'

It wasn't like Lloyd to mix a metaphor. 'Lloyd, you know something else, don't you?' The sense of dread had settled into her stomach, cold and hard. 'Tell.'

'It's probably nothing.'

'Lloyd . . .'

'OK, like I said, it's probably nothing. But I think there might be a connection to our own little mystery.'

'*Lloyd*!'

'Dimitri.' Lloyd said their colleague's name like it was obvious. 'I mean, he went absent today, too. And I think he may have been tutoring her.'

'In English?' Dimitri had only transferred to the department the past year. But her confusion was a small price to pay for the wave of relief that washed over her.

'Hey, even non-concentrators have got to take a few classes, right? Chaucer?'

'Actually not,' Dulcie admitted. Lloyd had come from Yale, and, in comparison, Dulcie was a little embarrassed for her Alma Mater. Besides, Dimitri's area of expertise – the hard-boiled detective fiction of the 1920s and '30s – barely overlapped with the basic canon. 'But, maybe she took something for fun. His noir seminar or something. At any rate, are you sure?'

'No, I'm not. But I seem to recall him saying her name. And he'd just arrived. Maybe he got saddled with her somehow.'

'Could you find out?'

'Yeah, sure. I think I've still got those assignments in my email.' He reached for his laptop and, in the process, knocked over a travel mug. 'Damn!'

Dulcie leaped up and reached for the pile of blue books. Lloyd, meanwhile, pulled a cache of paper napkins from a drawer and began mopping his desk.

'I'm sorry, Lloyd. I shouldn't distract you.' Dulcie placed the blue books on the dry side of the desk. 'Besides, you've given me an idea.'

As Lloyd left the office to fetch some paper towels, Dulcie powered up her own laptop. Email – of course – the modern equivalent of the telegram. In general, Dulcie tried to avoid contacting students electronically. Not because of the illusion of accessibility it created, although Dulcie had heard enough grumbling to know that some undergrads did think their tutors should be available 24/7. No, for her, it was the strange lack of affect in an email. However, in this case . . .

Or was she copping out? Even a phone message had more emotion in it. A few clicks settled it. The university directory listed an email for a Carrie A. Mines, but no phone. Off-campus students weren't on the university exchange. Just as well, Dulcie told herself. The police would have tried to call. And in truth, she admitted as she opened a new window, she didn't want to phone the girl. What would she say to a student she hadn't seen in a year? Email would be perfect.

*Hi Carrie*, she typed. *Don't know if you remember me, but I wanted to touch base. Is everything OK?* As Lloyd came back, a wad of damp towel in his hand, she hit send, and then opened another note.

*Corkie – Sorry to have missed you. We have midterm reports due! Let's resched?* Simple, sweet, and to the point. But no blinking reply came, and she was still staring at the screen when Lloyd, with a loud sigh, dumped the coffee-colored towels in the wastebasket. He looked harried, and although she had grading of her own, Dulcie sensed he'd be happier by himself. Besides, sending those emails had freed her.

'So, Corkie isn't coming back, right?' He nodded, distracted.

'Great!' She jumped up and grabbed her bag. This time, she meant it.

Halfway up the stairs, she paused to thumb in the digits. Corkie was a good student – not as brilliant as Raleigh, perhaps, but bright and amenable to hard work. If anything, Dulcie thought, the fresh-faced student had been a little too enthusiastic. The previous year, she'd told Dulcie, she'd let herself get overextended; it was easy, with so many extra-curricular competing for attention. And fresh off academic probation, Corkie couldn't really afford to miss their weekly tutorials. Dulcie would have to keep after her. But since the errant junior had canceled and wasn't responding to her tutor, Dulcie was going to seize the moment.

'Sweetie? It's me.' She wasn't being grammatical, but Chris wouldn't care. 'My day just opened up. Wanna have lunch?' She paused. 'Breakfast?' With Chris's crazy schedule, it was always possible that he had gone back to sleep. But when they'd talked earlier, he'd made some noise about being free, hadn't he?

That had been before Dulcie had brought up her latest theory, and before he'd dashed it to the ground, leaving her a little too miffed to want to make plans. But he'd been tired, and even with his new tutoring gig he'd been stressed about money recently, too. And she, Dulcie could now see, had been a little overzealous. After all, Chris had been right. Dulcie had been through a couple of run-ins with the police recently. The last one, which had resulted in the retirement of her first thesis adviser, Professor William Alfred Bullock, had nearly taken her life. Now that she had a little distance on the morning's conversation, she could see how maybe she had gone too far. Well, that was fine. As soon as she saw Chris, she'd explain. Or, no, she'd apologize. As soon as he called her back.

She'd reached the top of the stairs as the church bells sounded the hour, and she stood to the side, letting the rush of students pass by. A steady stream flowed into the Science Center, its glass and chrome livened by the variety of their late-winter attire. Ahead of her, dozens of students took to the paths across the Yard, funneled on to the pavement by the mud and last patches of melting snow. One student, either braver or running farther behind than his colleagues, took off across what would soon be lawn, splashing up brown water as he ran. Over by University Hall, a young woman waved as he made it back to solid ground and took her in his arms. The campus was alive, and Dulcie loved it.

The sound of an old-fashioned telephone ringer broke her reverie, and Dulcie put the phone up to her ear. 'Chris?'

'Why? Is he in trouble?' The voice on the other end rose in concern.

'Hi, Lucy.' Dulcie rarely called her mother by anything but her first name, but that didn't stop her mother from worrying about her only child. 'No, everything's fine.'

'And you two?' Lucy paused, and Dulcie imagined she could hear the wind through the trees. In truth, Lucy would probably be calling from the commune's kitchen, since the eco-friendly yurt they had shared didn't have a phone. But whenever Dulcie thought of her home, she thought of the great, stately pines that had served as her first study hall.

'We're fine.' Dulcie paused. Knowing her mother wanted her to ask didn't make it any easier. 'Why? What's up?'

'Nothing, dear.' Dulcie could hear her mother fussing with something. Had she called while cooking? 'Nothing important.'

'Mom . . .' Lucy Schwartz undoubtedly missed her daughter, but her means of expressing her empty-nest loneliness could be annoying at times. 'Did you have another dream? Did Karma see something in the I Ching?' Another silence. 'Were you two doing peyote again?'

'It's a vision quest, dear. When you say it like that, it sounds somewhat tawdry.'

Dulcie waited. If Chris was trying to reach her, she'd hear the call-waiting tone and cut her mother short.

'I think of it as assisted dreaming, really. Castaneda wrote quite a bit about it back in the seventies, Dulcie. Don't you remember any of your early reading? I could send you his books.'

'Lucy, I'm waiting for a call from Chris.' Also, she realized as her stomach growled, she was hungry. 'And this must be costing you a fortune. Was there something you needed to tell me? I can call you back tonight—'

'No, no, tonight we've got our circle. It's the full moon, you know.' Dulcie didn't. In the city, she tended to lose track of the lunar calendar. 'And now that I have Merlin, I want to make sure I observe the correct ceremonies.'

'Merlin?' Dulcie hesitated. Her mother hadn't had a boyfriend for years. She supposed she ought to be happy for her. 'Is he new to the community?'

'Oh, Jane – Moonthrush – couldn't handle him any more. He hissed and spit at her.'

'Merlin's a cat.' Dulcie found herself smiling. Her mother had a pet!

'In this life.' Lucy was back on solid ground. 'I'm quite sure he's an old soul, though. He has so much to teach me, you know. I've been dreaming, and I'm even thinking of taking out my tarot cards again, which I'm sure came from him. In another century, the authorities would have said he was my familiar. Did you know that as many cats were burned as witches as women were, both in Colonial times and back in England?'

'Yes, actually I did.' Lucy's predilection for books on magic had overlapped with the basic English department curriculum on Puritan New England. 'Let me guess. Is Merlin a black cat?'

'I knew you had the gift! I had my first visions at a much younger age, of course. But your father—'

Dulcie nodded, not really listening. The longer her father was gone, the greater his mythology had grown. Dulcie remembered him as a skinny, nervous man who had left Oregon on a quest, before settling down in an ashram in India. To his ex-wife, Dulcie's mother, he was alternatively a prophet who would one day return or a wandering spirit who had passed through only to give her Dulcie and to teach them both the importance of a female-centered world. As Lucy rambled on about the latest news – apparently a semi-coherent letter had arrived – Dulcie realized that all these interpretations might have some validity.

'Merlin came from him, actually.' Lucy seemed to be winding down. 'He didn't spell it out, but for those of us functioning at this level of consciousness, literal communication is no longer necessary.'

'I'm glad you have a pet, Lucy.' An adult cat, especially, Dulcie thought, remembering Esmé's bad behavior. 'Wait, does Merlin hiss at you?'

'Not at all. I believe he was simply unable to communicate with Moonthrush, and she didn't understand why he wouldn't wear the cute little hat she had made.'

'Poor cat.' Dulcie hadn't meant to speak out loud. She checked her watch; Chris wouldn't have a shift for several hours yet.

'It wasn't only that, dear. He needed to get to me. And last night, he sent me the strangest dream.'

Finally, Dulcie thought. Lucy's calls almost always had a message. After, should she drop by Chris's? Maybe pick up some bagels on the way?

'You see, it's all about commitment. Care and commitment, Dulcie.' Lucy waited, to make sure her daughter had heard her. 'That big black cat sat right on my chest, and he told me that as a teacher, you have to take your responsibilities seriously. And that you could be a great teacher, Dulcie. You. He practically said your name out loud. But you are facing a great danger from someone with commitment issues. From someone tangled up in the idea of love.'

It's empty nest syndrome, Dulcie told herself as she walked across the Yard a few minutes later. She wants me to find myself, to make my mark as a scholar and a teacher. But she's lonely, and she's worried about me. After all, look at how her own marriage turned out.

Our life will be different, she thought as she walked toward the street. But even as she formed the thought, some dark part of her mind countered with a question. *Will it?* After all, both she and Chris were headed toward academic careers, and those were notoriously difficult to plan. What if he won a position at UCLA – and she could only get on the tenure track at Brown or Tulane? The idea of a cross-country romance made her cringe. Would she have to give up her dreams? Would Chris? Was there any sense in staying together now, when in only a few years—

The gust hit her like a slap, fragments of ice and small stones raking across her face like, yes, like claws. And just as suddenly, it was gone. That was March for you: leonine for as long as it could be. Unless . . . Dulcie laughed to herself. Lucy's cat might be speaking directly to her mother, but Mr Grey had his methods, as well. That March wind – that was Mr Grey in action, cutting her off when her emotions threatened to drag her down.

'I'm sorry, Mr Grey,' she said out loud. 'You're right.'

She looked up at a sky that suddenly shone a clear blue. 'I'm just hungry and, well, everything has been freaking me out recently. If I only had the sense of a cat, I'd learn to live in the moment. Not worry so much about love.'

Across the Yard, a cloaked figure froze and turned to stare. It must have been the stillness, the sudden stop, that caught Dulcie's eye, but as she turned, the figure also pivoted, away from her, so that its face was hidden by the deep hood. Well, so she'd been caught talking to herself. Harvard Square was filled with weirdos. Some of them were geniuses, and some of them communed with ghosts.

Dulcie felt her better spirits buoy her up as she made her way down Mass. Ave. It didn't mean anything that Chris hadn't called her back. He'd probably crashed for a few hours of sleep and turned off his own phone. He'd call her when he woke up, and if he didn't ring soon, she'd get his favorite – peanut butter and jelly on a raisin bagel – and surprise him at his place. Yes, she had told Suze she'd go to the police, but in the light of day, she was no longer even sure what she'd seen. The cops probably had hundreds of people calling, people who had real information about the missing girl. Besides, how sweet would it be if, just for once, she and Chris were both more or less awake at the same time? The possibility of a romantic interlude began to take shape in her mind, and she felt herself blushing – and speeding up just a bit on her way to the bagel store. Mr Grey, she was sure, would approve.

Chris must be on her mind, she thought as she queued up to cross the street. For a moment, she almost thought she was seeing him on the other side of the street. Tall and gangly, with straight brown hair that fell over his face in bangs, her beau had a look that wasn't uncommon among the students and bohemians of Cambridge. But that scarf, orange with a black zigzag, seemed familiar, too. It looked like one of Lucy's offerings: the one she had knitted for him during their first visit out West. It would match his aura, Lucy had said: warm and somehow electric.

'Chris?' It was her sweetie, she was sure. And while she couldn't understand why he hadn't returned her call, she was filled with joy. As short as she was, however, joy alone would not catch his eye. 'Yo! Chris!' Dulcie jumped up and waved, earning a nasty look from a large man in a tweed overcoat. 'Sweetie!'

The wind was blowing again, though not with the clawing ferocity of a few minutes earlier. Her words were getting lost. 'Chris Sorenson!'

And with that he turned, prompting Dulcie to squeeze her way past the tweed overcoat and through a gathering of Japanese tourists. 'Chris!'

He was laughing as she made her way through, his wide mouth open in the generous smile she had come to love. 'Dulcie,' he said. But as she drew near, expecting one of his equally generous hugs, she found herself stopping short. Standing to his right, and looking down at her with a frankly critical expression, was a woman about their age. Only, she was as tall as Chris, with the kind of silky auburn hair that Dulcie could only dream about. There were freckles on her cheeks, too, but beyond that, all similarities went out the window. This woman was slender and graceful, and dressed in a camel-hair coat that probably cost more than Dulcie's computer. And she had slipped her hand around Chris's elbow, holding on to the tall geek as if she owned him.

'Chris?' Her mouth suddenly dry, Dulcie didn't know if the word was even audible.

'Dulcie. I thought you'd be stuck tutoring all day.' Chris was still smiling. Dulcie looked from his face down to his arm. The hand had been withdrawn, but she could picture it: kid-leather glove and all.

'I had a cancellation.' She choked out the words. 'I called you.'

'I've had my phone off.' He was talking as if it were the most natural thing in the world. 'I was trying to get Rusti through her fractals program, and we were both having trouble concentrating.'

*I'll bet.* The words came unbidden, and Dulcie bit her lip. 'Rusti?' She'd heard the name. Knew that Chris had taken on a private student to earn some extra money. 'I assumed . . . with the name . . .'

'Ah, you thought that anybody looking to place into Applied Math would be male, didn't you?' His smile was broader now, and Dulcie's heart jumped just a bit. He didn't seem to be taking this seriously. She had made a silly – a *sexist* – assumption.

She shrugged. 'I guess I did. Glad to meet you.' She held

out a mittened hand and waited while Chris's student reached to shake it. Was there a slight hesitation? Dulcie couldn't trust herself to judge.

'Charmed.' The tall woman had a slight twang to her voice. Alabama? Texas? Somewhere warm, that was for sure. Somewhere where sports were important. 'You must be the girlfriend.'

'Yup.' Dulcie knew she was nodding like a fool, but she couldn't stop. 'That's me. I, I mean.' She looked from Rusti to her beau, wondering if she could salvage the situation. 'I'd actually just called Chris to see if he wanted to have some lunch. I mean, I have a little time free. Maybe you'd join us?' Her smile was as genuine as she could make it.

'Oh, sweetie, I'm sorry.' Chris seemed to be backing away. It didn't make sense. 'We grabbed a bite at the Bagelry already, and I've booked some time for us in the Science Center. We've got to run. Besides, weren't you going to stop by the university police?'

'Um, yeah.' She choked it out, her smile setting into concrete on her face. 'Call me?'

'Of course.' He bent to kiss her, a quick, almost formal buss. 'Later, Dulce.'

She stood there and watched them cross the street. A matched pair, they bent their heads together. Another wind brought her the sound of a woman's laugh and a small, sharp pain, like tiny kitten teeth sinking into her heart.

# SEVEN

On autopilot, Dulcie headed to Lala's. Bagels had lost their appeal, and now nothing but a three-bean burger with Lala's famous hot sauce would do. If only Chris's student hadn't been so slim. She slid into a seat at the window counter and ordered without thinking. If only Chris's student hadn't had that accent. If only Dulcie hadn't been so preoccupied with Mr Grey and Esmé. She gulped down half her water and nearly choked it back up again. If only she'd been more available.

If only— Dulcie realized she was staring at the window, but not seeing anything. People were walking by, going about their lives. Over by the curb, a couple were holding hands. She looked down to see her burger. She took a bite, barely tasting the spicy sauce. If only she hadn't been so obsessed. With her cats. With her thesis. With an unknown author who'd been dead for two hundred years anyway.

'Tough morning?' Lala herself was standing beside her. 'Because I know that burger isn't as dry as you make it out to be.'

Dulcie swallowed with a start and realized she'd been chewing the same mouthful of burger for several minutes by then. 'No, really. It's great.' She swallowed again as something stuck in her throat.

'Here.' Lala reached over to the counter to hand Dulcie her glass of water, grabbing a handful of napkins as well. 'Wanna come into the back and tell me about it?'

Dulcie blinked and nodded. Why couldn't Lucy be like this?

'We can take your burger.' Lala reached for the cardboard platter, and Dulcie turned to hand it to her. But as she did, her eye was caught by an olive-green cape, its hood up, moving like a specter along the curb. And right beside it, Dulcie recognized her student, Corkie. The junior was easily a head taller than the figure beside her and clearly visible, talking a mile a minute and waving her hands.

Dulcie stood up to watch as her student stopped at the corner, still gesticulating. As more pedestrians gathered, waiting for the walk signal, Dulcie could see the top of Corkie's head and, occasionally, her hands. She probably hadn't checked her email yet.

'You OK, honey?' A blast of horn. Someone had run into the street.

'What? Oh, yes, thank you, Lala.' She looked up at the kindly face of the chef, and then back out the window. The light had changed, but she could still make out Corkie, her sleek brown hair pulled back in its customary bun. In a moment, she'd disappear, beyond Dulcie's reach. 'But I think I've got to get one thing right today.' She shrugged her coat over her shoulders and headed to the door.

'Hang on!' Lala shoved a hastily wrapped package into

her hands, the paper bag already turning translucent from the dripping sauce. 'Go get him!'

Dulcie didn't bother to correct her, but with a smile and a nod, pushed her way through a waiting group and out on to the street. But she had lost her.

'Corkie?' Dulcie called and heard her own voice thrown back by the wind. 'Corkie? Philomena McCorkle!' A couple in front of her turned, and Dulcie ignored them. Couples! 'Corkie?'

The light was in her favor, and Dulcie crossed, heading toward the Yard. Too late, she saw that the olive cape – a woman, it had to be a woman – was far down the sidewalk, making for the Coop or the T station beside it. Dulcie stopped in mid crosswalk and watched the green hood recede, trying to make out if Corkie was still with her.

'Lady!' The light had changed, and a cyclist maneuvered around her, his mood clearly not improved by the mud splattered all over his legs. 'Get out of the way!'

Dulcie jumped, landing on what appeared to be solid, gray pavement until her foot sank into it up to the ankle. Slush: the scourge of March. Shaking her foot free of the clinging, dirty ice, she made her way to the opposite side of the street.

'Watch it!' Another pedestrian knocked into her, and with a splash, she dropped the paper-wrapped burger that Lala had hurried to wrap for her. She looked down in time to see it run over, its orange-red sauce seeping out of the paper like blood. The final straw. Her foot was wet and cold. Her boyfriend AWOL. Her favorite student seemed to consider Dulcie's best efforts to keep her on track expendable. And now her lunch was roadkill. Dulcie bit her lip and fought back a sudden rush of tears. It didn't work, and she found herself blinking up at the sky until she could regain control.

Or be distracted. Sometimes, in the gray winter sky, she'd see one of the red-tailed hawks that had repatriated Cambridge. They made a majestic sight, like something that would have circled Hermetria's remote castle keep. Lonely, proud, and strong.

Today, though, the sky was empty of everything but mottled clouds. A depressing sky, good for nothing but hiding from. Or, Goddess forbid – at times of stress, Dulcie always heard Lucy's voice – snow.

Pulling her collar tighter, Dulcie plodded through the yard. The toes on her left foot were half numb, but she had dry socks in her office. If she put her boot up on the radiator, maybe she could dry out the worst of it before heading home.

Head down, to avoid any further mishaps, she made her way across the icy yard. Would this winter never end? But as she emerged near the Science Center, a flash – like a fleeting shadow – caused her to look up. Could it be one of the hawks? She never found out. For not fifty yards ahead, she spied Corkie, making her way up a side street to the new psych annex.

'Corkie!' The younger girl had a lead, as well as the advantage of longer legs, and Dulcie lost her in the crowd milling in front of the new building. The fountains had been turned off for the season, of course, but as Dulcie trotted across the stone courtyard, leaving dark, wet footsteps in her wake, she couldn't help but feel a bit resentful. The humanities never got new buildings. The English department in particular had had to lobby non-stop simply to have the roof of its departmental offices repaired. Martin Thorpe had been saving up mildewed theses for months to show the comptroller.

'Corkie?' A church tower tolled the hour, and the students scattered. Anyone heading back to the Square would have to hustle. Inside the glass-fronted lobby, Dulcie saw a coat and a door. An elevator. She was no longer sure it was her student, but followed anyway. At least she'd be warm.

'May I help you?' The guard looked Dulcie up and down with a skeptical eye.

'My student, Philomena McCorkle? Did you see her go by?' At the end of the lobby, one of the elevator doors closed.

'Your ID, please?' With a ping, the elevator began to ascend. 'Miss?'

At least he was being polite, but Dulcie could not resist a heavy sigh as she dropped her bag on his desk and began rummaging through it. Why, at times like these, was something as simple as a wallet so hard to find? 'Here.' She smiled in relief.

The guard took his time. 'Go on up,' he said finally, sounding resigned as he waved her by. But before she could get to the bank of elevators, before she could even begin to guess which floor her student had chosen, or why, a dull thud made them both turn. A truck going over a pothole, Dulcie told herself. Someone rough-housing into the glass. Or—

The afternoon was shattered by a piercing shriek.

'What the?' The guard turned toward the doors, one hand on the phone, the other on what looked like a baton at his waist.

'Corkie?' It didn't make sense, but Dulcie was suddenly seized by a horrible premonition. Her student was in danger. Her student was hurt. Her student – her charge, a young woman she should have taken better care of . . .

'It's Fritz!' A young woman ran in, eyes wild. 'Fritz Herschoft! He's jumped out of a top-floor window!'

# EIGHT

What happened next was a blur of noise and confusion. Unlike the multi-storey buildings in the modernistic science complex, the Poche Building didn't have special locks and alarms. It wasn't a skyscraper. It wasn't even that big. But, at seven stories, it must have been tall enough.

Trapped inside the glass foyer by the horror outside, Dulcie found herself slinking back. Until she came to the elevators. No, she didn't want to go there. Not up. Not now. Although she didn't have a clear sense of the man who had jumped, she felt the shock of his fall. What would make someone do that? Who was Fritz Herschoft? Who had he been?

Even as her mind reeled, she found herself thinking of a young professor, barely more than a TA. He'd had glasses and thick, dark hair that for some reason she thought of as greasy. He'd built a name for himself – something about the attention he gave his students – but when Dulcie tried to conjure an image, she remembered an ugly man, short, plump, and beetle-like. No, that wasn't fair. It wasn't his fault if his hair was greasy or his hands clammy.

Dulcie drew back her own hands, automatically, as if afraid to touch a memory, and dropped her bag. Bending to pick it up, she was jostled, as the elevator bays began disgorging the building's inhabitants. Somewhere, an alarm had gone off. She couldn't think about the dead professor now. She had come here for a reason. But even as dizziness threatened to overcome her, Dulcie kept enough of her mind focused to watch. Students, researchers. A coterie of lab techs, all still wearing their safety glasses, came down, alerted by the sirens and the panicked screams outside. None of them were Corkie.

Had she been imagining her? Seeing her student in a haze of heartbreak and hot sauce?

'Excuse me.' She pushed her way up to the guard again. In the tumult, he had gained authority. Students pressed against his desk, some crying. But their prior interaction also seemed to have bonded them, and he looked over at her with what could have been a shell-shocked smile. 'Is there another way out of here? A rear exit, perhaps?'

Corkie couldn't have been involved with this. No way. But Dulcie still wanted to talk with her, even if her reasons seemed very remote and far away.

The guard nodded. 'Fire exit around the back. Take the stairwell door to the right there, and follow it down one flight, to street level.' Dulcie grabbed her bag. 'Wait! Miss? The police might want to talk to you.'

Dulcie nodded and hoped she looked reassuring. 'I'll check in with them. I promise.' The guard was behind his desk, and that was surrounded by the crowd. With another nod, Dulcie turned and headed for the door.

Dulcie hadn't realized how tense she had been as she wound down the stairs, along a basement passage, and back up. Not until she shoved open that door and stepped into the alley did she find herself breathing freely. Even the cold seemed welcome. But although the rear of the Poche Building offered a relatively peaceful alternative to the front, it didn't help Dulcie with her search. The sirens were muted back here, contained by the bulk of the building. But even as Dulcie saw people scurrying on the nearby sidewalk, none of them looked like Corkie. She headed for the street and realized that a dumpster had obscured her view of the crowd.

'Corkie?' There was no way anyone in the milling throng could have heard her. The buzz from the crowd was loud. At least one woman was sobbing. 'Corkie?'

People were moving in panic, some running away. Others, confused or curious, rushing in. Among the latter, Dulcie noticed a small figure, slight, in olive green, jostling furiously through the crowd.

'Wait!' Dulcie called again. It wasn't her student, Dulcie was sure of that. But her voice seemed to mean something to her, and the woman froze, then turned and disappeared.

'Hey!' Who was that woman, and why did she keep turning up? 'Wait!'

But as Dulcie pushed forward, she found herself running into the yellow reflective arm of an emergency worker.

'Please, miss, step back.' Another yellow jacket – a cop or something like – was herding three other onlookers back. 'We need to clear the area.'

'But I'm looking for someone.' Being short had some advantages: Dulcie ducked under the outstretched arm.

'Miss, please!'

And stopped short. The police hadn't succeeded in entirely clearing the plaza. One young man was leaning against the building's steel pillars, head down with either sorrow or sickness. And a knot of down parkas surrounded another emergency worker, his broad gestures doing little to disperse them. None of them seemed to be wearing that particular shade of green. But just beyond, strangely lonely on the patterned stone pavement, she could see a hand. Palm up, fingers curled, it made the only still point in the whole tableau.

Dulcie gasped. She hadn't thought – not really – what all the hubbub had meant. She hadn't realized. And then she did. The stone of the plaza wasn't patterned. Those two thin stripes, dark against the gray, were too shiny. They were blood.

Back behind the building, Dulcie sat on the curb, gulping in air. Head down, she reminded herself: *breathe*. Her imagination was running wild. Blood? It had looked dark, thick. Shouldn't there have been more? But as she sat there, the horror of what had happened began to sink in. Blood. A body. A member of the university community sprawled on the pavement. Blood.

It was several minutes before her vision cleared. At least she hadn't finished her lunch.

It was cold, sitting on the curb, but Dulcie didn't quite trust her legs. Instead, she dialed Chris's number.

'Chris?' His voicemail seemed so distant. 'There's been an accident.' No, that was wrong. 'An incident. Call me?' She hung up before she could start to cry. Mr Grey, that's who she needed. But although she could picture the gray cat, she knew she couldn't summon him. Increasingly, in fact, he had only made his presence felt back at her apartment, when she was on the edge of sleep.

Sleep. Dulcie knew her nerves were too jangled, but the idea of crawling into bed with the kitten beckoned. Or maybe just a cuddle on the couch, a mug of hot cocoa, and warm, clean socks. Thinking of Esmé, of how her cat could distract her, was comforting. Maybe it was time to unveil the felt mice Lucy had sent, the ones stuffed with home-grown catnip.

Lucy. Dulcie had a sudden strong urge to call her mother. To tell her everything. But, no. Lucy's heart was in the right place, and Dulcie knew her mother loved her. But she'd muck this all up with her mongrel mysticism. What Dulcie didn't need right now was the kind of advice her mother would give, about karma and the circle of life. Likewise, there was no way she was going to gather sage and charcoal now, not to make a circle around the Poche Building. Not to exorcize a spirit who had, she hoped, already gone on to better things.

Speaking of moving on, Dulcie noticed how the damp of the curb had begun to seep through her jeans. Her nausea had abated. It was time to get going. Home. The kitten. Cocoa. One of the emergency vehicles drove past, no lights, no sirens. Well, there was little need for them now. Still, when her cell phone rang, Dulcie jumped.

'Hello?'

'Dulcie, glad I caught you.' She should have looked at the number. She'd hoped for Chris, or some other friend. For Corkie. Even, she admitted, Lucy. Instead, she had Norm Chelowski, her thesis adviser. 'Are you on campus?'

'Well, I was on my way home.' For once, Dulcie wished she found it easier to lie. 'You see, I stepped in a giant puddle and—'

'No problem, then. I've just had a breakthrough that I think might help you with your work. Might help you get back on track. Why don't you come on by now?'

'But, my feet—' She couldn't tell him about the body. The blood.

'I bet Nancy has a towel. Maybe even some extra socks. See you in a few.' He hung up, leaving Dulcie with no recourse except to call him back and explain – or to meet with him. Neither had any appeal, not when home and a kitten waited.

But the little clapboard building had been her shelter before, and it was closer than her Central Square apartment. Besides, Dulcie told herself as she plodded down the street, even Norm Chelowski couldn't make things any worse. Could he?

# NINE

At least Nancy got it. As soon as Dulcie walked into the departmental offices, the motherly secretary took one look at her and bustled her into a chair. She had heard the news – a university-wide text blast had gone out announcing the closure of the building, and the student network had quickly filled in the rest.

'You poor dear.' She pushed a mug into Dulcie's hands and wrapped her own sweater around Dulcie's shoulders. From where she was sitting, Dulcie could just see the note board. A flier advertising a futon had gone up in the last twenty-four hours, its banner headline – pillows included! – covered the bottom of Carrie Mines' face.

'Thanks, Nancy.' Dulcie grasped the mug tightly, hoping to still her shaking hands. On the wall, Carrie Mines' eyes looked out, wide and surprised.

Nancy tut-tutted. 'I'm only sorry I don't have something stronger to add to that.'

'There you are!' Norm Chelowski appeared in the doorway, ducking his head as he always did to avoid hitting the lintel. 'You wouldn't believe what I just saw.'

The phrasing, his voice, sent a wave of nausea over Dulcie. She closed her eyes and leaned back in the chair.

'Norm, can't you tell she's had a shock?' Nancy's warm hand made Dulcie aware of how cold she felt, as well. 'She's shivering.'

'A little distraction will be just the thing.' Norm smiled as he shrugged off his own coat. It was an odd smile, slightly too wide to look natural. 'Shall we?' He held out one pale hand, and Dulcie winced.

'Norm.' Nancy hustled the balding man off into a corner, leaving Dulcie to nestle into the sweater. It smelt of Nancy's perfume. Sweet, a little old-ladyish, and comforting. From the opposite side of the room, she overheard the word 'shock' again, along with 'witness' and 'incident.' When Norm looked back at her, his interest seemed more genuine. At least the weird grin was gone.

'Oh my, you have had a day, haven't you?'

It wasn't a question, but Dulcie nodded.

'But since we're both here . . .'

If Nancy could have leveled the man with her eyes, she would have. Dulcie felt her gathering her resources for a fight.

'I'm OK, Nancy.' She stood up, still cradling the mug. 'I'll be OK.' She handed the scented sweater back to the secretary and immediately regretted it.

'You keep that.' Nancy pushed it back. 'You can give it back to me when you leave.' With a parting shot at Norm, she relinquished her charge, and Dulcie followed her adviser up the stairs.

'I've been in the library all day, but Nancy told me what happened.' He'd settled into his seat. Behind him, Dulcie could see the Poche. She closed her eyes and tried to breathe.

'Sorry, sorry.' He got up and pulled on a cord. The shade stuck halfway down, and he fussed with it for a moment, finally bunching his coat up on the sill.

He was hopeless, Dulcie realized. Forget the weasel. This man had the social graces of a reptile, but he was her thesis adviser. For the first time in a while, she thought fondly of her first adviser. Professor Bullock had had his own problems, and plenty of them. But at least the ancient professor had a kind of old-world gallantry. 'Pretty bad, huh? Have they released any information?'

She shook her head, avoiding even an explanation. If he wanted information, he could join the twenty-first century and get text updates like everyone else. 'You said you found something that would relate to my thesis?'

'Oh, I did. I do.' He reached into a canvas book bag and

pulled out a handful of Xeroxes. 'It's lucky I caught you today.'

She really was going to lose it, but he pushed the papers toward her until she made herself reach for them. They were copies of broadsheets, the type smudged and archaic. 'I'm sorry, Mr Chelowski. I don't understand.'

'The New World, Ms Schwartz! That's your missing piece!' He pointed at one of the pages and pushed it closer to her.

She shook her head slowly. The papers in front of her weren't that hard to read, not for a scholar. She just had to focus. She read the masthead, making out the words: *Philadelphia* and *Evening Standard*.

'Your radical theories? Your missing author? You've just been too narrow in your focus. Read those. Look at the dates.'

She did: 1801, 1802. 'These are later, and they're American.' Her head was not working. 'They're not by the author of *The Ravages*.'

'Of course they're not by her!' Chelowski shook his head at her confusion. 'But they're not that much later, Ms Schwartz. And if you check out what they say, you'll see many of the same ideas.'

Dulcie tried to read – *A woman, when educated, gifts to her children a bounty more to be priz'd than jewels* – but Chelowski kept talking.

'It's all the same ideas, Ms Schwartz, and they are all over the American press. The period after the Revolution and before the War of 1812 saw a flowering of ideas – all those radical émigrés, all that New World opportunity as trade reopened. Your author may have had some minor literary merit in her day, but as you can see from these essays, she was hardly a revolutionary thinker. Her colleagues across the Atlantic were writing along the same lines, more freely even. Therefore, your author would not have been murdered or hushed up or what have you. There'd be no reason! She probably lost her publishers as the New World became ascendant, and then faded away. *Quod erat demonstrandum!*'

He wasn't making sense. None of this was making sense. And to top it off, her chills were getting worse. She closed her eyes and felt the building sway. 'I'm sorry, Mr Chelowski. I don't understand.'

'Of course, of course. The day you've had.' He was standing

beside her now, pulling the papers toward her and patting them into a pile. 'I shouldn't have pressed you to meet with me today, but I wanted to finally put that silly idea to rest. Are you capable of walking home? Should we call a taxi for you?'

It was an out. But if the author of *The Ravages* wasn't exactly original, she also didn't believe in fainting heroines. 'I'm fine. It was just the shock.' She would leave with dignity. She put the papers into her bag and stood up. The room regained its mooring. Still, she let him help her on with her coat.

'Must have been horrible. Horrible,' he said as he held the door. 'I guess it's not a surprise, though. Psychology and all.' Curiosity got the better of her, and she turned to face him. He was grinning again, that weird, self-satisfied grin. 'Nobody in *our* department ever defenestrated themselves.'

Dulcie made it to the curb before she lost what little lunch she'd eaten, the shadow of the Poche Building adding to the late winter chill.

# TEN

Sometimes the modern world simply wasn't worth it. All Dulcie wanted was to get home, to crawl into bed, and to dream of nothing but cats. If Mr Grey was looking for a moment to comfort her, this would be it, she thought as she dragged herself toward home.

Instead, her phone rang. It was Suze, calling from work, but at least she provided Dulcie with a chance to unload.

'It was horrible, Suze. You can't imagine.' She wanted to think that the silence on the line was sympathy, but her room-mate had been so busy recently, she couldn't be sure. 'You there?'

'Yeah, I am. It does sound awful. I wish—' Dulcie heard voices and knew what was coming next. 'I wish I could get home and see you.'

'It's OK.' For all her misery, just hearing her friend's voice helped. 'At least you're not gloating, like Chelowski.'

'Why did he insist on seeing you right then anyway? You don't think—' Suze said something else, but it was eaten up by the sound of traffic. Dulcie didn't want to stop walking, and so she put one hand up over her ear.

'I don't know, Suze. He's just an odd duck, and when he wants to meet with me, he calls. But it was weird, like he felt superior because it hadn't happened to someone in English. Like it was something that would reflect badly on the department.'

'It might, actually. I mean, from what I heard, Fritz Herschoft was a rising star in developmental psyche. Everyone expected him to get tenure, and I gather most of his students loved him.'

'Love—' Dulcie sidestepped as a couple, oblivious to their surroundings, made their way down the sidewalk. 'Just goes to show, love isn't always enough.'

'Uh oh.' Suze knew Dulcie well enough to ask. 'Is this about Chris's hours?'

'It's not just the hours, Suze.' Dulcie paused. It had been only a short while since she'd seen Chris with his student. His tall, slim, red-haired student. Her head began to spin again.

'I wonder why he did it.' Suze's voice broke through the fog.

'Maybe it was just lunch. I mean, I'd said I was busy.'

'What?'

Dulcie shook her head to clear it. 'Sorry, you're talking about Herschoft?' In some ways, it was easier than thinking about Chris.

'Uh huh, and about what your jerk of an adviser was saying. Maybe it *was* something to do with the department. I mean, maybe he was in some kind of trouble.'

Trouble. 'Would have to be pretty bad to push him that far.' What had people been talking about? 'Suze, you think maybe he was the Harvard Harasser? Maybe somebody knew and was threatening to expose him?'

'Could be.' Suze sounded thoughtful. 'Or maybe it was getting worse, and he couldn't stop himself.'

Dulcie cringed, and as she did, she remembered a pair of eyes wide set – perhaps in fear. 'Suze, did you think this has anything to do with the missing girl, Carrie Mines?'

'Carrie who?' With a start, Dulcie realized that she hadn't

talked to her room-mate since the night before. Their dinner together – and their warm apartment – seemed light years away. Picking up the pace, she filled in her room-mate on the morning meeting and the flier on the departmental bulletin board.

'And the photo – I'm pretty sure it was the girl I saw yelling at that guy, under the arch.'

'Well, what did the cops think?' Dulcie didn't answer, and Suze knew her friend well enough to know what that meant. 'Dulcie,' she said with a bit too much emphasis. 'I thought you were going to go tell the cops what you saw.' Suze sounded a bit short. She was at work, after all.

'Suze, please.' Dulcie was embarrassingly close to tears. 'I just didn't have time, and the way my day went . . .' She paused, remembering. 'Actually, I was about to, but then I'd seen this student of mine, who had sort of blown me off—'

'So, you haven't.' The line grew noisy, and Dulcie heard someone calling her room-mate's name. Suze was losing patience. 'Did you say anything to them, you know, at the Poche?'

Dulcie paused on the sidewalk to catch her breath. 'Suze, I left. I mean, before the cops got to me.'

Silence. Dulcie wasn't sure if her room-mate was disgusted or just dealing with another emergency. 'I mean, they don't know who I am.'

'Didn't the guard log you in?' Suze came back loud and clear.

'Well, he looked at my ID.' Dulcie tried to recall if the guard had written anything down.

'I know that guy, he's a gorgon. You better go; you don't want them thinking anything.

'But I was in the lobby when he— When it happened.'

'You were in the lobby desperately trying to get upstairs.'

Dulcie swallowed, the weight of the day sinking in. 'Suze, would you go with me?'

'Oh, honey, I wish I could but . . .' It was the same story she'd been hearing for months now. Work, work, work. And besides, she was an adult, wasn't she? As Dulcie passed through Central Square, Suze rang off, leaving her alone in the center of the city.

\*    \*    \*

It was with great relief that Dulcie finally labored up her own front steps and into the apartment. Closing the door behind her, she leaned back and took a deep breath. She'd made it, for what that was worth. If she could only get up the stairs to the kitchen, she could make herself a cup of tea and fall asleep on the couch. Sleep would probably be the only comfort she'd get tonight.

As if on cue, Esmé's face appeared at the top of the stairs. 'Meh?' she asked, and Dulcie did her best to smile.

Without waiting for more of an invitation, the kitten trundled down to greet her. She was learning to handle the apartment's stairs, Dulcie noted, bouncing down them without tumbling much.

'So, what's up, little one?' As soon as the words were out of her mouth, Dulcie starting tearing up. 'Little one.' That's what Mr Grey called her. Mr Grey, the real cat of her heart. But before she could sink any further into that particular black hole, Esmé responded, reaching up to sink her claws into Dulcie's leg.

'No! Bad kitty.' The prick of the kitten's claws hurt, but as Dulcie reached down for her, she also realized that she'd needed the distraction. 'Did you do that on purpose, Esmé?'

The kitten only looked at her and blinked, and Dulcie held her small body up to her face, snuggling close, and then carried her up the stairs.

'If only I could understand you.' Dulcie collapsed on the sofa and set the kitten down beside her as she stripped off her wet footgear. Jumping to the floor, the kitten bounced around and then flopped on to her back, exposing her white belly. It was too irresistible, even for an exhausted scholar, and so Dulcie slid to the floor to play. But when she reached to pet the downy fur, the tiny beast grabbed Dulcie's hand and bit. Hard.

'Ow!' Esmé looked up, unfazed, at Dulcie's shout. This time, she hadn't needed the pain. 'Bad!'

But even as she shook her finger at the little cat, white paws reached up to pull her hand back. Dulcie sat back, exasperated. 'My finger is not a cat toy, Esmé.' The little cat tilted her head, looking for all the world like she was trying to understand. 'Mr Grey –' Dulcie addressed the air above her – 'what am I supposed to do with this cat?'

But no answer was forthcoming – not that Dulcie could hear, anyway. And, lying back on the sofa, she fell asleep.

# ELEVEN

*Writing, writing still. Outside, it is dark, but there is no rest to be had this night. Instead, there is pressure. The wind rattles the panes, desperate to get in. Reaching for her, threatening to flood o'er all. The storm is only one more sign of all that looms over her, of all the forces aligned against her. She must finish, and soon. The woman at the desk works furiously, her pen scratching away. Suddenly, a huge peal of thunder causes her to jump. The ink blots. It is too much. She puts down her pen and buries her face in her hands. This is not what she wanted, but she sees no choice. Reaching for her knife, she takes up her quill again. One swipe, two, sharpening the edge. Thunder again, louder than before. Despite herself, she jumps. The sharp blade knicks her finger, but the pain is good. It forces her to focus. She must get back to work. Soon, she knows, she must leave it all.*

The sound of the wind woke her, rattling the window like an angry spirit. Dulcie sat up and realized she'd been asleep on the sofa for hours. Her socks had dried, more or less, but her neck had a crick in it that made turning around painful. And the taste in her mouth was hideous. She'd been dreaming, she knew, but the specifics eluded her. The woman at the desk. A woman at risk. The storm. She didn't know if this was about her author any more or herself. Or the missing girl – the one she'd seen only briefly, in the dark, before she'd disappeared.

Upstairs, a floorboard creaked. 'Suze?' Something about the house was too still. Too quiet. Her room-mate hadn't come home. Dulcie had no real reason to worry. These days, Suze barely stopped by, using the apartment only as a base between her crazy hours and Ariano's place. The floor creaked again, and she started to worry anyway.

'Esmé?' As quietly as she could, Dulcie got to her feet and

slowly, step by step, made her way to the stairwell. 'Mr Grey?' She mouthed the words silently. 'Is that you?'

Dulcie had always thought she loved privacy. Growing up in the arts colony, time alone had been rare, and she'd lived for those afternoons when she could escape to the woods with a book and an apple. But that had been a different kind of solitude. A country solitude. Peaceful with the company of nature. Things were different in the city. Thoughts of the strange attacks on campus, of the missing girl . . . Of a young professor driven to desperation . . . It all made the dark apartment suddenly foreign. The quiet, menacing. 'Esmé?'

And then with a sudden thud and rattle, the kitten came bounding down the stairs, moving so quickly that she ended with a somersault at Dulcie's feet.

'Mew!' The bright yellow-green eyes looked as surprised as Dulcie felt, and Dulcie burst out laughing as the energetic little animal raced back up the stairs, desperate to conquer whatever had caught her fancy. Leaning heavily against the wall, Dulcie heard her careening around. That must have been what woke her, she realized. In a way it was a blessing. Yawning, she felt her neck crack. She'd do better sleeping in her own bed, particularly once she brushed her teeth.

Above her, another soft mew sounded, and Dulcie waited for the next thud – or the sounds of breaking pottery or glass. 'At least she hasn't injured herself,' she muttered to the air.

Unless— The sight of the little kitten tumbling down the stairs brought back the scene at the Poche, and Dulcie had to close her eyes. It was ridiculous. Esmé was a healthy young cat. She just needed to be trained. Dulcie was a teacher, wasn't she? And the thought hit her. Maybe that was why the authorities were looking for Carrie Mines. Maybe that was what that fight had been about. Maybe the girl was at risk of hurting herself. Now she was missing. . . . The girl had been a sophomore, according to the poster. Still new to the city, to the university. Probably not even twenty years old.

From Dulcie's own undergraduate days, she knew the confusion, the disorientation that could throw students – freshmen particularly – into a funk. For her, the academic pressure had been welcome. After the artificially non-judgmental atmosphere of the arts colony, it was kind of nice to have someone tell her to work harder. Nobody on the commune had ever given Dulcie a B-minus, and she had relished the challenge of getting that grade up to an A. But the social pressure – that had been unpleasant. Looking around to realize that her Indian print skirts and home-knit sweaters were not the norm. Hearing the giggles as she went to her first house social in a tie-dyed wrap dress. She'd had Suze then as a support – both to guide her to some of the more budget-conscious boutiques in the Square and to get her to laugh at the most outrageous of the preppies. Did Carrie have someone like that? In the back of her mind, Dulcie vaguely recalled that someone she knew worked as a peer counselor. Try as she might, she couldn't remember who, though. Was there somebody else she should call? Suze had wanted Dulcie to go to the cops. Well, she would. First thing in the morning.

As she brushed her teeth, Dulcie checked her phone. Chris had called, hours before. He'd be up – working. Or so he'd said. Dulcie paused with her finger on the callback button. It had only been lunch with a student. She should trust him, she knew that. But right now, she was too tired to think straight. And if there was bad news – if – it could wait till morning. With a sigh, she slipped on her old flannel nightgown and climbed into bed. She could hear Esmé on the stairs and was pleasantly surprised when she felt the kitten jump up beside her, even when she started washing right by her ear. 'Good kitten. You'll learn.' She couldn't be bothered to reach for the kitten, and simply hoped that the small beast would settle down. 'Won't you?'

'*She will, little one. She will.*' But Dulcie was already asleep.

The rest of her night was blessedly dreamless, and Dulcie woke with a sense of purpose. Carrie. The cops. And, realizing that she'd checked her phone, but not her email, Dulcie booted up her little laptop and searched through the usual spam. Nothing from Corkie. She was going to have to keep after that girl. But there was one real message in the in-box, and the sender was one CMines.

*Thx for asking*, *I'm fine*, it read, and the flood of relief that swept over Dulcie was matched only by her gratitude that the young woman had indeed left the department. Email grammar, such as it was, was another reason she preferred the phone. *Boyfriend trble :)*

'Boyfriend trouble?' Dulcie turned toward Esmé, but if the kitten had any answers, she wasn't sharing. 'That could mean anything from a missed birthday to a real fight.' The smiley face, she knew, was supposed to reassure her. But memories of the confrontation in the archway weren't so easily dismissed. 'Boyfriend trouble' could be dangerous. As she dressed, Dulcie mulled over whether to respond. Better not, at least until she'd spoken with the police, she decided. At her feet, the kitten looked up with anticipation.

'You want me to play, don't you?' Dulcie smiled and reached to pet the smooth black head. Her pet had successfully distracted her from the horror of the day before, but today was a new day. 'I'm sorry, Esmé, I've got work to do.'

The kitten looked up, quizzical, as Dulcie pulled her gloves on. As tempting as it was to remain with the kitten, Dulcie donned her coat. She felt rested and ready, relieved to finally be going to the police. Yes, Carrie had emailed her back and that was great. But for whatever reason, the police wanted to know about her. Dulcie had information, and maybe she could put a few minds at rest.

Speaking of inner peace, her own was next on the list. After the cops, she would call Chris and arrange to get together. Suze was right; his hours were taking a toll on their relationship. Chris needed to work, but Dulcie had to make him sit down and talk with her, too. She wasn't the jealous type, usually, but she was having a rough time and that made her more vulnerable. They'd both seen too many couples torn apart by the pressures of academia: Trista and Jerry flashed through her mind, and she swept thoughts of her friends aside. She and Chris were solid. They would make it. They only needed to clear the air. A talk and a little time together would clear everything up.

'Wish me luck, kitty,' she called as she descended the stairs, a spring in her step. 'I'm going to set everything on the table today. And to start with, I'm going to the cops.'

The kitten didn't say anything, not that she heard. But as she locked the door behind her, Dulcie glanced up the stairs. At the top, a black and white face was staring down, the yellow-green eyes wide with concern.

# TWELVE

The castle keep loomed large and gray. Its stone walls impenetrable, even to the biting wind. But as Dulcie approached the university police headquarters, a skinny redhead bolted ahead of her to hold the glass door open. And the imposing fortress was breached.

'Hey, you're Dulcie Schwartz, aren't you?' The redhead towered over Dulcie by at least a foot. 'I heard you speak on conventions of metaphor and the pathetic fallacy. You were great.'

Dulcie colored slightly. The talk had been a small affair, one of a series encouraged by the department for students with theses in process. To Dulcie, it had been a bit of a coming out, her chance to defend some of her more original theories about *The Ravages of Umbria* even before she really got started writing. 'You did? I mean, thanks.'

The redhead smiled, making dimples in his freckled cheeks. 'My pleasure.' He held out a hand. 'Merv, Merv Copeland.'

'Merv?' Something must have showed in her face, because the smile grew wider still.

'Yeah, I know. Just think of the old TV guy.'

'Hey, my full name is Dulcinea.' It felt good to make a full confession. 'My mom, well, she's basically a hippy. A hippy with a lit degree.'

'Peace, love, and Cervantes?'

'Kind of.' Dulcie realized that she was grinning back, and that they were both standing in a large anteroom, obstructing traffic. 'I'm sorry. I'm keeping you.'

'Hey, I interrupted you. So, uh, ladies first.' He half bowed, and Dulcie felt her cheeks getting redder. Still, after as gracious a curtsy as she could manage, Dulcie walked by him and up to a large woman in uniform behind a desk marked 'Information.' Around her, flat-screen displays blinked and glowed.

'Can I help you?'

Dulcie winced. This was a university, after all. Shouldn't the employees know the difference between 'can' and 'may'?

'Yes, please,' she said, rearranging her face. 'I'd like to speak to someone about the missing student?'

'You have information?' The woman's eagerness won Dulcie's forgiveness.

'Just a little,' she said with regret. The more she thought about the missing girl, the more she worried. Boyfriend trouble, indeed. 'I saw her two nights ago, I think. And, well, I may have seen something going on.'

'Hang on, please.' The woman turned and shouted: 'Gary!' So much for high-tech communications. 'Detective Rogovoy will be with you in a minute.'

In less time than that, Dulcie was startled to see a large creature lumbering toward her. Man-shaped, if you didn't count the nose, it waddled across the room, and Dulcie revised her initial impression. This wasn't a castle. It was a fortress, ready for war. And the creature approaching her was an ogre. She half expected him to growl.

'Miss?' The hand that reached out to her was certainly paw-like, large and lined, but the voice was soft. Blinking, she refined her opinion again, nodding to the tired-looking middle-aged man who ushered Dulcie around the front desk. 'Come with me, please, miss.'

She started to talk, but he was already walking. Although portly, his pants tight around his waist and hips, he moved fast, and Dulcie struggled to keep up. At the end of a long hall, he opened a door. Dulcie looked in and saw a battered table and four chairs. There was no window, and the harsh lighting made the room look a little like a cell. Maybe her initial fantasy hadn't been that far off. Ogre or man? She hesitated as he held the door for her. The detective waved her in with the folder, his voice still soft. 'Miss?'

She went in and watched as he put a leatherette folder on the table and then took a seat. With a slight shudder of trepidation, she sat in the chair opposite.

'So, you think you saw something?' Now that they were away from the bustle of the reception area, she heard the Boston accent in his voice, a brassiness that accented the first verb so strongly that Dulcie knew he doubted her.

'Well, I'm not sure. I've been doing research into another disappearance, and my boyfriend tells me I've got murder on my mind.' She was going on, she knew it. The cop – and this room – had flustered her. She should never have allowed herself that fantasy.

'Murder? You have something to tell me? There's been another disappearance?'

'No, no, nothing new.' He was looking at her, waiting. 'I mean, the disappearance that I was studying happened about two hundred years ago. If it happened at all.'

'All right, then.' The detective slid back his chair as if he were going to get up.

'But, no, I do have something current. I saw Carrie Mines. I saw a fight.' That got his attention. 'I mean, I think what I saw was a fight. An argument, really.'

'You saw the missing woman fighting with someone?'

She nodded.

'All right, let's start at the beginning.'

And so she did, explaining her distracted state as she left Widener and her initial reluctance to interrupt what she'd first thought was a romantic interlude. Only when the portly detective waved his hand did she realize that, once again, she was embellishing a story.

'It was probably around four, maybe a little later. It was getting dark.' She mentally kicked herself. Specifics were key. She was a scholar; she knew that. She should stick with what she knew for a fact. 'I didn't get a long or a close look at her, but I am pretty sure Carrie was who I saw.' On point at last, she ran through what she had seen the night before. 'And she yelled something. "No" or "I won't do it," or something. And she shoved him off her and ran away.'

'And you didn't get a look at the man?'

'No.' She shook her head, and another thought hit her. 'But this was just Monday, late afternoon. I didn't even know she was missing till Tuesday, till yesterday. And, well, this morning I found out she's fine.'

'Oh?' From the look he gave her, Dulcie realized she should have started with her latest news.

'Yes, well, I think she is.' Quickly, Dulcie explained about emailing the student. 'And her response said she was fine, but that she was having "boyfriend trouble."' She paused. 'So, well, I guess maybe that was her boyfriend I saw her with. And maybe it's nothing serious. But, well, have you tried to email her?'

He ignored her question. 'You've been in contact with a missing student, and you didn't think to let us know until now? You wouldn't happen to have that email with you, would you?'

A bit taken aback, Dulcie pulled her laptop from her bag. She hadn't thought of showing it to the police, but then, she hadn't thought she'd have to defend her actions either. While the computer started up, she kept talking. 'I only just saw that she'd gotten back to me this morning.' The program opened, and she clicked over to email. Detective Rogovoy didn't have to see her latest collection of cat picture screen-savers. 'Here.' She turned the laptop toward the burly man. He reached for the keyboard, and she winced. That got her a look, and she bit her lip until he stopped typing and reached for a pen and pad instead.

'Isn't this good news?' she asked. 'I mean, she must have had a fight with her boyfriend and taken off. That's what you're concerned about, right?'

'Not necessarily, Ms Schwartz.' The detective leaned forward again and tapped a few more keys. 'For example, did you notice the date of this response? It's from yesterday. Less than an hour after your initial email.' More key strokes. 'But she's not on the university grid, that's for sure.'

'She's probably over at a friend's house or something.'

He looked up. 'Look, Ms Schwartz, since you do seem to be in touch with her – or with someone using her log on – why don't you help us out here? Why don't you type her another message, asking her to get in touch with me, at this number?' He wrote down ten digits in a blocky hand.

Dulcie looked at the number and at her laptop, which Rogovoy had turned back to her. 'Tell her to call the police?'

'Tell her we want to talk with her. That's all.'

'But she's OK, and—' Dulcie wasn't sure what she'd been about to say. That she wasn't a stool pigeon. That she didn't work for the police. But one look from the hefty detective stopped her.

'Your friend was "OK" yesterday, Ms Schwartz, but now it is today. Please, you have to take me serious here. I'm not at liberty to discuss the circumstances around Ms Mines' disappearance. Let's just say that we are concerned. But the policy with missing adults, and Ms Mines is of legal age, is that we do not investigate unless a family member files a report, which they haven't, or we have reason to believe she is at risk.'

'At risk, like, she might hurt herself?' Dulcie thought of that little smiley face, and of the failings of email.

He nodded.

'But if you thought she'd been . . .' She paused. *Boyfriend trouble*? 'Hurt, or something, then the city police would be involved, too. Right?' Dulcie scanned his face, looking for clues.

'Look, Ms Schwartz.' He leaned in, and she did, too, hoping for a confidence. 'Your name was familiar, so I did some asking around. I know you're a smart girl, and I heard about what happened last summer with your room-mate . . .'

She caught herself nodding and stopped, waiting. She really didn't want to get into those horrible memories. Never again would she rush into a summer sublet.

'So, what part of "I'm not at liberty to discuss the circumstances" don't you understand?' He sat back, and Dulcie made the effort to close her mouth. The heat in her face let her know that she was blushing again, with a vengeance. Her initial impression was correct: the man was an ogre.

But once again, his voice turned soft. 'Miss, I'm sorry, but this really is confidential. And we'd really appreciate you doing us this favor.'

She nodded, appalled at the tears that had suddenly filled her eyes.

'Look, it's OK. I mean, it's probably nothing.' He had dropped his voice. 'This isn't even about her any more, OK?' She nodded. 'There's been another incident, and we just have some questions for her. And even that might not be anything more than what it seems. An accident, maybe. Or a suicide.'

Dulcie swallowed, the tears gone. 'I know about—' She couldn't bring herself to say 'incident.' Such a cold little word. 'About what happened at the Poche Building. I was there. There, too.'

That got the officer's attention. 'You weren't by chance with the recently deceased?'

She shook her head, hoping to shake loose the image. 'No, no. Not at all.' She paused and remembered the guard. Her ID. 'I was in the lobby, looking for one of my students, when, well . . .'

'Did you give a statement to the officer on the scene?'

'No,' she told the floor. 'I needed to leave.' He had to understand, didn't he? After a moment of silence, she looked up. He was still staring at her, his face unreadable. 'But, I'm here now.' She heard the quaver in her voice. 'And I'll do what I can.'

'Thank you, Ms Schwartz. If we can find this girl, she's – well, let's just say we need to talk to her.' He waited, and with a nod, Dulcie reached for the laptop.

*Glad 2 hear it!* That sounded casual, didn't it? *But folks are worried. Call?* She typed in the number, took a deep breath, and hit send.

When she looked up, Detective Rogovoy was nodding. He was also holding an oversized Manila envelope. Dulcie could have sworn that hadn't been on the desk a minute before. 'Thank you very much, Ms Schwartz. And one more thing.' He pulled a white sheet out of the envelope. 'That man with the girl? The one you didn't see?'

He leaned in as he slid the sheet toward her on the table. It was slick and shiny. 'It wouldn't be this guy, maybe, would it?'

He flipped the sheet over to reveal a glossy photo. A man's face, close up. Dimitri.

# THIRTEEN

'I don't know if he was actually an ogre, Dulcie, but I'd say your initial instincts were right on. You were played.' Dulcie had called Suze as soon as she'd left the police station. What her friend was saying did not make her feel any better. 'That cop sounds awfully good at his job.'

'But Suze, I was trying to help. I mean, I told him about the email. So we know she's alive. And maybe what I saw did mean something. You were the one who said I should go down there.' She looked around. The tall red-haired stranger was nowhere to be seen, and Dulcie realized she was a little disappointed. She could have used a knight.

'No, that was the right thing to do. I should've gone with

you, though.' Suze was at work, and Dulcie could hear a baby crying in the background. 'I'm not at all sure about him asking you to email that poor girl. The legalities of that are iffy.'

'You've got your hands full, Suze. I thought I could handle it. But, Suze? The officer said something about Carrie that really worried me. I mean, he said they want her for questioning. But I think she's in trouble, like somebody is after her. You don't think it's Dimitri, do you?'

'Hang on.' The line went dead.

'Suze?'

Her friend came back, talking fast. 'I wouldn't worry about Dimitri, Dulce. I mean, you recognized him, but you didn't see him with that girl. You didn't see them fighting. Maybe there's some connection. She did say "boyfriend trouble," right? But maybe they're asking about him for something entirely different.'

That thought didn't make Dulcie feel any better. She knew she had blanched at the sight of Dimitri's pale and smiling face. After that, she'd had to identify her colleague, and even though she swore up and down that she didn't think he'd been the one in the passageway, she didn't know if Rogovoy believed her.

Meanwhile, Suze was still talking. 'Maybe it's simply that they're worried about her. You know, these things can be contagious.'

'What things? I'm sorry, Suze. I was distracted.'

'Suicide. You know. One person does it, and the idea goes around. Especially on a college campus.'

'*What*?' It was too late. Dulcie heard the phone clatter on to a desk and waited. She was standing outside the police headquarters, leaning into a cornice to hear. 'Suze! What do you mean?'

'Sorry. Crazy as usual.' Suze was back. Dulcie tried to interrupt, but her friend kept talking. 'Hey, I'm probably not coming home tonight. Let me make some calls, see what I can find out.'

'Wait, Suze. Suicide?' It was too late. The line was dead, and Dulcie didn't even know if her friend had heard her. Suicide was contagious, like a cold? And Carrie? No, it didn't make sense. That email had sounded so chipper, and, more to the point, the detective had said that they hadn't thought Carrie Mines was 'at risk.' Still, she wondered as she made her way across the Yard, could you really tell someone's mood from an emoticon?

And what role, if any, did Dimitri play in all of this? Walking down the Memorial Hall steps to the tiny office she shared with Lloyd, Dulcie thought about their absent colleague. Dimitri Popolov might sound like the name of a Russian gangster, but the quiet scholar Dulcie knew was anything but. Slim, pale, and soft spoken, Dimitri looked more likely to be a victim of violence than its perpetrator. True, his area of expertise – Raymond Chandler and his ilk – was bloody. But that kind of dichotomy wasn't that uncommon. After all, she – Dulcie – considered herself an extremely rational person, a fan of detailed proofs and abstruse arguments. And here she was, studying highly emotional Gothic fiction.

*'And talking to ghosts.'*

Dulcie started. 'Mr Grey?' The basement room was always dim, but today less light than usual came from the high-set window.

*'Yes, kitten?'* A swirl of dust, a slight movement in the shadows, drew her eye, and Dulcie realized she was holding her breath. Recently, it had seemed that her late cat had manifested only in the apartment, and even then, only to instruct Esmé. It wasn't that she was jealous of her own kitten, or not exactly. But if she was going to have a conversation, she wanted to make sure of whom she was talking with.

'That is you, isn't it?' She couldn't help the peevish note creeping into her voice, even as she reached toward the corner with the darkest shadow. 'It's been so long. And, well, you never come to the office any more.'

*'Dulcie!'* She wasn't the only one who could sound annoyed. And if there was any question of who the shadowy presence was, a sharp scrape – like a slap with unsheathed claws – caused her to pull back her hand.

'Sorry.' She slumped into her desk chair, head in hands. 'It's just been horrible, Mr Grey. Professor Herschoft. The police. The missing student.' She didn't know how much he knew, but as a living cat, he'd always been able to pick up on her moods. Surely, he would now. She waited, but when the only response was a little chirp – part purr, part inquisitive – she went on: 'I thought everything was going to be fine, but now, I don't know. Suze was telling me about how the idea of suicide can spread, and, well, maybe that's happening here.'

The full implications of what she had just said hit her. 'I might have been the last person to see her, Mr Grey.' She paused, swallowing the end of her thought. 'The last to see her alive,' she choked out. 'I should have gone straight to the cops, I know I should have. But there's so much going on. Chris, Chelowski. And I didn't want to get more involved in this, Mr Grey. I have my own life.'

The silence that followed lasted so long, Dulcie was sure he had gone. She had chased him away with her whining. With her refusal – she nodded as the truth hit home – to take her responsibilities seriously. Did it matter if the girl had dropped her class? Dulcie was a teacher. She was another woman on campus. She had an obligation to help. To get involved. 'I'm sorry, Mr Grey. I guess I've just let everything get to me. And, well, Suze is hardly ever around any more, and Chris is always busy.' She didn't even want to go into her fears about her boyfriend. Luckily, she didn't have to.

*'I'm here for you, Dulcie. Never forget that.'*

She breathed a sigh of relief and reached out, once again. Sometimes, if she was lucky, she could still feel the long, silky fur of her late pet.

*'Teaching is always part of it.'* She felt a passing touch of a damp nose, the brush of a soft muzzle – and then teeth. *'There are connections, Dulcie. We touch those we teach. We always touch them. But there are limits. A teacher has responsibilities beyond the text, Dulcie. And with responsibility, there must always be limits.'*

'But how can I tell—?'

Before Dulcie could finish her question, the door opened, raising a cloud of dust that sent Dulcie into a coughing fit. Lloyd entered, fanning the dust out of his own face, and scrambled over to pat her back.

'I'm fine, Lloyd,' she managed to choke out. 'Fine.'

In truth, she was more confused than before. Had Mr Grey been interrupted in the middle of his message, or had he said all he'd meant to say? Sometimes, Dulcie suspected he knew what was about to happen and timed his appearances accordingly. At other times, he seemed to enjoy being enigmatic.

Maybe those were the last vestiges of his mortal feline nature. Or was it just that he was so far above her, both as a cat and as a spirit? That final comment about teaching gave her pause.

And raised some other possibilities. As Lloyd retreated to his own desk and Dulcie rummaged through hers for a tissue, questions floated about like dust motes. Had it been Dimitri she'd seen with Carrie under the arch? Had Dimitri been the missing girl's teacher? But what kind of pedagogical inter-action would have resulted in the scene she had witnessed?

Could it have anything to do with the section she had dropped – that Dulcie had *let* her drop? No, she tried to reas-sure herself. That class had been a year ago. Whatever it was that had sparked Monday's confrontation, it was current. Plus, it was more likely something personal, rather than academic. And that, given the cloistered environment of the university, probably meant romantic. There was a history of this kind of thing. Heloise and Abelard. Lloyd and Raleigh. It didn't really matter, she realized, blowing her nose. None of this absolved Dulcie of her responsibilities.

She had a moral obligation to look into this. But how? She looked over at her office mate. He was humming, flipping through yet another blue book, with a pile of about thirty others before him. Clearly, he was better at keeping up with his grading than she was, and she hated to disturb him. Still, he was the logical starting point. Not only might he have some information on who taught what classes, because of his own complicated – and forbidden – relationship, but he might also have other insights as well.

She paused. That wasn't exactly fair. Their situation was different from any that might have pushed Carrie Mines into danger. Raleigh wasn't that much younger than Lloyd, and they had started seeing each other when she was in a different department, which meant the romance had initially been kosher. Still, it was a link. Who knew? Maybe there was a secret fraternity of scholars who were involved with their students.

Dulcie was mulling over this unlikely possibility when her phone rang. 'Suze!' she answered. 'Did you learn anything?'

But the caller wasn't her room-mate. 'I can't believe you ratted out Dimitri to the police.' The voice on the line was furious. And female. 'And you call yourself a friend and a colleague. You're nothing but a rat, and you know what happens to rats.'

The line went dead, and Dulcie found herself staring at the phone. Whoever had called had blocked the number from being recorded.

# FOURTEEN

'I didn't "rat out" anyone.' Dulcie couldn't believe she was defending herself. 'I went to tell the police what I'd seen. And, yeah, I recognized Dimitri from the photo. But I never said he was the man I'd seen. I don't understand it.'

'Who uses the phrase "rat out," anyway?' Trista focused on the etymology.

Lloyd sat opposite Dulcie, his attention rapt. Twenty minutes after the strange call, Dulcie felt angry rather than frightened. But his suggestion that they leave the office for some air and a snack had been welcomed anyway. Trista had seen them on their way into the Square and was now clearing away their empty plates to place another, with three more chocolate chip cookies, on the café table.

'It sounds like something from one of Dimitri's stupid books,' Trista added. Dulcie couldn't disagree.

'I think you should call the cops,' Lloyd said. 'After all, they got you into this.'

'No.' Dulcie was firm. 'No way. I don't need any more of this.'

'Wait, catch me up here?' Trista broke off a piece of one cookie to dunk in her mug. 'You went to the cops this morning?'

Dulcie went through it all again. The fight on Monday night, the misery of yesterday.

'Chelowski,' Trista, who had heard some of this, muttered under her breath. She and Lloyd made eye contact and he nodded. Dulcie wished she hadn't seen that.

'You guys know something about him?' The words stuck in her throat. She didn't need more problems.

'He's just—' Trista waved a hand in the air. 'Weird.'

'Let's be fair,' Lloyd added. 'He's not likeable, but we all would rather have someone smart and on point than someone who panders, right? He's just sort of competitive with the other departments, that's all.'

Dulcie nodded, remembering his callous comments about Herschoft. 'Besides, it was a female voice.'

'Oh, I didn't mean that he—' Trista and Lloyd fell over each other explaining, until Dulcie interrupted.

'No, you were both just sympathizing with me. I've got the dregs of the department now, I know.' She swallowed again. Hard. 'Actually, Lloyd, I didn't even tell you the worst.'

The look of horror on both their faces made her sorry for her phrasing.

'No, it's not that bad. It's just that he thinks I'm on a wild goose chase. He thinks I'm *malingering.*'

To her surprise, neither rushed to disagree.

'What?' She looked from one to the other.

'I've been thinking about it.' Trista shrugged, as if to soften her words. 'And you have been getting a little off topic. You've got some great stuff with the text, but then you get into that whole disappearing-author thing.'

'Great.' Suddenly her coffee tasted bitter, and Dulcie pushed her mug into the plate of cookies.

'Hang on a minute here.' Lloyd, the peacemaker, centered the plate. 'We all have the right to complain about our thesis advisers. I mean, I lost Bullock, too, when he retired, and it could have been me, stuck with ol' Norm.'

Dulcie nodded and reached for a cookie. 'But you think he's right?' She broke the cookie, not wanting to look up at her friends.

'Honestly, Dulce? I don't know.' Trista answered for them both. 'It is kind of scary to think about finishing, about going out into the world.'

'But you've got Jerry.' Dulcie looked at her friend and waited. There had to be a reason she hadn't come to the pub with Jerry the week before. 'Tris, is everything all right with you?'

'Yeah.' She made a face that moved all three of her piercings at once. 'Men, you know. Sorry, Lloyd.'

He shrugged, and Dulcie turned back toward her friend.

'But Jerry's a sweetheart.' Silence. 'I mean, I know both

he and Chris have been really busy recently, but . . .' She let the sentence hang, open and inviting. Trista didn't respond, and Dulcie suddenly didn't want to know more.

'Kids? Shouldn't we stay on point here?' Lloyd was trying again. 'Dulcie was acting like a responsible member of the community. She's had a horrible experience already, and now someone has scared her with a nasty phone call.'

'I don't know if I was scared, per se.' Dulcie was loath to admit how much the anonymous caller had shaken her.

'You were freaked out. I saw you.' Lloyd looked to her for confirmation. 'OK, at the very least, it was harassment.'

'Maybe it was the Harvard Harasser?' Trista didn't look that engaged, but Dulcie was willing to make peace.

'It was a woman, a girl.' Of that, she was sure. 'And it was specifically about Dimitri. That I had "ratted him out." But I hadn't. I mean, I identified him. But they already knew who he was. And it wasn't like I said he was the man I'd seen arguing with Carrie. If it weren't for the cops and now this call, I wouldn't have any reason at all to connect Dimitri to that girl.' Dulcie moved the cookie plate toward Trista. 'I mean, does anyone know if they were dating or anything?'

Lloyd shook his head, and Trista shrugged. 'Relationships. Who knows? They're complicated.' For a moment all three were quiet. Finally, after breaking apart the last cookie, Trista started talking again. 'Anyway, Dimitri can take care of himself. The person I want to know more about is that missing girl.'

'Well, I had her in my English 10 section last year, but she dropped out.' Dulcie tried to ignore how those words made her feel. 'But I don't remember, I don't know *why*.' This wasn't any better than talking about relationships. She swallowed. That last bit of cookie had been too dry. 'I don't think I asked.'

Trista shook her head while she chewed. 'I remember,' she said at last, unfazed by the sweet's consistency. 'I was helping with the scheduling last year, you know, when everything was being rejiggered.'

Dulcie waited with a growing sense of dread.

'She didn't drop the course, though. Only your section. She claimed she had some conflict. Some other prof wanted her to work in his lab every morning or something.' Trista took another piece of cookie, then slid the plate back across the table.

'To be honest, it seemed fishy at the time, but I figured she just wanted to sleep in on Monday mornings. At any rate, I remember slotting her into an afternoon section. Dimitri's.'

Suddenly, the rest of the cookie didn't look so appetizing. 'So, she was in Dimitri's section last year.' Lloyd spelled it out. 'But so were, like, two dozen other freshmen.'

Trista shrugged. 'I know, but, well, you asked.'

The friends sat in silence for a moment, and Dulcie found herself relaxing. The vague feeling of nausea she'd had since the phone call was fading to the point where the idea of one more chocolate chip began to appeal. By that point, however, Tris had pretty much denuded the remaining cookie of its chips, leaving Dulcie to wonder how her blonde friend remained so slim.

'Yeah, I did.' She fingered the remaining crumbs. 'So, do you think there was anything going on? I mean, was she trying to get into Dimitri's section?' Students changed classes for any number of reasons. Later hours were a common one, but Dulcie and Trista both had had experience with students having crushes on them – or on fellow students. Sometimes it seemed that the entire undergraduate student body was running on hormones. 'Or be with someone else in that section?'

Trista bit her lip. 'I don't think so,' she said after a moment's pause. 'I don't remember really well what happened, but I don't think she was eager to transfer *to* another section, if that made sense. There was something off about the whole thing, like maybe she was trying to avoid talking about something.' She looked across the table, a guilty look on her wide-set blue eyes. 'To be completely frank, I do remember wondering if she was trying to avoid *you*, Dulcie.'

'Great.' That last bit of cookie sat in her belly like lead. 'Just great.'

'So, to bring it back around.' Lloyd turned in his seat to focus on Dulcie. 'I know you didn't identify the man in the passageway as Dimitri. But maybe someone else saw them together that night. Maybe Dimitri *has* done something.'

Trista looked up. 'Maybe Dimitri is the Harvard Harasser.'

Lloyd and Dulcie turned toward her, but neither could think of anything to say.

# FIFTEEN

'I could be totally wrong, Tris. It could all have been nothing.' Trista and Dulcie were gathering their coats and bags to go. Lloyd had already taken off. They all had papers to grade. 'I mean, it was one phone call. An anonymous phone call. A prank.'

Trista looked at her. By this point, she didn't have to say anything.

'I know,' Dulcie admitted. 'And I know I should go back to the police. I just hate the idea of digging Dimitri in any deeper, when I can't be sure.'

'You can be sure about one thing.' Trista checked her phone. 'Things are getting worse with the Harvard Harasser. I just got a text: somebody slashed some poor girl's coat to ribbons in the Union cloakroom.'

'Creepy.' Dulcie shivered. 'Suze keeps warning me about that. Says that things like this can escalate.' Neither of them repeated what Trista had said. That it might be Dimitri who was responsible.

'Wonderful.' Trista zipped up her own leather jacket. She might not be dressed warmly enough for this weather, but she certainly looked like she could take care of herself. 'The way things are going, someone's going to get away with murder.'

Dulcie crossed the street, heading toward the office. Lloyd would be halfway to Mather House by now. And while she feared she was too distracted to get any of her own work done, she also knew that student papers didn't grade themselves. Head down against the wind, she realized with a shiver that she was walking through the same gate where she had witnessed the – what? The fight? The confrontation? Pausing, for a moment, she looked at the arching brick, the slate beneath her feet, hoping to see some sign of Monday night's interaction.

'And I heard that it wasn't suicide at all.' Two women, deep in conversation, pushed by. Dulcie stepped to the side to avoid getting smacked by a navy-blue knapsack. 'Served him right,' the other said, her voice magnified by the odd acoustics of the brick tunnel.

'Wait, what do you mean?' Dulcie stepped toward the pair. 'Hello?' She waved, but the two had moved on, and once out of the arching gate, their voices faded. Dulcie paused. Herschoft – they must have been talking about Herschoft. And it hit her: if another student's coat had been vandalized, then there was no way the late psych professor could have been responsible. Herschoft hadn't been the Harvard Harasser. Those girls must not have heard about the latest attack. Not that it mattered now. Dulcie felt a pang of sympathy for the poor man. Something else had driven him over the edge, but to some students, at least, he was already guilty.

That would change when word got out. Spinning on her heel, she walked back through the arch and into the bustling city sidewalk beyond. She needed to talk to Dimitri. Maybe there were amends to be made, and Dulcie was woman enough to make them. Maybe she'd end up apologizing for her suspicions. And maybe, just maybe, she'd get some answers.

Dimitri, if Dulcie recalled correctly, had a tiny studio on one of the side streets not far from the Square. Its space, or lack thereof, was made up for by its proximity to classes, libraries, and the various bars that all the grad students liked to haunt.

'Besides,' Dulcie could remember the tall Russian whispering to her one evening, 'this room is what you would call pretty big by Moscow standards.' She'd smiled back at the time, unsure whether the new transfer was joking or not. He'd come from London most recently, and seemed as assimilated into Western society as any of them, despite a slight discomfort with American colloquialisms. Even his slightly stilted way of speaking probably owed more to hours with Dashiell Hammett than to a real accent. A little odd, maybe, but not criminal.

Dulcie ducked down a side street, past an overpriced pen shop. It was amazing anyone could still live here in the heart of Cambridge. Dimitri was smart. He knew how to take care of himself in a strange city. He'd understand why she had identified his picture, and he'd have a good explanation for why the police were asking about him. Maybe he would even have an idea about who had made that phone call.

Buoyed by the thought, Dulcie nearly skipped the remaining block. Only when she turned on to Dimitri's street did she stop short. Partly, it was the wind, fresh off the river, smacking her in the face. And partly it was the sight of two police cruisers parked in front of the ancient brick building, which housed a used bookstore and an art gallery in its tiny front rooms – and Dimitri's apartment above.

'What's going on?' A small crowd had gathered, but Dulcie squeezed between the parkas to where a uniformed cop was standing.

'Miss, please, step back.' The man barely glanced back, simply held out an arm to bar her way.

'But Dimitri's my friend—' Too late, she realized what she had said. The cop turned to look at her.

'Miss, would you mind waiting over here, please?' He motioned toward the picture window that fronted the gallery. If she stood there, in front of two expressionist paintings of dubious quality, she'd be separated from the crowd, unable to sneak away. There was still the possibility that the two cruisers were parked here for another reason. A break-in at the gallery, perhaps, though Dulcie couldn't imagine anyone wanting to steal anything she could see there. A heart attack in the bookstore was more likely. But the way the cop was staring at her was making that possibility evaporate.

'I'll just come by later.' She waved her hand as a combination farewell and dismissal and started to back away. Clearly, the cop had been stationed here to hold back bystanders. He couldn't go after her, could he? She stepped back once, and then once more.

'Miss!' He raised his hand and began moving toward her. Dulcie froze – and was saved by the crowd. This was Cambridge, and he was blocking one of the narrow brick sidewalks. A large woman in a camel hair coat started to walk by. 'Wait! Ma'am?' As he turned back to stop the woman – she seemed intent on the art gallery – Dulcie bolted.

'Miss!'

It was too late. Dulcie had made it to the end of the street, where she ducked around the faded brick of some historic building or other. A school, of course, she read on the blue plaque. The city was lousy with them. But now that she had her breath, and her freedom, Dulcie needed to focus. The way that cop had reacted had confirmed her initial suspicion: they were there for Dimitri. And they were there in force. Two cruisers to bring in one grad student? Even if they suspected him of being the Harvard Harasser, that seemed excessive.

But if they thought Dimitri was actually dangerous, well, that would be a different story. Dulcie thought again of the fight she had witnessed. It had been an argument. Heated, sure, but the only contact she had seen was when the woman – Carrie Mines – had pushed the man away. Had he been brandishing some kind of a weapon? Had she expected violence, perhaps experienced it in the past from that man? Could that man have been Dimitri? She pictured the tall, slim grad student and tried to match up the image in her mind to the shadow in the archway.

As if on cue, she heard a shout from around the corner. She peeked around in time to see Dimitri, hands behind his back, being walked to one of the cruisers. Dulcie saw a pale face above the blue. Dimitri, his glasses askew. He seemed to be looking right at her, but she resisted the urge to wave. That look might have been imaginary, or it might have been full of accusation. Had she helped the police arrest him?

Dulcie was still staring as the second cruiser took off, leaving a void in a crowd that had grown to overflow the sidewalk. As she watched, it closed in, filling the space that had been held by her friend and his entourage. And as the people moved about, she recognized a figure in olive green. Only, this time the hood was thrown back, and she could see the wearer's face. Wild curls. Dark eyes, wide with emotion – fright? Rage? It was Carrie Mines.

# SIXTEEN

'Carrie! Carrie!' Dulcie waved as she ran. 'Yo!' For a moment it seemed the young woman looked at her, and Dulcie waved again frantically. 'Carrie!' But while Dulcie usually didn't think much about her height, or lack thereof, when she hit the small crowd, she found herself at a distinct disadvantage.

'Excuse me! Excuse me!' She tried to push through the sea of people, most of whom towered above her. 'Coming through!' With a last shove, she parted a couple deep in conversation to find clear sidewalk in front of her. Carrie Mines was gone.

That, in itself, didn't mean anything, Dulcie kept telling herself as she headed back to her Central Square apartment. The girl might not have seen her. Or not realized that her former, temporary section leader wanted to talk to her. Maybe, Dulcie thought, she had simply become invisible.

Not to everyone, however. Dulcie opened her front door to see Esmé tumbling down the steps to greet her. 'You OK?' Dulcie scooped up the tuxedoed feline and buried her face in the downy fur. Esmé responded with a resounding purr, but no other comment.

'Well, I guess that descent didn't do you any harm.' The kitten began kneading as Dulcie held her to her shoulder and ascended to the kitchen. 'And it is nice to be greeted.'

There was no sign of her human room-mate around. But as she placed Esmé on the floor, Dulcie noticed a green sponge beneath the kitchen table. 'Is this your work?' The kitten stared up at her, silent. 'Is this your new toy?' Mr Grey, she remembered, had had a fondness for kitchen sponges. Suze had thought that the food remnants on the squishy plastic had been the lure. Dulcie suspected that her dignified gray cat had toyed with the cleaning supplies just to amuse her.

'Did Mr Grey suggest this to you?' The kitten kept silent, and Dulcie felt her throat close up with unshed tears. 'OK, never mind.' She rescued the sponge and replaced it in the sink. 'How about some tea?'

As Dulcie waited for the water to boil, Esmé chirped – and took off. Esmé, Dulcie had come to realize, was not a quiet cat. Since her earliest days in Dulcie's life, she'd expressed herself by a series of squeaks, mews, and howls that often had Dulcie jumping out of bed at the oddest hours – and left Suze muttering. Mr Grey, in contrast, had been a fairly silent cat in life. But even though Dulcie firmly believed that Esmé, like the spirit of Mr Grey, could speak to her in comprehensible terms, could use the same kind of mental projection her departed pet could, she found the little black and white cat frustratingly uncommunicative. At least, in the manner to which she had become accustomed.

'Mrrup!' From the third floor, a small thud, followed by the rapid patter of fleeing paws, announced another of the kitten's misadventures. Minor, Dulcie hoped. There had been no sound of shattering, and Dulcie decided to ignore it. Whatever had fallen, if it was breakable it was already too late. Besides, there was little left to break. Although Dulcie despaired of training the kitten, Esmé's accident-prone antics had succeeded in training her and Suze. Dulcie looked at her mug: she'd automatically slid it toward the center of the table, where it was unlikely to be knocked off. Likewise, in the living room, the only surviving potted plant had been set as far back on the window sill as possible, a brick from the stoop set in front for the inevitable times that Esmé decided that she had to squeeze herself into just that one puddle of sun that the poor begonia occupied. That thud couldn't have been from Suze's room, could it? Dulcie realized that, in truth, she simply didn't want to know what fresh damage the kitten had wrought.

Mr Grey had never acted like that. Suddenly, the weight of the day seemed too much to bear, and Dulcie sunk into a kitchen chair. 'Mr Grey, I miss you so much. It's not that I don't love Esmé, I do, but she's not you.' Dulcie closed her eyes and leaned over her mug. The warm steam felt soft, like the touch of fur. Almost, she could imagine her beloved cat. But more and more, she was coming to believe that he was gone. Gone for good. Perhaps, she thought, one tear escaping to roll down her cheek, he had never really come back. Maybe it had all been her fancy, finding a lost friend in the comforts of home, in the warmth of a teacup. In her dreams.

'*Dreams are all well and good, Dulcie. But you can't live in them.*'

'Mr Grey!' Dulcie sat upright as her heart leaped.

'*You can't live in them. But you can learn from them – and move on.*'

'Mr Grey?' Like that, she knew the presence was gone. Dulcie slumped back in her seat. It was so unfair. She missed him so much, and it seemed like he could come and go at will. Unless . . . She paused, the thought sending a cold shiver down her spine. Was it possible? Was Mr Grey fading? Could the presence of Esmé in her life have chased him away?

'No, that can't be,' she said aloud. Mr Grey had approved of the kitten, had encouraged Dulcie to adopt the little foster as her own. Perhaps he was trying to warn her. Perhaps *he* was the one who was ready to move on.

Of course, Esmé wasn't the only new development in Dulcie's life. Since the winter break, she and Chris had grown more serious, as well. At least, she thought they had. Chris had even started talking about the two of them living together. Suze would be graduating from law school this spring, and it seemed likely that she and Ariano would move in together. They were even talking about moving: New York, Washington, San Francisco. The timing would be right, Chris had pointed out. But Dulcie had hesitated. Chris didn't know how hard it had been for her mom after her father had left.

Also, although she didn't dare admit it, she wondered about Mr Grey. He had been saying something about connections the other day, before Lloyd had come in. He might have been talking about Chris, but he also might have been about to tell her something about the special bond they had shared. Damn, Lloyd! She wished she could summon her spectral pet now, at least for clarification.

It was time to acknowledge the truth. It wasn't only his voice coming more infrequently. The physical manifestations – when she could feel the brush of his proud flag of a tail or the weight of his body as he jumped up to the bed – had become even rarer. And they only came when she was alone, here, in the house that she had shared with Mr Grey. If she moved, would she lose that? If she lived with Chris, even here in the apartment Mr Grey had lived in, would she be shutting out the comforting spirit?

Was that what Mr Grey had meant? It was true that she and Chris loved each other. They had something beyond shared grad school angst. Her brief encounter with her boyfriend suddenly came back to her. The student. The cool kiss goodbye. Perhaps she had waited too long. Perhaps Chris had had enough. Her stomach knotted, and the smell of the mint tea suddenly seemed noisome.

Another thud distracted her. Something heavy; probably a book. She looked up. Or maybe Mr Grey's message meant

something else entirely. Maybe Mr Grey was helping her with
another problem: the mystery of the missing author.

'W–ooo–w!'

Dulcie's reverie was broken by a howl.

'Esmé, are you all right?' Dulcie raced up the stairs. 'Esmé?'

No blood greeted her. Not even any shards of glass or
pottery.

'W–ooo–w!'

The howl took Dulcie's breath away, but when she looked
toward its source, she saw the little cat sitting quite serenely
in the door to Suze's room. She turned toward Dulcie and
blinked once, mewing more softly this time. 'W–ooo–w?'

'Oh, kitten, I don't get you.' Dulcie reached for her pet –
and noticed the disarray inside. Unlike Dulcie, Suze tended to
keep a neat room, and it was easy to see Esmé's work. A
dictionary had somehow been pushed off the desk and, as Dulcie
went to retrieve it, she saw an opened pair of scissors and a
letter opener beside it on the floor. A gift from Suze's mother,
they made up part of a nice leather desk set that Suze was rather
fond of.

'Esmé! You've got to be careful.' She retrieved the scissors
and letter opener and replaced them in their leather sheath.
'These are not toys. And they're not yours.' Neither the shiny
metal nor the soft leather seemed to be scratched. 'Besides,
you could have been hurt.'

She finished neatening up and closed the door behind her,
first making sure that the little cat was out of the room.
Oblivious to the trouble she had caused, Esmé was in the
kitchen sitting calmly on the window sill, and Dulcie joined
her pet in contemplating the view outside. In a few months,
there should even be greenery. For now, though, the view was
as bleak as any in *The Ravages of Umbria*, if only the rocky
crags had been replaced by the neighbor's triple-decker and
the circling eagles by pigeons.

'What was Mr Grey talking about, Esmé?' Dulcie stroked
the smooth black fur. A low rumble grew into a purr. 'You
and me? Chris? Or was he trying to tell me something about
*The Ravages*?'

The kitten turned once toward Dulcie and then back to the
window, before letting out a series of low, chattering noises.

'That's not an answer, Esmé.'

'Meh–eh–eh.'

'It's almost as if she expects me to learn her language,' Dulcie said in exasperation.

'Who?'

Dulcie almost jumped. But the voice coming up the front stairs belonged to Suze. 'You're home!'

'Just for a pit stop. Seems it's spring out, suddenly.' Suze peeled off her sweater as she passed through the kitchen on her way up to her room, and Dulcie felt a rush of relief that she'd been able to tidy up after the kitten. 'So whose language are you learning?' Suze's voice carried down the stairs.

'Oh, it's nothing.' Dulcie felt a rush of self-consciousness, and then berated herself. Suze had been her best friend for years. 'I mean, I was thinking about Mr Grey and then about Esmé here.' Silence. Perhaps Suze hadn't heard her. 'I've been feeling kind of out of sorts. Like, maybe, because I've been so busy, with Chris and everything, I haven't been taking good care to train Esmé.' Silence. Suze hadn't noticed anything, and so Dulcie continued: 'And that, well, maybe Mr Grey is moving on.' There, she had it out, and she swallowed the lump in her throat.

'And you think that would be a bad thing?' Suze came back down the stairs, buttoning up a cotton blouse. 'Spending more time with your boyfriend than with the ghost of your last cat?'

Suze saw the look on Dulcie's face and gave her a quick hug. 'It's not the end of the world, Dulcie. I swear it isn't. But maybe, well, maybe it is time for you *both* to move on.' And then, grabbing a light jacket, she was gone.

# SEVENTEEN

*T*he room is the same. A small, ill-lit chamber dominated by a writing desk, papers. A quill. The wind makes its way through the rattling panes, causing the candles to flicker. The woman at the desk looks up, staring for a moment at the rain on the windows, at the darkness. Her hand aches. But as she stands to draw the drapes, a gust makes its way down the chimney, raising a shower of sparks. The papers *she has just left shift, and she turns with a gasp to grab them as they fall. The movement opens the cut on her finger, and she watches as her blood despoils a page.*

*Does it matter? The question echoes through her head. There are connections to be made: a woman, a young girl. There has been so much she's left unsaid. What did one small spot mean, already spreading, already turning dark as ink? So close to being gone ...*

'Mrrow!' Dulcie woke to find her hand wrapped around Esmé's tail, the kitten turning on her in dismay.

'Sorry, kitty. Sorry.' Dulcie sat up. The dream had been so real, the feeling of desperation so palpable. Dulcie's heart was racing, and she took a deep breath to calm it. This was natural, this anxiety. It had to do with approaching the end of a project. Her thesis. An author's novel. It didn't have to mean death. It didn't necessarily mean suicide.

Or did it? Dulcie felt, rather than saw as the kitten settled down again at the foot of the bed and proceeded to groom. The emotions of the other night's dream had been clearer – and more fearful. Tonight, the woman had felt despair. She had also been nervous, true, but had it been for herself – or for some young girl? A character? Carrie's face sprang to mind, those strange, light eyes wide open in fright, or ... No, she was mixing her messages. There had been something else as well: a desire to get something done. To make some kind of move. To write, probably, before the feared doom fell. That could be a deadline, or it could have been – could be – something more physical.

That was it. If Dulcie had been toying with the idea that her dreams were not about the mysterious author, she dismissed those hesitations now. This wasn't some fancy created out of half-remembered novels or last night's salami-sausage pizza. This was real.

'What do you think, Esmé?' In the dim light, she could barely make out the kitten's black body at the end of the bed. But even in the pre-dawn, her white muzzle shone, moving rhythmically as, wrapped around herself like a pretzel, she worked away on the fur of her lower back. Dulcie waited. She watched as that tongue moved on to her white booties, spending an awfully long time on each foot. The kitten could

hear her. She just had to find a way to make herself understood. 'Does this mean I'm on the right track?'

Bath done, her companion curled up for a nap. 'Great.' As
Dulcie lay back on her own pillow, she realized it was damp
with tears.

From the time Suze had left last evening, Dulcie had been
on edge. She'd meant to tell her room-mate about the strange
phone call – more confident in Suze's advice than in anything
Lloyd or Trista could say. After all, Suze knew the legal ins
and outs of the university, and knew about Dulcie's unfortunate interaction with the police, too. But Suze had run out too
quickly, and Dulcie had felt odd about ringing her when she
knew her friend was either heading back to work or to some
rare private time with her boyfriend. In the normal course of
things, she'd see her again soon.

And besides, Dulcie had had her own work to do. After
Suze had taken off, Dulcie had tried to settle down, although
the passage of time hadn't made her feel any easier. Promising
herself some couch time with the kitten and with a new collection of essays – *The Female Domestic, Continental Views* –
she had tried to turn her mind to grading. She'd gotten through
three papers before she'd quit in disgust and ordered that
pizza. Why did students bother with literature, she'd thought,
if all they cared about were the grades? Didn't they know
there were no 'right' answers in the arts?

The irony of her own complaint had hit her. How long had
she been researching – searching, really – for some kind of
truth? And how much writing did she have to show for it?

'But that's different,' she'd said out loud, waking Esmé.
'I'm trying to find out what happened to a real person.' The
kitten had grunted and rearranged her tail, and Dulcie had
taken the book to bed.

The essay by Dulcie's author wasn't the only piece of
interest in *The Woman Question*. The anthology, a collection
of pieces by her author's contemporaries, had been extremely
useful in placing Dulcie's subject, and many of them supported
her ideas about the novelist's philosophy. But reading them
last night had only made her feel more lost. Three centuries
later, and how much progress had been made? Even worse,
Dulcie had to admit, was the disregard in which the great
fiction of the day was held. Nobody seemed to care about the

great Gothic novels any more. Sure, they were over the top, with their ghouls and specters, their romance and abductions. And they were fun, acknowledged Dulcie, feeling that slight niggling desire to justify her academic interest. But they were also one of the first incidences of popular fiction written largely by and for women. For all anyone knew, the author of *The Ravages of Umbria* had been as big as Danielle Steele in her day.

And about as respected, Dulcie had realized last night, with a sinking feeling. 'Not that anyone at Harvard will care about her in two hundred years either.' In fact, if anyone cared now, she'd mused, it was only in some semiotics pop-culture sense that would have the textural purists in her department running for cover in the depths of Widener.

'Can I help it if I'm ahead of my discipline?' Dulcie had called out for the kitten. 'Well, can I?'

The kitten hadn't answered. In fact, nobody had, and as the evening had worn on, bringing with it a windy rain that lashed at her own twenty-first century windows, the silence had begun to wear on her. The only time the phone had rung, Dulcie had jumped to answer it. It was Lucy, calling with an urgent message that she claimed had been channeled by her new spiritual cohort, Merlin:

'She's found a guru, dear. Something about a guru.' Her mother had a tendency to start conversations in the middle, as if Dulcie had been participating all along.

'She? I thought Merlin was a male.'

'He is, dear. Don't be dense.' A loud bang and some very un-PC cursing could be heard in the background. Lucy kept talking, and Dulcie decided to ignore it. At least her mother wasn't involved in one of the community's feuds. 'The message is about a woman – a "she" – and so I immediately thought of you.'

'A guru?' Dulcie looked at the clock. Eleven. If Chris were going to call, it probably wouldn't be until midnight. 'You mean, like a teacher?'

'Yes, that's it exactly. It was about the teaching. All the teaching and the students, how distracting they can be.' Lucy must be calling from the communal space again, Dulcie realized. At least the cursing had changed to something sing-song. Chanting. 'Maybe not the teaching. More the students.'

'They do take a lot of time.' Dulcie thought with regret about the remaining ungraded midterm papers. Tomorrow, she promised herself. Besides, she needed to reschedule that meeting with Corkie. Something was going on, and the junior could too easily put her academic career in danger. Dulcie not only liked her, she also had an obligation to her as her tutor.

'It's more than that, dear. There is something going on. Oh, Hecate.' Dulcie heard another crash, and a mental image of a falling soup pot flashed through her mind. Despite Lucy's best wishes, Dulcie wasn't psychic. She simply remembered the turmoil whenever the commune – the arts colony, she corrected herself before she slipped up out loud – prepared for its monthly moon feast. 'May I call you back, dear? It's all gone— Oh!' And the line was dead.

After that, Dulcie had kept her phone turned on as she'd read, waiting for her mother's breathless explanation. Knowing that the night would only grow more frantic, she hadn't been overly surprised when no call had come. But now, in the growing morning light, she realized the phone was still beside her. Still turned on and charged. And still silent.

Chris had never called back.

'*You didn't call him, either.*' A much lighter pressure, barely perceptible, announced the presence of another feline at the foot of her bed. From beneath the quilt, Dulcie could feel the feather-light footfalls as they made their way up the bed.

'Mr Grey?' She ought to get out of bed. From where she lay, she could see the clock. It didn't matter. 'Are you still there?'

A gentle purr greeted her, along with the light rhythmic pressure of paws kneading, just out of sight.

'Mr Grey?' She wasn't sure how to ask. Or, really, if she wanted to know the answer. 'If Chris and I— If we grow closer, will you still be there for me? Will you still be here?'

The purr only deepened, and she had the uncanny feeling that her spectral pet knew she was evading her real question. 'You see, Chris was talking about me moving in with him. Suze is almost done with her degree, and the end of the semester is coming up. And, well, I think he feels like we're at some kind of crossroads. Only, I haven't been sure. Not about Chris, but about moving in. And now—' The memory of the previous day flashed before her eyes. Chris and his student. His tall, slim student. 'Now, I'm afraid maybe I waited too long. Maybe it's too late.'

'*And why would you ever think that, little one?*'

The feelings came in a rush. In a way, it was easier to talk about her fear of losing Chris than about her fear of losing Mr Grey. Hadn't she lost him once, already? Whereas Chris was real. He was here. Except that, more and more, he wasn't.

'*Don't be so quick to judge, Dulcie.*' The quiet voice, deep and calm, had picked up on her question before she had voiced it. '*What is absence, anyway? What is presence?*'

'Well, spending some time with me would be a start.' She heard the peevishness creeping into her own voice, even before she felt the slight, sharp slap of a leathery paw. 'I'm sorry. I'm just lonely. And I think, maybe, I did something wrong.'

Again the purr, softer now. And while Dulcie had the strong feeling that Mr Grey knew exactly what she was thinking, she also sensed that he wanted her to acknowledge the problem that was eating away at her.

'You were telling me about connections, Mr Grey. About responsibility. At least, I think you were. And, well, I think I may have let a student down. I think maybe I was too focused on my own work, on my own life. She was a freshman, and I . . . Well, she's in some kind of trouble now. And maybe I could have made a difference. Only, I didn't.'

The soft thud of a cat hitting the floor was followed up by a slight creak as her bedroom door opened ever so slightly. Mr Grey was gone, though Esmé was still sleeping at the foot of her bed.

'Thank you, Mr Grey. You're right. Whatever I may have messed up in the past, it's not going to help me now if I don't get to work.'

# EIGHTEEN

But the scene that greeted her as she came down the stairs was not conducive to work. Sometime during the night, Esmé had gotten behind the metal screen that blocked off the apartment fireplace. And then, curious or just plain bored, she had proceeded to explore the kitchen, leaving dark, sooty footprints on the counters, around the sink, and on the kitchen table. Dulcie pulled over a chair to examine the top of the refrigerator. Yes, greasy paw-prints had made their way across the top and had circled the pile of takeout menus the room-mates kept there, too. Apparently, at night the kitten had taken the liberty of exploring everywhere that she was forbidden to go.

'Esmé, it's no use hiding.' Dulcie called for the kitten. 'The evidence is piled up against you.'

No wonder the kitten had been grooming so assiduously. Steeling herself, Dulcie started her own exploration. Sure enough, the paw prints were all over the kitchen and – yes – along every window sill. It was a wonder that Suze's remaining begonia had survived.

Then, as she approached the ground-floor bathroom, she gasped. The tiny half bath off the kitchen had its door ajar, and a trail of toilet paper emerged. Partly shredded, it led her to the roll, and to a pile of tissue that had been unspooled by the kitten's claws. Between the spill of paper and the tufts of shredded tissue that still floated in the air, the bathroom was a mess, and Dulcie shook her head. Mr Grey had never done anything like this. Mr Grey—

Dulcie caught herself. Mr Grey had been an adult cat, who had lived with two students. Esmé had been home alone most of the day. 'I guess I'm not the only one who has been feeling abandoned, huh, Esmé?'

From the other side of the pile, the kitten pounced, and Dulcie couldn't help smiling. At least somebody had started the day on a productive note.

Dulcie looked over at her own mess: the pile of papers that formed a gentle, disorderly hillock on her desktop. Although she'd spent the better part of an hour cleaning up the apartment, she'd still gotten an earlier start than usual. And although she had half promised her friends that she would report the anonymous phone call, she couldn't resist stopping by the office first. She had the basement space to herself this morning, but the memory of Lloyd's diligence hovered. It wasn't that she was shirking her civic responsibility; she was just focusing on her primary tasks. Hadn't

Mr Grey himself said something about the duties of a teacher?

It sounded weak, even to her own ears. But after a half hour, two blue-books and most of a student essay, she felt sure she was doing the right thing. What was she going to say to the police anyway? That someone knew the police were asking questions about Dimitri? For better or worse, they had him now.

That thought didn't help her peace of mind. She pulled the essay closer and straightened up in her seat. With the door closed, the small room was blissfully quiet, insulated from the hum of activity outside. Weak sunlight from the one high window warmed the overhead fluorescent, and Dulcie switched on her desk lamp as well. But the additional illumination didn't help; the paper lay in front of her, inert and only one of many. She had let too much work go too long.

Teaching was a serious obligation, as well as a big part of being a grad student. Not only did it provide real-world experience in what she'd be doing once she got her doctorate, it also gave the university something back – labor in return for all those grants. But recently the teaching had become the monster that ate her days. A giant looming presence; a shadow over the pure joy that was research.

It was hopeless, and Dulcie slumped back in her wooden chair, pushing the essay away as if she could clear her mind along with her desk. As she did, something fell off the other side of her desk with a small flutter, and she felt her eyes fill up in response. This was ridiculous. There was just too much to do. What Lucy had been saying, whether through her cat or not, made some sense. Her teaching was eating up an increasingly large part of her time. Eating into her work, in fact. And suddenly Mr Grey's words took on a new meaning. The idea of limits, of dreams and moving on. Maybe she was the woman at the desk, in the rain. Maybe she was the one desperate to write, frantically putting down words before it was too late.

'So you think this is all about your thesis?' Trista hadn't quite dismissed the idea, and Dulcie could have kicked herself. Why was she talking about her dream when she needed to get back to work? But Trista was into it. 'Could be stress related. Did I tell you I met this psych TA the other night? Sort of a surfer dude to look at, but we went over to the Harvest for drinks, and he was telling me about this study . . .'

The connection wasn't great, and, Dulcie had to admit, she didn't really want Trista to continue anyway. So she interrupted. 'It's not about stress, Trista. I mean, it felt . . . strange.' She'd been about to say 'real.' But that sounded too much like something Lucy would say.

Trista hadn't even heard her interruption. 'I mean, dreaming about your thesis happens to everyone, and worrying that you'll never finish, well, I had one nightmare . . .'

At least she wasn't talking about some strange guy. Still, Dulcie had a hard time listening. Trista's dream was one of the more common ones: the long hallway. The test room with the door that wouldn't open. The questions printed in an unreadable mix of symbols and numbers. Dulcie had to smile as she heard her friend's particular take: a blue book already cluttered, like some Victorian novel, with illegible longhand, spidery and dense. But maybe her own dreams were as obvious, with the Gothic castle replacing the locked exam room, the quill and paper replacing the blue book.

If that was what her dream meant, she should get back to work. The papers before her weren't going anywhere. And if she could squeeze an hour in Widener into her schedule, then maybe she could get back on track.

Chelowski was wrong about her not wanting to finish her thesis. And he was wrong about her theory being a digression, too. Dulcie knew that she was on the trail of a literary mystery. The author of *The Ravages* had stopped writing for some reason, and Dulcie was going to find out why. The proof – as was always the case for her in all her years of study – had to be somewhere in the text.

She stood to go and looked down at her desk. All those midterm papers. Well, she could she read them at home, on the sofa tonight. Couldn't she? A brief flash of Esmé, diving into a pile of papers, made her smile. OK, such a scenario would have its challenges. Overall, however, the minor distractions of the little cat might make the work go more easily. And Mr Grey, she just knew, would approve.

Trista was still talking: something about how, in her dream, her pen never had ink. And so, with what she hoped was a supportive 'huh,' Dulcie shoved the student papers into her bag, almost losing one over the side.

'Gotcha!' She folded it in half.

'What?' The disembodied voice almost made her drop the paper again.

'Sorry, Tris.' She'd almost forgotten Trista was on the line. 'Something fell off my desk.'

'Your desk, yeah. I believe it. But be careful. I almost lost a very important contact that way, if you know what I mean.'

'A note from Gullingham?' Trista's thesis adviser was almost as senior as Bullock had been.

'Nope, something a lot more fun.' There was a warmth in Trista's voice that Dulcie hadn't heard before. Certainly not when she spoke about Jerry. Suddenly, Dulcie didn't want to hear any more.

'Hey, Tris? I've got to run.'

'Oh, well, do you want to meet us later?' Dulcie wasn't sure who 'us' was any more and made some vague excuse as she ended the call. Tris and Jerry had started seeing each other about six months before she'd met Chris. Was this the natural life cycle of a grad school romance?

She couldn't think that way. It was too crazy. She needed to get to Widener. But as she stood to go out, she noticed a pink Post-it on the floor. It must have been buried in the mess of her desk until she'd accidentally pushed it off.

*Ms Dulcie Schwartz!* The handwriting was immediately recognizable: Corkie still wrote with the loopy letters of the girl she had been not that long ago, and the use of the little sticky note only enforced its goofiness. The day before yesterday – was it really only two days ago? – Lloyd had said Corkie 'was going to' leave a note. Either he hadn't noticed that she had, or Dulcie had misinterpreted his use of the past continuous as a dubious subjunctive. Well, she'd been distracted lately, and as she bent for the single Post-it, she felt a strong urge to just shove it in her bag and bolt. But it would get lost again, she knew, and so she unfolded it.

*I'm sorry I have to cancel today. I know I'm behind, really!!!* Only an undergrad would use that many exclamation points, thought Dulcie with a smile. The next line wiped it off. *But this is an emergency, a real emergency! Can't explain – I'm not the only one involved – but please don't give up on me! Please!!!*

# NINETEEN

That was it. Dulcie wasn't going to let another student down. Racing up the stairs, she dialed Corkie's cell number. 'Corkie? It's Dulcie. I got your note. Call me?' She paused. Corkie might be girlish, but she was usually steady. This note sounded rattled. 'Any time, day or night.'

Surfacing just at the hour, she found herself surrounded by students, most of whom towered over her. Even if she knew where to look for her beleaguered charge, she probably wouldn't be able to see her. There had to be a way. Lucy, she knew, would come up with some conjuring spell. Not that it would work, but it would pass the time while she waited. If only she had the girl's schedule.

Dulcie could have slapped herself. She might not have Corkie's schedule, but the department would. A quick call to Nancy would put her in touch with her elusive student.

'I'm sorry, Dulcie.' Nancy sounded as disappointed as Dulcie felt: Corkie was not scheduled for any classes this morning. 'I do remember her saying something about keeping Thursdays open. I believe she has a job.'

'Thanks.' Nancy was trying to be helpful, but that could mean anything. More than half the students on campus worked, and Corkie could be doing anything from filing library books to waitressing at Lala's. No, although the thought of Lala's made her mouth water, Dulcie knew that going out for lunch at eleven would put her on the road to perdition. Besides, Nancy was still talking.

'I'm glad to see you're out and about, but don't push yourself, Dulcie.' Her voice dropped a notch. 'Personally, I think it was unconscionable for Mr Chelowski to call you in for anything less than an emergency. In fact, I was thinking of having one of the student counselors come in to talk about suicide and loss. That new peer counseling group has offered an outreach program.'

That was it! Corkie worked as a peer counselor. 'That's a great idea, Nancy.' Dulcie didn't bother to explain. 'Thanks!'

And as Nancy began to ask her about possible times, she
hung up. With a small twinge of guilt, Dulcie grabbed her
bag and headed back into the yard. Below the Stairs had been
a student-run space since her own undergrad years, but over
the last few semesters, somebody had turned the basement
coffee-house into an informal counseling center. Although
the university health services kept a hand in – training interested students and providing leaflets about individual and
group therapy – Below had become the first line of defense
for many beleaguered undergrads. With its worn sofas, weekly
rap sessions, and two private offices carved out of what used
to be coffee house's kitchen, it was an unthreatening alternative. A place where the harried student could just drop in,
no appointment necessary.

Corkie had drifted into working there when she'd come
back to school, she'd told Dulcie. Accustomed by her rural
Iowa upbringing to hard physical labor, she'd been thrown by
the hustle and bustle, the politics, and the sheer press of urban
life when she'd first arrived at the university, she'd said. She'd
needed help to make the transition, and both before and during
her semester off, the center had been there for her. Dulcie
hadn't known her then, but the Corkie she had met upon her
return seemed both focused and happy. Like a student who
wanted to give something back. One who usually kept her
appointments, come to think of it.

Something had broken up that new-found equilibrium,
and Dulcie was determined to find out what. Head down,
Dulcie made her way through the student swarm to the side
of the brick administrative building and grabbed the iron
rail of the stairs.

''Scuse me.' A young woman, eyes swollen from crying,
was making her way up from the basement entrance. Well,
maybe the tears had done her good. Dulcie stood aside as she
passed, wiping one glove under her nose, then descended into
the concrete stairwell that served as the center's front door.
The private entrance – one that didn't force students by a
security guard – was definitely one of Below the Stairs' selling
points.

'May I help you?' An elegant dark-skinned woman looked
up as a set of chimes rang. 'We've got a group starting in ten
minutes, or just help yourself to some mint tea.' Her smile

countered the formality of her voice, and Dulcie found herself smiling back.

'Thanks, I'm actually looking for someone? Philomena McCorkle?'

The other woman shook her head. 'I'm sorry, Corkie isn't here right now. Would you like to speak with someone else?'

The idea was tempting. Between the police and Dimitri, the strange phone call, and that awful moment at Poche Hall, Dulcie could use a shoulder to cry on. And she certainly was having trouble getting to work on her thesis. But no, if she wasn't actually helping a student then she needed to get to the library – not spend time hashing over the same old issues.

'No, thanks.' She paused. 'But maybe I could leave her a message?'

As the smiling woman looked for a pad, Dulcie surveyed the room. It really had changed since its coffee-house days: three very squishy-looking sofas lined this outer room, with a low coffee table and two bean bags filling up most of the rest of the space. Some vintage posters gave it color, and the sweet scent of mint offset the damp basement funk she remembered too well. This was a comforting place. Well, good for them.

It was also a private place, Dulcie realized, as she thought about what to write. Much as she saw Corkie as her responsibility, she also didn't want to intrude. After all, tracking a student down to her workspace, particularly when her work involved counseling, might be a bit much.

'You know, I don't think I'll leave a message.'

The other woman raised her eyebrows. 'Everything here is confidential, you know. You can just leave a first name.'

Dulcie's smile widened. 'I'm not here for – oh, never mind. Would you tell her that Dulcie is looking for her? Dulcinea Schwartz?'

It was a measure of her professionalism, Dulcie thought, that the woman didn't even chuckle as she wrote that down.

But any of her attempts at discretion were moot when, not ten seconds later, Dulcie ran into her charge on the stairs.

'Corkie!'

'What? Oh!' The younger girl blinked, clearly distracted.

'I'm sorry, I didn't mean to surprise you.' Dulcie felt again that perhaps she had overstepped.

'No, no problem at all. Below the Stairs is open to all. Us female students in particular have reason to want a safe space where we can talk freely about the issues in our lives.'

Corkie's voice had the ring of a memorized speech, but Dulcie admired how well the lines were delivered. 'This does seem like a good place, Corkie. And I'm really impressed that you're working here. But, actually, I was just looking for you.'

'Oh?' Corkie's eyebrows arched, confusion registering in her round face.

'You cancelled? I emailed you, but never heard back. And that note you left?' This was some seriously distracted student. As the door chimes rang softly behind her, Dulcie heard alarm bells going off in her own head. Corkie had already had to withdraw from the college once. 'Are you OK, Corkie? Are things getting out of control for you?' She paused, not wanting to add the obvious: 'Again.'

'No, no, I'm fine.' Corkie backed against the stair rail to let an exiting student pass. 'Really, you didn't have to come here.' Her voice rose with a note of what sounded like panic.

'Do you have a moment? Could we go talk somewhere?' Dulcie wasn't convinced.

'I'm really busy.' She ran a hand over her tightly bound hair, and Dulcie saw how pale she was.

'Just two minutes?'

'OK, but not here.' Corkie led her tutor back up the stairs and around a corner. Sheltered slightly by the brick building, she started to talk. 'I am sorry I blew off our tutorial, and I'm really sorry I didn't get back to you. I mean, I know I've just been let off academic probation and I've got to keep at it. Only, things have gotten crazy now. They've gotten really hectic here –' she nodded back toward the building – 'and they need me.'

Dulcie bit her lip and took a good look at her student. It wasn't just the pallor; everyone looked pasty by March. She'd gotten so used to thinking of her student as a healthy farm girl that she'd not noticed how much weight she'd lost, or how dark the rings under her eyes had grown.

Corkie was aware of her scrutiny. 'I'm doing good work here, Ms Schwartz. And I love it.'

Dulcie nodded. 'I believe you, Corkie. I just want to make

sure you're keeping things in balance. After all, you're no good to Below the Stairs if you flunk out.'

Corkie rolled her eyes. 'Don't I know it. I feel like I spend half my time trying to get girls to stick with it. To stay in school. And sometimes, I don't know. Maybe it's not the best thing for them.'

That was a red flag. 'Come on, Corkie. You can't mean that. I mean, we all have our problems, but an education is a way out. It can be a solution.'

Corkie shrugged. 'Yeah, but sometimes things around here can be part of the problem.'

Dulcie had to nod. The pressure – and now the extra burden of grief. She remembered what Suze had said about suicide. How it could become contagious. 'Are you hearing a lot –' she didn't even want to bring it up – 'about what happened?'

Corkie looked at her blankly, and for a moment, Dulcie wondered if it was possible that she hadn't heard.

'I mean, the situation with that young professor, Fritz Herschoft? You know, the chubby one?'

'Oh, lord!' The volume, the tone of Corkie's exclamation startled Dulcie, and she stepped back. 'That one! You don't think there's a connection, do you? I don't even want to—'

From Memorial Church, a bell sounded. Quarter past the hour.

'Look, I'm sorry, Ms Schwartz. I'll make up the work, really. But I can't talk about that . . . that *creature* right now. And I've got to go.'

With that she turned and raced back down the stairs, leaving Dulcie open mouthed in shock.

# TWENTY

'He wasn't an attractive man, but . . . but . . .' Dulcie was talking to herself, and even though she was aware of it, she felt unable to stop. Corkie was a caring girl. She worked as a counselor. And yet her reaction to Fritz Herschoft had been callous in the extreme. Dulcie was dumbfounded. And she was still muttering as she made her way back across the Yard, which probably explained why she nearly ran into her colleague.

'Dulcie!' She looked up to see Dimitri, her tall, pale classmate, now looking slightly more skeletal and even more pallid. For a moment, she started – could he be a ghost? – but his wide smile reassured her that, even if he were, he was of the friendly variety.

'Dimitri?' Even as she said his name, she half expected the figure in front of her to waver and dissipate.

'In the flesh.' His smile grew more crooked, and he reached up to adjust his glasses. 'I love your American colloquialisms. I mean, how else would I be here?'

She smiled back, rather than answer, and then felt her smile melt away. If he knew that she had identified him – she tried not to think of the phrase 'rat out' – his cheerful good will just might evaporate into the ectoplasm.

'I'm just glad you're here.' That came out wrong, and she tried again. 'I mean, not in jail.' That wasn't much better, but Dimitri didn't seem to notice.

'So you heard?' He was shaking his head, apparently oblivious to how the color had drained from Dulcie's face. 'That was . . . unpleasant.'

She could see his Adam's apple bob as he swallowed and felt an overwhelming urge to confess. 'I didn't mean to say anything to them, really. I almost didn't. But I had seen Carrie, the missing girl, the night before, and then when I saw the posters, Suze – that's my room-mate – told me I had to go talk to them.'

He was looking at her as if he didn't understand what she was saying. Since, despite his heritage, he was also a doctoral candidate in English, Dulcie realized the fault lay in her explanatory skills.

'There was an argument going on – when was that? Three nights ago? Anyway, I was leaving Widener and I heard two people fighting.' He didn't need to know her initial impression. What mattered was the way the confrontation had ended. 'The woman was Carrie, Carrie Mines. And when I went to the police, they showed me a picture of you and asked if I knew you.'

'Ah, so that is what happened.' He looked down, then took off his glasses to clean them. 'My . . . friend Lylah was quite upset.'

Dulcie couldn't help but notice the pause. Odds were, she knew, Dimitri was being discrete. After all, perhaps his friend was simply that, or the liaison was too new to be qualified in any way. But just a little, she had to wonder. Had Dimitri brought up another woman's name because she had mentioned Carrie? A bit of misdirection from a reader of crime fiction, perhaps?

'Lylah? I don't think I've ever met her.' Dulcie felt sleazy asking.

'You would not have. She matriculates at the School of Public Health.' Dimitri turned toward her; his eyes, behind their gunmetal gray frames, looked wide and concerned. 'Why me?'

'I don't really know.' Dulcie shrugged and tried to think back. 'It took me a while to get over to the police. I mean, there was the, um, what happened over at the Poche Building.'

'What happened at the Poche?' He leaned in, his friendly face suddenly intent. 'Dulcie, tell me.'

How could he not have heard? She took a deep breath and began to speak, hoping to get the worst over with quickly. 'Someone jumped. Someone jumped and died, Dimitri. It was – it was awful. Terrible. I don't know if it was an accident, or—'

'*Who*?' He interrupted her. ' Dulcie, tell me. Who jumped?'

'Herschoft. He was a professor,' she said. 'Fritz Herschoft.'

'Oh, him.' Dimitri seemed to collapse into himself, suddenly looking even more tired than before.

'Did you know him?' Concerned, she reached out to take his arm. 'I'm so sorry, Dimitri. Was he a friend?'

'What? No.' Dimitri seemed to be fading as he spoke. 'I know *of* him. Friends of friends, is that the saying? Odd, really, thinking of a person that way. Other than that . . .' He shrugged, clearly beyond caring. 'Look, Dulcie, I am wiped out. The police were not unprofessional, but the experience of being questioned was draining.' He turned toward the street, and Dulcie wondered if she should offer to walk him home.

But one question still lingered, and she kept her hand on his arm. 'I understand. But Dimitri, would you tell me what happened? Why did the police want to talk to you?'

He shook his head. 'It is private, I cannot. Other people are involved. Even the police asked me not to talk about it. I am sorry, Dulcie. It's not – I am not the bad guy here.'

She nodded, unsure of what to say. She didn't know Dimitri well, but he seemed like any of her colleagues – a nice, normal guy. Who, right now, looked positively exhausted.

'Well, I'm sorry if I got you in any trouble.' He turned, and Dulcie was struck by how sunken his eyes were. 'And I'm sorry to be the one to break the news.'

'The news?'

'About Professor Herschoft.'

'Please, that man was a monster.' He spat the word out like poison. 'All I can say is, we are all better off.'

Lucy would probably have an explanation, Dulcie thought as she headed back toward Widener. Lucy always saw patterns in the stars.

But even Lucy would have been surprised by what Dulcie found once she descended into the stacks. For starters, someone had been using her carrel. True, other students often sat in empty carrels while doing their own reading. But a kind of honor system ruled their usage. When the assigned student showed up, you vacated the little mini office. And you never, *ever* left a mess. So Dulcie was both troubled and surprised to find her books disturbed: some missing, and one on the floor. And horrified to realize, as she pulled herself into the seat, that that same interloper had put a large wad of chewed gum under the table, just where it was bound to stick to her jeans.

'Oh, *great*.' She kept her voice low, but inside she fumed. This was not the peaceful study break she had hoped for. Rubbing the gum off the best she could, she got up to search for her books. The two she'd left out were common research works; she'd have put them in the re-shelving carts otherwise. But she couldn't find either. In fact, where *Bulwich's* should have been was a book she'd never seen before. In frustration, she took it down and started leafing through it. It seemed to be a collection of essays and letters. A few looked quite standard: journal entries. And then something hit her. There was something about the style, a clarity of language despite the age.

*A woman press'd must make use of her mind . . .* Yes, that

was it. A defense of women as thinkers, as philosophers and writers. This sounded like *The Ravages*, like the other works of her anonymous subject that she had been tracking down. Dulcie kept reading. *A woman of thoughtful turn must do her work. Such a woman must turn her own hand to the creation and education.* She skimmed ahead. How could she not have read this piece before?

*For if the woman thinker be swept aside, she will have no choice but to abandon all. Not her family, nor her virtue, as has commonly been assumed. But all else, fleeing as she would a noisome beast to cross beyond.*

Could this be her author? Dulcie felt her pulse quickening as she took the volume back to her carrel. Sitting carefully, to avoid touching the desk's underside, she pulled out her laptop to begin making notes. What was that phrase? Something about 'noisome beasts,' about a woman thinker being 'swept aside'? Could that be the missing threat? The last note of desperation?

First things first. Using a piece of loose-leaf as a book-mark, she flipped to the front of the book. *The Woman Question: 1793–1803.* This was very promising. Why hadn't she read this before?

*Volume 2.* She read on: *Women of the Americas.*

Dulcie shut the volume with a thud, her hopes deflating like a balloon. This was the right sentiment and the right language. But it was the wrong continent. What she had thought was special must have been as common as grass. Maybe her heroine hadn't been the groundbreaking thinker she had hoped. Maybe Chelowski was right.

# TWENTY-ONE

'*D*e mortuis nil nisi bonum.' It always surprised Dulcie when Chris spoke Latin. 'Speak no ill of the dead. So much for that old chestnut, huh?'

'But it's more than not saying anything but good.' She'd reached her beau during her walk home. But although she was hoping to talk about them – or about his willowy student – Dulcie couldn't get her mind off that strange conversation with Dimitri. 'I mean, I didn't really know the guy, but this was something else. Corkie sounded positively dismissive, and she's supposed to be all empathic. And Dimitri looked like he hated the guy. Like he could've pushed him out of a window himself.'

'You don't think . . .?' Chris might be more logical than Dulcie, but together they had survived some strange occurrences.

'Dimitri? No.' Dulcie quickly dismissed the idea. 'Besides, I'm sure the police checked his whereabouts.' She'd almost said 'alibi.' 'Besides, it was suicide.'

'I'm not so sure, Dulcie. The Harvard cops had a forensic tech guy down at the Science Center. I heard they were checking his passwords, looking for emails and the like.'

'But they'd do that if it were suicide, wouldn't they?' Something was scratching at the back of her mind. Something disturbing.

To her surprise, her boyfriend chuckled. 'Are you telling me you aren't campaigning for it to be murder? That would be a change, Dulcie.'

'Chris.' She knew he was teasing. Right now, she couldn't take it. 'Please, it's not a story, OK? I was *there*.'

'Oh, honey, I'm sorry. I sort of forgot.'

'You forgot because we didn't *talk*. I only left a dozen messages.' She could hear her voice ratcheting up. She wasn't being rational. She didn't feel like being rational. 'He had clammy hands. That, and the greasy hair. That's all I knew about him. That's all anybody said. And now he's dead. He's *dead*, Chris, and nobody seems to care. And my thesis adviser hates me, and someone has been using my carrel, and now I think maybe he's right to hate me and I've been on the wrong track all along. And yesterday—' She was as close to breaking as she'd ever been. She could hear it, but she couldn't stop. 'Yesterday, Chris, you didn't call me. After everything that happened, you didn't call me back.'

Luckily, Chris understood. 'I know, I know, Dulcie, and I'm so sorry. I've taken on too much: these private students expect you to be on call constantly . . . Look, I can get Jerry to cover for me tonight, at least for a few hours. Why don't I come by in an hour? I'll swing by Mary Chung's?'

She sniffed. He was complaining about his private tutoring. The storm passed as quickly as it had sprung. 'Would you get the dumplings, Chris?' Suze might not approve, but then, Suze was hardly around these days. And Dulcie felt like she deserved something: he hadn't called, and she had kept herself from mentioning that girl, even after he brought up tutoring. 'And the scallion pancakes, too?'

'You bet, sweetie. I'll be over there by eight.'

Chris was better than his word, showing up not only with one big white bag from Mary Chung's, but with another from Toscanini's, which held two pints of ice cream. Without even looking, Dulcie knew they'd be his and hers pints: her favorite chocolate brownie mint chip and his mocha peanut butter crunch.

'Do you think every couple has routines like this?' They were on their dessert by this time, each with a spoon and a pint.

'Do you mean, do some couples put their ice cream in bowls?' He reached over to dig into her pint. Chris might have his favorites, but all ice cream was good to him.

'I mean, Chinese food and ice cream after a bad day.' Dulcie took a taste of his. Coffee and peanut butter could almost work, when united by chocolate.

'Maybe.' They hadn't spoken about the events of the last few days – about Herschoft or even about his student – instead settling into a companionable silence as they ate. Chris had the sports section unfolded in front of him. Dulcie found herself staring into space. Somewhere, Esmé was probably brewing up trouble, but for now the apartment was free of thuds, squeals, or crashes.

'Do you think that's a bad thing?'

Chris looked up. 'What do you mean?'

'I'm not sure.' Dulcie took another spoonful, letting the sweetness melt on her tongue. 'I guess I'm just wondering if we should talk more.'

Chris raised his eyebrows. 'Is this about Dimitri?'

'Not entirely.' Dulcie sucked on her spoon. Now that Chris was here, her fears had faded. Still, Chris's student had taken up an awful lot of his day. Rusti. That was her name. Tall, slim, *pretty* Rusti. 'I guess I was just thinking about relationships.'

'But didn't you say that Dimitri wasn't involved with, what's her name, Carrie Mines?'

'That's what he said. He says he's got some girlfriend from the School of Public Health, but nobody's ever seen her – and I did see Carrie at his place. She was in the crowd when the police took him in for questioning. And she wasn't just passing by. She looked intent. Involved, somehow, and she made a point of disappearing before they brought him out.' She spoke quickly, before Chris could interrupt. 'There's something going on, Chris. I know you think I create fictions, but there was a look on her face. Like, she was waiting. She expected it. It was all very intense.'

'So you think she called them?'

'Maybe.' Dulcie tried to put it together. 'But I'm not sure. I mean, supposedly she's missing. Nobody can locate her. But there she is, out in public. So is she hiding from something – or someone – in particular? Is she in some kind of trouble? And if she is, why show up in a crowd in the Square?'

'Maybe it's all a big mistake. You know, like someone reported her missing because she blew off a deadline.'

Dulcie shook her head. 'No, the cops are taking it seriously, and when I called to her, she took off.'

'And you don't think that was because she dropped your class?' He caught Dulcie's look. 'OK, forget that. Maybe it is something with Dimitri. Do you think he was the one you saw arguing with her? Maybe he hurt her in some way.'

'No.' Dulcie rejected the idea with a quick shake of her head. 'Dimitri's not like that. He's—' She paused, searching for the right words. 'He's a nice guy. Civilized. But there was something going on – more than he told me, anyway.'

Chris shrugged. 'So maybe they are involved, despite the regulations. Wouldn't be the first time. Not even for your department.' He ate more quickly than Dulcie, and his spoon was scraping against the bottom of the pint.

'You don't seem that upset about it.'

He shrugged again. 'Relationships happen. People aren't set in stone.'

Thinking of Trista and Jerry, Dulcie found herself nodding. Whatever was going on with those two, something was certainly changing. They'd been together forever. Longer even than she and Chris, but if Trista could meet someone new, even while she was supposedly deeply involved with

Jerry, then . . . Suddenly, the ice cream was too much. Dulcie put the pint down. 'What do you mean, relationships happen?'

'Well, you always talk about how good a couple Lloyd and Raleigh are.'

'Yeah?' She was waiting.

'That's all.' He looked at her quizzically. She waited. 'You going to finish that?'

'It's all yours.' She smiled, her face stiff with the effort.

# TWENTY-TWO

D ulcie woke the next morning to a scream.

'Suze? You OK?' Suze was not normally a screamer, but as Dulcie threw off the covers and made her way to her room-mate's bedroom, the voice was unmistakable. Chris had left around midnight for the rest of his shift, and Dulcie wondered, for an awful moment, if he'd left the door unlocked. Perhaps let someone in. One more yell, though, and Dulcie registered that Suze was more angry than scared.

Dulcie stood in the hall. From the grumbling that had followed the initial shout, it seemed neither life nor limb were in danger. 'What's happening?'

'That – that *cat*!'

Dulcie turned to see Esmé sitting on the top of the landing. The small cat only blinked once, but when Suze flung her bedroom door open, she turned and quickly trotted down the stairs. Dulcie swallowed. 'What did she do?'

'Come here.'

Dulcie took a careful step into Suze's bedroom. Suze was pointing to her desk. Dulcie could see the leather accessories, the scissors and letter opener, where she had replaced them. But across the top, over the tan leather case and the desk's blotter, were perfect little paw prints, black with greasy soot.

'Oh, that's from yesterday.' Dulcie had feared more break-ages, or something worse.

'Oh?' Suze turned to Dulcie, fixing her room-mate with what Dulcie privately called her prosecutorial stare. 'You knew about this?'

'Yeah, it was later, during the night, so after you'd come home to change—' They both turned in unison to where Suze had thrown her winter-heavy clothes on her bed. Without a word, Suze picked up the discarded sweater to reveal more paw prints. Esmé had apparently made herself at home on it, after circling several times.

'Well, if you weren't going to wear it.' As soon as the words were out of her mouth, Dulcie bit her lip. The old Suze, the friend she'd come to love, would understand. But this new work-obsessed Suze? The cat had walked over all three of her pillows as well.

'That cat . . .'

Dulcie waited, not daring to breathe. They'd been friends for years. 'I could . . .' She tried to think of appropriate compensation. She couldn't get rid of Esmé. The little cat might not be Mr Grey, but she had made a commitment.

And then Suze started laughing, and Dulcie collapsed into Suze's desk chair.

'Watch out, Dulce! I don't think I looked there!'

Now they were both laughing.

'I'm sorry, Suze. Really.' Confession was good for the soul. 'I thought I cleaned everything up. I didn't know she got into your room, too.'

'She takes after you, I guess. Into everything.' Suze shed her clothes and reached for her bathrobe, giving it a good once-over first.

Dulcie watched her friend, relieved to see her still smiling. 'Well, she's usually a little better about marking her progress.'

'Uh oh, what's up?' Suze belted her bathrobe and nodded toward the door. 'Tell me over coffee?'

'It's Chelowski. Though, with everything else going on, it almost seems minor. You really want to hear it?' Dulcie didn't even wait for an answer as she followed her friend down to the kitchen. Esmé was amusing company, but it was nice to have breakfast with someone human for a change.

'So, he thinks I'm just avoiding writing. But, Suze, I know something happened to her. I just know it.' By the time Suze had scooped up their scrambled eggs, Dulcie had filled her room-mate in on her latest thesis woes.

'Hot sauce?' Suze took her seat as Dulcie passed the bottle. 'It sounds doable.'

Dulcie considered her room-mate. 'I think you're the only person I've talked to who has said that.'

Her friend smiled. 'Maybe I know you better than some other people. Maybe you just need time. I mean, you've had some other things on your mind recently.'

'No kidding.'

Suze paused and examined her room-mate. 'Has something else happened?'

'Not really.' Dulcie thought back over the odd exchanges with Corkie and Dimitri. 'It's just that nobody is reacting like I expect them to. And, well, I'm getting the feeling that maybe, somehow, that missing girl is linked to the professor who killed himself. There's the timing, and I feel like everyone who talks about her has something to say about him, too.' Even to Suze, she didn't want to mention Mr Grey.

Suze raised her eyebrows. 'Interesting. Of course, that could be said of you, too, Dulcie.'

That prompted an answering glance from Dulcie, which set Suze off laughing again. 'Oh, hey, I almost forgot. There's a message for you on our answering machine,' she said when they'd both caught their breath. 'A detective from the Harvard police wants you to call.'

The smile disappeared. 'Great.'

'Maybe they just want your help. I mean, Dulcie, you are good at finding things out.'

'In the library.' The memory of her last few hours in Widener surfaced. 'And maybe not even then.'

'Come on, Dulce. You know you can do it. As a certain small being just proved, everyone leaves some kind of tracks.'

Suze took the first shower while Dulcie plopped on to the sofa and, with an air of resignation, dialed the number for the Harvard police. The message had been from Detective Rogovoy, and she was put through immediately.

'We'd like you to come in again,' said the voice on the line. It wasn't even ten, but the voice sounded tired. 'We need to ask you a few more questions.'

Dulcie didn't mean for her sigh to be quite so dramatic. 'Today? I'm sorry, I can't.' She leaned back against the old pillows, thoughts of the day ahead already weighing on her. 'I want to help. Really. But I've got work to do.' The image of all those ungraded papers loomed. 'A lot of work. We just had midterms, you know.'

There was a grant application, too. Not to mention her research. Yesterday had been a total waste, and if she was going to get Chelowski off her back, she'd have to come up with something solid. She closed her eyes, tired just thinking about it.

But the detective on the other end had his own problems.

'I understand the academic schedule. But we just had a suspicious death, young lady.' The detective's tone caught Dulcie off guard. So did that word.

'Suspicious?' She remembered what Chris had been saying.

'Undetermined, let's say. Look, we need you to come in.' Rogovoy's voice had lost its edge. 'I promise this won't take long.'

Dulcie wondered how late he'd been working on this case, and if he'd been to bed at all. While some of her colleagues might have scoffed, Dulcie felt a wave of sympathy for the detective. He was dealing with bigger issues than deadlines or even grant applications. For a moment she wavered, her sense of duty weighing against her own concerns. And then – for just a moment – she felt it. The brush of fur against her outflung arm. She almost turned to look, but just then a small thud and the rapid patter of a running kitten confirmed her suspicions. Esmé was upstairs.

'Mr Grey?' She closed her eyes and felt the smooth, firm push as a spectral cat butted his head against her hand.

'Excuse me?' On the phone, the detective sounded even more fatigued.

'I'm sorry.' Dulcie didn't move her hand, but she did try to concentrate. 'I got distracted. I do understand.' Dulcie ran through her day's duties. 'I've got a few things to take care of, but I can come by in about an hour.'

'I'll be here,' said the detective. Dulcie had the distinct feeling that he never left. As she hung up the phone, she heard a gentle thud as if a cat had jumped off the sofa. But the sound of a purr lingered.

Suze took one look at her face and stopped in the hallway, still toweling her hair. 'What?'

'I'm going to talk to the cops. Again.' Dulcie was thinking hard. 'But I don't want to just answer their questions. I want to find out what the deal is with Carrie, and why they picked up Dimitri. I just can't believe he's done anything.'

Suze raised her eyebrows, but didn't say anything as Dulcie walked past her into the bathroom.

'OK, maybe he's involved in *something*, Suze.' Dulcie gave her that. 'But not . . . Not whatever they think.' She hung up her robe, pausing as the thought came to her. 'I wonder if someone is trying to frame Dimitri, and if somehow my student – or my ex-student – is involved?'

# TWENTY-THREE

C orkie was the key. Suze had been skeptical when Dulcie outlined her plan, but a half hour later as Dulcie walked to the Square she became more and more convinced she was right. Something very odd was going on, and her way in was through her junior tutee. Then, once she knew a bit more, she would go see that detective. A little bit of preliminary sleuthing would serve both their causes.

Head bent against the wind, Dulcie went over the facts: Corkie knew Carrie; Dulcie was pretty sure that was who she had seen her student talking with outside of Lala's – and that was after the younger girl had supposedly gone missing. Corkie was involved in something unusual, something that had taken her away from their regular meeting. And Corkie, bless her, was likely to open up to Dulcie in a way that neither Dimitri nor the elusive Carrie would.

After all, Corkie had already confided in her tutor. During the semester they'd worked together, Corkie had talked about being overwhelmed when she'd first arrived. In many ways, Dulcie saw the big girl as a younger version of herself. A much taller Midwestern version, but with the same mix of enthusiasm and, yes, innocence. The thought made her smile, and she fished an errant curl out of her mouth. She, too, had been eager, a little wide-eyed. It had taken a while before she'd found her footing.

Still, she had to admit Corkie had reacted strangely at their last meeting. Since she'd canceled their tutorial, Dulcie realized, and Dulcie had seen her on the street – deep in conversation with Carrie Mines. Could her work at Below the Stairs be part of that? Was listening to other people's troubles weighing on her, setting her natural empathy against her zest for life?

One way or another, Dulcie was going to find out. And since the Square was getting closer, she dug out her phone to call the mysterious junior. As if on cue, it rang, and Dulcie stopped short when she saw the incoming number.

'Lucy?' It wasn't yet ten on the East Coast, and Dulcie's mother was more a moon-goddess type than a sun worshipper. 'Is something wrong?'

'Of course not, dear. Merlin just insisted that I get in touch.'

Dulcie smiled. She'd always been grateful that Mr Grey wasn't an early riser. Lucy, it seemed, wasn't so lucky in her choice of pet. 'And he said you should call me?' Then again, Merlin probably had more wildlife around to get excited about. Here, well, it was all squirrels and pigeons.

'He did. He said you should watch out.' Dulcie surveyed her surroundings. She was standing in the Yard, the stone steps leading up to Widener to her left. Memorial Church to her right. A steady stream of students broke around her, making their way to the nearby lecture halls. 'You should watch the skies.'

'Always good advice.' Dulcie glanced upward. It did look like rain. Perhaps Merlin had meteorological instincts? 'So how are things back at the com— Arts colony?' Lucy did not appreciate Dulcie's cavalier references to their home. Dulcie, her mother was quick to remind her, had been born in an actual commune, and Lucy had been more than ready to move out of the shared farmhouse by the time her daughter was three months old.

'Well, it's interesting that you ask, dear. Or maybe not, considering that you are an Aries.' Static broke up the line, and Dulcie looked up at the sky again. Definitely rain. 'Look out for something.' The line was breaking up, and Dulcie walked over to the Widener steps. Elevation wouldn't mean much to her cell connection, but if those clouds let loose, at least she could bolt for the library foyer.

'Keep your eyes open.' Up a few steps, the sound was no better. But looking out over the intersecting paths, Dulcie caught sight of a familiar bobbing head. Corkie! It looked like the undergrad was hurrying over to the basement counseling office.

'Lucy, I've got to go.' As if to lend credence to her urgency, a fat raindrop landed on Dulcie's head. Another followed. The gray marble steps began to gather dark blotches. 'It's started to rain. I'll call you soon. Love you.'

Trotting down the stairs, mindful of how slick they could become, Dulcie thought about her mother's parting words. A warning. Trouble from above. She smiled. Only Lucy could make fortune-cookie pronouncements sound so serious. No, she corrected herself, only Lucy's cat could do that.

The last few steps were treacherous, the rain turning to something like sleet, and Dulcie had to concentrate on her footing. By the time she reached asphalt, Corkie was too far away.

'Corkie!' She called anyway, knowing it was futile. Halfway across the Yard, a head bobbed up, but didn't turn. 'Bother.'

Grabbing at her scarf to hold it tighter, Dulcie started to run. At least she'd found her student – and the weather gave her a perfect excuse to duck into the basement center. But as she descended the stairs, she realized that Corkie might have plans of her own. The girl might not have been hurrying only because of the weather. She might have patients to see. Clients, whatever they were called.

Sure enough, the waiting room was empty when she came in, and Dulcie approached the window where she had checked in before. 'Hello?'

Nobody answered and she looked down the hall. That gentle chime would have alerted anyone here to her arrival. 'Corkie!' Her student was ushering someone into an office: a slight figure in olive-green wool.

'Ms Schwartz!' Corkie stepped back into the hall, pulling the office door closed behind her. 'May I help you?'

'Um, yes, actually.' Now that she was here, Dulcie realized how vague her plan was. 'I have a few questions for you.'

Corkie glanced back at the door. 'Can this wait?' Her voice sounded tighter, more anxious than Dulcie had ever heard.

'Of course.' Guilt washed over her. Here she was, barging into her charge's private life. 'I'm sorry. I'll wait.'

'Is there a problem?' The receptionist had reappeared in the window. 'Do you need an appointment?'

'No, I'm fine.' Dulcie began, only to be interrupted by Corkie.

'This won't take long, Reneé.'

The black woman smiled, and Dulcie had the distinct feeling that it was Corkie's assurance, rather than her own, that made her finally turn away, sit at her desk, and start typing.

Thirty minutes later, Dulcie was deep into an article on hair ties when a hand on her shoulder caused her to jump.

'Fashion conscious?' Corkie smiled down at her, and Dulcie, a little flustered, threw the magazine back on the low coffee table. 'I'm free now.'

'You are? Great.' They were alone. Dulcie felt sure she would have heard the chime, even if she'd been too engrossed to see someone walk by. Then she remembered the receptionist's sudden appearance. The basement must have a back exit, perhaps into the main part of the building. 'Can we talk in private?'

'Sure.' Corkie looked anything but as she led her back to the small office, barely big enough for a tiny sofa and a comfy-looking chair. A table up against the wall held a pile of files and a bottle of water. Corkie, following her eyes, grabbed an empty clipboard from the floor beside her chair and put it on top of the files, obscuring the labels. 'Please, have a seat.'

'Thanks.' Dulcie realized she should have spent her time trying to figure out how to broach the topic. 'Look, Corkie—'

Corkie began talking at the same time. 'I should warn you—'

They both laughed, and Dulcie nodded. 'You go first.'

'Thanks.' Corkie had settled into the padded chair and folded her hands in her lap. She looked, Dulcie realized, older this way. More professional. 'What I was going to say is, you should always feel free to come here. Below the Stairs is a free peer-to-peer counseling center, open to all members of the university. And, especially after such a tragic death, a lot of people have felt the need to talk, to air their feelings. But—' She paused.

Dulcie nodded for her to continue.

'But, well, you're my tutor. So, um, I'm not entirely sure if I'm the best person for you to talk to. I mean, I understand that you know me, so maybe there's a comfort factor . . .'

'No, no.' Dulcie shook her head as she interrupted. 'I'm sorry. I must have given you the wrong impression. I'm not here for counseling. Not that there's anything wrong with counseling,' she added quickly. 'I'm here because of another student. Because of Carrie Mines.'

Dulcie had hoped for a reaction, but Corkie's voice was calm and professional. 'Are you worried about this student?'

'Well, yes. Yes and no.' Dulcie tried to frame her thoughts. Had that been Carrie just now? She'd had a glimpse of a green wool coat, that was all. 'You know Carrie was reported missing, right? That the police want to talk with her? In fact, I believe I saw you talking with her, out on Mass. Ave.' Corkie's face gave nothing away. 'Look, maybe it's none of my business. But if you know where she is, you really ought to tell the cops.' Again, nothing. 'And, well, I think she may be involved with another student I know. A colleague, who's in trouble. So, even if you don't want to go to the authorities, I need to find her. Or at least find out what's going on with her. I emailed her and got one quick response. But that was a few days ago. Since then, nothing.'

'And you've tried calling?'

That took Dulcie aback. 'Well, she never got back to me after the second email. And her phone isn't listed in the university directory. But I've seen her and called out to her. She runs away.'

'Maybe she doesn't want to talk to you.'

'Well, obviously.' Dulcie was losing her, she could tell. 'But I think she's in trouble, and I think she's getting in deeper – and dragging other people in as well.'

'So, you'd like her to come forward?'

'Yeah, I guess.' It was little enough, but Corkie clearly wasn't going to talk. Maybe she could get Carrie to come forward and clear Dimitri – and shed some light on what was going on. 'I mean, she should get in touch with the police. But if she doesn't want to, she could call me.'

Corkie nodded, satisfied. 'Well, I can't say whether or not I know this student, and I certainly can't provide any information that we may have in our files to you. But I could try to pass along your message. Tell her you'd like to chat.'

'That would be great.' It would be something, anyway.

Corkie stood up. 'So, I have your number. Again, I can't promise anything, but—'

'Wait, Corkie.' Dulcie had an idea. 'May I give you a note for her? I mean, I understand that maybe you don't know her and never will or anything. But just in case?'

Corkie's smile looked real this time. 'Sure, and thanks for understanding.' She looked around. 'Hang on. I'll get a pad and some paper from Reneé.'

She walked out of the room, pulling the door half closed behind her. Dulcie could hear her voice, talking to the receptionist. She looked around. It was bad. The wrong thing to do. But she couldn't resist. That olive green; it *might* have been Carrie. And the pile of files was sitting there, almost asking to be opened.

'You don't have to say it, Mr Grey,' she muttered into the silence. 'This makes me glad you're not here.' She pushed back the covering clipboard to look at the top file. CARRIE MINES. The name jumped out at her. She paused – and opened the file.

'What?' The voice in the hall made her jump. 'Tell her five minutes, tops!'

It was too risky. Dulcie started to close the file. But as she did, a piece of paper fell out, and Dulcie reached for it. White notepaper, about half the size of a sheet of typing paper, it was blank on one side. On the other, Dulcie saw a curious block print: *I'm sorry,* it said. *This cannot continue. No one is to blame, but I've got to end it.* And that was all. Someone had torn off the bottom – the signature – but the meaning was clear. *I've got to end it.* What more needed to be said?

If suicide was something one person could give to another, like a cold virus . . . Suddenly, Dulcie remembered her talk with Dimitri. He'd been so tired, but he'd come back to life when she'd mentioned a suicide, that someone had jumped from the Poche. But when she'd told him that the jumper had been Professor Herschoft, he'd waved it off, like he didn't care. At the time, she'd been taken aback. He'd sounded a little insensitive, to be honest, which was not how she thought of Dimitri. Now it all made perfect sense. He didn't care about

Fritz Herschoft because he wasn't worried about Professor Herschoft. He *was* worried about Carrie. This was serious.

A laugh right outside the door alerted Dulcie that Corkie's conversation was winding up. Without thinking, Dulcie grabbed the note. She had just time enough to shove it in her pocket and slide the clipboard back on top before Corkie walked back in, smiling. 'Here you go.' She handed a legal pad and pen to Dulcie. 'I can even dig up an envelope for you, if you want.'

'That won't be necessary.' A letter would take too long. It was too chancy. She should call – or email. Memory slapped her like a blast of frost: she had emailed Carrie only days before, but in that email she'd urged her to call a number that really belonged to the police. If Carrie, fragile and distraught, had reached out and found herself being interrogated . . . No, it didn't bear thinking about. All she could do now was try to make amends.

*Carrie – Call me please!*, she wrote. *I can and will help you – no matter what has happened.* She underlined the note to give it an emphasis email would never convey and signed her name, finishing the note with every number she could think of: cell, home, the departmental office. Carrie Mines had been her student once, and now she was considering suicide. She had to do anything she could.

'Thanks so much, Corkie.' Dulcie rose to leave.

Her current student looked at her, her ready smile disappearing. 'Are you OK?'

Dulcie nodded.

'Because you really can talk with someone, you know.'

'Thanks, Corkie.' Dulcie shrugged her bag over her shoulder and patted the pocket with the note. 'I think you're doing great work here, but I'm not the one who needs your help.'

Corkie walked her to the counseling center's door, still looking confused. Dulcie nodded to the receptionist and stepped outside, into the stairwell. Her one-time student, her charge, was at risk, and she may have made her situation worse. She had to do something. But what?

And then everything turned black.

# TWENTY-FOUR

As the light came back on, Dulcie became aware of a horrible pain in her head and of a large pink face leaning over her.

'I didn't think this was how you meant to keep your appointment, Ms Schwartz.' The face had a bit of stubble and an unfortunate nose. She blinked, unable to place the large face. 'I'm Detective Rogovoy.'

'Oh, right.' She started to sit up and was stopped both by the shooting pain and by Rogovoy's hand on her shoulder.

'I don't think you should do that yet.'

She let herself be pushed back down. She was on a bed, in a curtained alcove. Hushed voices and lights carried from the outside world. 'Where am I?'

'University health services.'

She nodded, a little. It hurt. 'And?'

'You were hit on the head with a piece of brick, coming out of the basement of Weld.'

She put her hand up to where the pain was coming from and felt dampness. Rogovoy reached over to a table and grabbed an ice pack. 'I'm supposed to tell you to leave that on for twenty minutes at a time.'

She nodded again, a mistake. 'An accident?' The pain was making her nauseous.

'There's no loose masonry in that stairwell.' He looked at her, his tired eyes sharp. 'You don't remember seeing anything? Hearing anyone?'

'No.' She worked to keep her head still, but the thoughts were coming fast. 'The Harvard Harasser?'

Rogovoy tightened his mouth into what could have been a smile. 'That nickname. Makes him sound harmless, doesn't it? This fits with the other attacks, but we won't know anything until we find out more.'

'OK.' In her current state, that had almost made sense. 'So what happens now?' The ice was helping. If she spoke softly it didn't hurt so much.

'So I take your statement, such as it is, and then I pretend you just woke up and call for the nurse.'

That was her cue, she decided, to close her eyes and wait.

The next time she opened them, it wasn't Detective Rogovoy's nose that greeted her, but Chris, looking more pale than usual.

'You OK?' Dulcie asked, sitting up. It didn't hurt as much.

'Me?' His thin face broke into a grin. 'Dulcie, you had us all so worried.'

'Us?' She risked turning her head to look around. They seemed to be alone.

'Me, Suze. Even Trista came by.' He reached to stroke her cheek. 'But never mind all that crap. You're awake.'

'Yeah.' He was always pale, and it was March in New England. One sunny day didn't change that. Still, something was up. 'Chris, how long have I been out?'

'You've been in and out for a couple of hours. The doctors say you probably have a concussion.' He slumped back in his chair, leading Dulcie to wonder how long he'd been perched over her. 'They kept saying it probably wasn't serious, but you were so still.' He turned away, but she saw him wiping his face. 'I was scared.'

'Oh, Chris.' Despite the pain, she smiled. It was nice to be cared about. But something was bothering her. 'Chris, I found something.'

'Oh, no, you don't.' Her boyfriend sat up in his seat. 'You are not playing cops and robbers. You're in no shape.'

'I know.' It was a relief to admit it. 'But there's something I found. Would you hand me my coat?'

He looked around until he found it and then gently laid it on the bed.

'I shouldn't have taken this, I know, but—' She reached into the pockets. She pulled out a mitten. One mitten, and that was it. 'Oh, hell.' She caught herself. 'Goddess preserve.'

'What?'

'This is all that was in my pockets?' She held up the ragged knitting.

He shrugged. 'The Coop's having a sale. I'll pick you up some new ones before you get out.'

She closed her eyes. Was he being dense? 'It's not the mitten. It's what else was in there. A note. A suicide note.

I think Carrie is at risk, and that somehow Dimitri is involved.
And maybe that professor, too. I had it. In this pocket.'

She looked up to see Chris staring blankly, like she wasn't
making sense. Behind him, stood a gray-haired woman in a
white coat. 'You've decided to come back to us?'

Her professional calm was too much for Dulcie. 'Yes, I'm
back. And I need to know what happened to the note that was
in my pocket.'

'Hang on.' The woman reached to lift Dulcie's eyelid, and
it was all Dulcie could do not to shake her off.

'We have to talk before you rush off. Don't blame your
boyfriend.' The white coat cut off Dulcie's protest and moved
on to her chest. 'He's been a real stalwart here. You gave us
all a scare, young lady.'

Dulcie smiled at the description. Emotionally, it was apt
anyway. And then Chris saw her smile and the worried look
fell away. 'Yes, she did,' he said to the nurse. 'But I think
she's back.'

'If that's the case,' Rogovoy interrupted, appearing in the
doorway, 'then I would like to have a few words with Ms
Schwartz here.' He looked at the nurse, rather than Dulcie,
for confirmation and must have gotten it. She turned to leave.

'Chris stays,' Dulcie put in before anyone else could. The
detective nodded as if his head were heavy and pulled up a
plastic chair. Looking at her with tired eyes, he started to take
down her statement, writing longhand on a yellow pad just
like the ones Suze used. Dulcie gave him an abbreviated
version, ending with her waking up in the infirmary.

'So, what's the note?' He'd been listening.

She paused. It wasn't just the content, a cry for help, it was
how she had gotten it. 'I . . .' She paused, unsure how to
proceed. 'I happened upon a note that I believe was written
by Carrie Mines. A note that sounded like she was on the
verge of something. Something desperate.'

He nodded, and Dulcie had all the confirmation she needed.
'You knew she wasn't really missing, didn't you?'

'Wait a minute. Dulcie?' Chris started to protest.

Rogovoy raised a hand. 'Please. You're here on sufferance.'

Dulcie nodded. 'It's OK, Chris.' And, with a sigh, began
again. 'I don't know what's going on, but she's not missing.
I've seen her. A few times.' The way Rogovoy was nodding,

Dulcie figured this wasn't news to him. 'I thought I saw her going into the counseling center.'

It wasn't the whole truth, but it wasn't a lie either. She looked up at the detective and waited for his response. When none was immediately forthcoming, she asked: 'You saw that she emailed me.' She paused, the memory of her own complicity almost too painful to bear. 'I assume she didn't call you?'

'She did not, and she hasn't gone back to her apartment or responded to subsequent phone or email queries. We have made it clear through all resources that we'd appreciate her coming in to answer some questions.' Rogovoy chose his words carefully. 'We believe she may have information on an ongoing investigation, but there is not an active alert out for her. I probably shouldn't even be telling you this, but she has a history of what we call "voluntary missing." She always turns up, and her parents aren't worried. That said, yes, we would like her to come talk to us.'

'You'd *like* her to come in.' That was food for thought. Dulcie had always assumed a summons from the police was as good as law. But maybe the university cops didn't have the clout that city police had. Either way, she realized, Lucy would be appalled at her blind acceptance of authority. 'What is this about, Detective Rogovoy? I think you owe me an explanation.'

'No, I don't.' But from the way he shifted in his seat, Dulcie knew something would be forthcoming. 'But I think you've figured out that there was a connection between Ms Mines and the professor who . . . who died.'

'Fritz Herschoft.' He nodded, and she was hit by another thought. 'Suze, my room-mate, said that suicide can be contagious.' She started to get up. 'And if somehow I scared her off, scared her away from her therapy session . . .'

'Relax, Ms Schwartz.' Rogovoy held his big hands out, as if to calm the air. 'We're not concerned about Ms Mines' well-being right now. We don't have her listed as a person at risk. You were the one who was attacked, remember?'

'Well, yeah.' The sudden movement had set her head aching again. 'But wasn't that just the Harvard Harasser? My room-mate said she thought he might escalate, might really hurt someone.'

'I'd like to talk to your room-mate.'

Dulcie thought for a moment about Suze, ace law student, under questioning. That thought alone was enough to keep her mouth closed – in a smile.

'Well, that's not a priority. What is, is finding out who attacked you and why. Because – and I am only telling you this because I want you to stay out of trouble, Ms Schwartz – we have begun to believe that the so-called harasser's attacks are not entirely random. The fact that something may have been taken from you while you were unconscious, something that may have a connection to recent events, is reason to suspect that this was not some random act.'

'But it wasn't a clue. It was a suicide note. A cry for help.' Dulcie paused and tried to remember exactly what the note had said. It hadn't been specific. Nothing about a date or time. But its tone had been desperate: the voice of a person driven to the brink. 'Wait, "*may have*"?'

'You were hit pretty hard, Ms Schwartz.'

Dulcie looked from the detective to Chris.

Chris nodded. 'You had your bag and everything when they brought you in.' He was trying to make peace. 'Maybe there was something, and it fell out of your pocket? They had to lift you out of the stairwell.'

She shook her head. A mistake. 'I don't know. Maybe.' She had to acknowledge the possibility. 'But it doesn't matter. I know what I read. And you've got to believe me.' She turned from Chris to the detective. 'Maybe the attack wasn't meant for me. Maybe someone is following Carrie. Threatening her. And maybe you're wrong about Carrie not being at risk. If she heard about Professor Herschoft or knew him . . . You should be looking for her – actively looking for her. Add it all together and she could be on the brink of suicide, just like Professor Herschoft.'

'Only that wasn't suicide, Ms Schwartz.' Detective Rogovoy looked from her to Chris, his dark eyes sharp. 'You'll be reading this in the papers soon enough anyway, so here goes. Despite the initial reports to the contrary, we now have reason to believe that Fritz Herschoft's death was in fact a homicide.'

# TWENTY-FIVE

'Oh, this is maddening!'

Chris smiled, but didn't respond. Dulcie had been raving since Rogovoy had left. The detective had refused to say any more, even after eliciting a promise that she turn over the note 'if it turned up.' Even Chris had given up arguing with her. So had the nurse, who had poked her head back in when the portly cop had took off. 'Overnight,' she'd said, finally. 'Doctor's orders.'

'Think of it as a chance to think about your thesis. Uninterrupted.' He had been trying.

Dulcie, however, couldn't get over Rogovoy's bombshell. 'Homicide, Chris. He'd told me it was undetermined, but now . . . So, does that mean someone pushed him out that window?' She was missing something – something important – but her head was aching too much to piece it together. 'Herschoft wasn't a big guy, but still.'

'Dulce, you have your own murder mystery to solve, don't you?' From the look on Chris's face, Dulcie suspected he'd been instructed to divert her. 'With that missing author?'

'You don't believe in that. Nobody does.' She was frustrated, and frustration made her grumpy. She wasn't being fair to her boyfriend and she knew it, but she could feel herself spiraling down. 'Even my thesis adviser thinks the whole thing is an excuse. That I'm trying to track the author of *The Ravages* because I don't want to actually write.'

'That's crazy.' Chris looked at her seriously. 'I know I've had my doubts about your theory, but saying that you don't want to write? That's just nuts. I'm sorry you have to deal with such a jerk, Dulcie. You'll prove him wrong. You will. And maybe this is the break you need. You can do some more reading.' He looked around. 'I could run over to Widener, get some books for you.'

'Like you would know which ones.' Her mood was growing

worse by the minute. 'Besides, I know you're only trying to distract me. It's hopeless, Chris. *I'm* hopeless. I find an important note, which is then stolen or—' She swallowed both the lump in her throat and the difficult truth. 'OK, that I lost. And I spend hours in Widener and only turn up this depressing essay that turned out to be a total dead end. I know she was on the edge, I know it from my dreams, and it's been driving me mad. Besides, what I *should* be doing is grading midterm papers.'

'Now *that* would be bad for your health.'

'I'm a captive of the patriarchy,' Dulcie grumbled, and then, aware of how silly she sounded, found herself breaking into a grin.

'Some patriarchy.' Chris saw the smile and chimed in. 'Considering that your doctor is a woman. I've met her. She's nice.'

'Oh?' Dulcie eyed her beau.

'Not my type.' He looked more like himself again. Still pale, but much more animated. 'I go for the bandaged type. The ones with big bumps on their heads.'

'Great.' She reached up to touch the tender lump and imagined how dried blood must look in her copper-tinged hair. 'I'm a freak.'

'You're *my* freak.' He kissed her. 'And according to the *matriarchal* power structure, there's no limit on what you can eat.' He saw her look and laughed. 'I mean, there are no dietary restrictions in place. So I was thinking, maybe I'd go get us some lunch?'

He wanted to leave. This was his second attempt at an excuse. But as she tried to think of a response, her stomach growled. Her traitorous stomach. And the clock on the wall did say it was past four. 'That would be wonderful,' she conceded, attempting something like a smile. 'Would you go to Lala's?'

'Or how about peanut butter and cream cheese on a toasted cinnamon raisin?'

'No, not bagels.' An image of a redhead, tall and lean, flashed through her mind. She looked up at her beau, suddenly aware of how she must appear. Muddy, bloody, and battered. 'Chris?'

He was putting on his coat, but turned at her voice. 'Yes?'

'Don't take too long, OK? I'm— I'm hungry.' It wasn't what she'd meant to say, but he nodded.

'Don't blame you,' he said. And he was gone.

After he'd left, Dulcie tried to remember what that stray thought had been. Rogovoy had said that Herschoft had been killed, and just at that moment, she'd thought of something. Something important.

It was no use. The harder she tried to think back, the more she became aware of how tired she felt. Outside the curtain, voices were murmuring softly. In the hall, hard soles clipped along a vinyl floor. But lying in bed, warm and quiet, none of this seemed to concern her. She felt herself drifting and closed her eyes. If she were home, she thought, then Mr Grey would come to her. She would feel him jump to the bed, register the soft thud as he landed and then the rhythmic motion of his paws kneading the bedspread. At one point, he had come to her anywhere: appearing like a phantom in her old thesis adviser's home. Making his presence felt deep in the stacks of Widener. Recently, however, his visits had been restricted to her apartment. *Their* apartment: the one where he had lived most of his life.

'Makes sense,' Dulcie muttered softly. 'He was a house cat. *Is* a house cat. A house cat ghost.'

If that were the case, what did it mean for the future? The end of the semester seemed a long way away, and there was no telling if Chris would bring up his proposal of living together again. He might have forgotten or given up, she thought. 'He might not want to live with a failure, an all-but-dissertation,' she murmured to herself. 'He might want a real redhead instead. He might be ready to cross over.' Her mouth formed the words, but no sound came out. Her eyes closed, which was why she didn't see the fat gray squirrel that had scampered up to her window. Her breathing grew more quiet, deep and regular, so she didn't see the furry beast cock its head and peer inside. And in seconds she was asleep, unaware of the soft thud at the foot of the bed.

When she awoke, just ten minutes later, Dulcie felt strangely refreshed. Chris hadn't returned yet, but she decided not to worry. The wait at Lala's could be intense. Instead, Dulcie realized, she had a choice. She could wallow in jealousy and self-pity. Or she could reach out to those who cared for her. She looked over at the note Suze had left, urging her to call. No, she knew that was only out of friendship. Suze was busy; she'd moved on. Like Trista had, and even Lloyd.

Work it was then. She might be dispirited, but she couldn't give up, not yet. Chris probably had been trying to distract her, but his efforts had worked. She was thinking about her thesis again – and about the mystery of the missing author. Maybe all her friends were right. Maybe Chelowski was, too, and she had been chasing a phantom, abandoning her legitimate textual analysis for some two-hundred-year-old mystery. But one thing her thesis adviser hadn't gotten right was her intent. She was Dulcinea Schwartz and even if she had wasted a month, two months, on a wild goose chase, she was going to write her thesis. And she was not going to let any more of her students fall through the cracks.

# TWENTY-SIX

D ulcie was released the next morning with a headache and a new resolve. This afternoon, she would catch up on her grading. Tomorrow, she'd go back to her original thesis idea. It was solid, based on an actual text, and she needed to start writing something. But this morning, before anything else, she was going to fulfill her obligations to Carrie Mines. She might no longer have the note in hand, but she had knowledge of it.

Rogovoy had promised that the department would follow up and find out who had attacked her. Their track record with the Harvard Harasser hadn't been great thus far, but maybe, if he really was escalating, they'd take their manhunt more seriously. Still, between that and their newly classified homicide, it seemed unlikely that the police would be able to expend any resources on a student whom they thought was simply playing hooky. And despite what the detective had said about Carrie not being a person at risk, Dulcie had a sense that the girl needed help.

But to do that, to reach the missing girl, she needed to come clean to Corkie about the note.

'What you need is breakfast.' Suze had come to pick her up, in a cab no less. The day was fine – cold again, but clear and crisp – and at first Dulcie had wanted to walk. But when Suze pointed out that the collar of Dulcie's shirt was stained dark with blood, Dulcie allowed herself to be herded into the yellow taxi and back to their apartment. 'You go take a shower,' her room-mate said as she paid the cabbie. 'I'm making pancakes.'

But before Dulcie even made it to the front stoop, she was stopped by a force of nature. Helene Duvoisier, their down-stairs neighbor, was out on the sidewalk in her hospital scrubs, her wide brown face creased with worry.

'There you are! You poor thing.' Dulcie allowed herself to be hugged, admitting after the first squeeze that the friendly pressure felt good. 'How are you feeling?'

'I'm OK.' She reached up to gingerly touch the knot on top of her head. 'But someone beaned me pretty bad.'

'So I heard.' Helene shook her head. 'You've got to be careful. Head injuries are funny things.'

'Don't worry, I've got a backup drive.' She meant it as a joke, but Helene did her best to suppress her smile.

'Very funny, young lady. So, is Susannah staying with you today?'

They both turned. Suze had already made her way in, and Dulcie could only hope those pancakes were in the works. 'No, I'm fine – really, Helene. And I've got work to do.'

Her neighbor raised one eyebrow. 'Work, huh? I wish you'd stick to the books.'

Dulcie felt herself smiling. 'And how do you know I'm not?'

'Too many people been by asking for you.' Her neighbor's broad face stayed serious. 'How do you think I knew what happened? And the cats – Julius and Murray – they wouldn't let me sleep all night. I bet your little girl is frantic.'

She was right, Dulcie thought as she took her leave. She had only been gone overnight, but the little cat greeted her at the door as if she'd been on safari. Having a cat twining around her ankles made it difficult to climb the stairs, however, so Dulcie hoisted the tiny body and carried her up to the kitchen. Suze was already at work, and the smell of melting butter made her realize just how hungry she was.

'Wow, do I have time to shower?' She placed Esmé on the floor and looked over her room-mate's shoulder at a mixing bowl that already held batter and what looked like granola.

'Ten minutes. Hurry up.'

'Aye aye, captain.' When the kitten didn't follow her up, she paused. Had it been affection that had prompted that greeting, or the possibility of butter?

Fifteen minutes later, Dulcie was enjoying Suze's pancakes. Her room-mate had indeed added granola, which made the cakes a little crunchy for Dulcie's liking, but with enough maple syrup they still tasted great.

'So what did Helene have to say?' Suze asked.

'Helene? She was just welcoming me back.' Dulcie sliced off some butter, reaching down to give it to Esmé.

'That cat is so spoiled.'

'She missed me. Helene said her cats did, too.' The little tongue made quick work of the butter, polishing off Dulcie's finger with rough, rapid swipes. 'She said they were worried about me.'

'You want more?' Suze was already standing, and Dulcie held her plate up.

'Thanks.'

'Here, take these last two. I should get going.'

Dulcie nodded, her mouth full. Suze had probably rearranged her schedule for her. 'Big day?'

'We've got this one landlord to depose. There's something going on in the housing project. We think he's insisting on sexual favors in exchange for rent.'

'Charming. You sure you don't want one of these?'

'No, thanks. Graciela is covering for me, but I should get down there.' She was already washing her plate. 'Can you take it easy today?'

'Don't want to.' Finishing the last bite, Dulcie stood. Suze had made breakfast; cleaning up was the least she could do. 'Let me do that. You go save the world.'

'Thanks.' Suze smiled as she relinquished the sponge and headed toward the closet. 'But really, take it easy. Head injuries are serious things.'

'I know.' Dulcie turned the water up high, enjoying the steam. 'That's what Helene said.'

'I wonder how she knew.' Suze's voice was muffled as she pulled a heavy sweater over her head.

'Excuse me?'

'Helene and her cats,' Suze said as she reached for her coat. 'I mean, I didn't see her last night. I didn't tell her you were in the health services.'

'Maybe Mr Grey told her.' The idea warmed Dulcie. 'Or told her cats.'

'I hope so.' The voice came up the stairs. 'I mean, I don't know if I like the idea of people talking about you.'

Dulcie knew Esmé didn't want her to go, and so before heading out, she decided to spend a few minutes playing with the kitten. The young cat was all energy, bouncing around the living room as Dulcie tossed and then retrieved a catnip ball. At times, she seemed almost too energetic, throwing herself into the sofa and against the wall in her fury to get at the toy.

'Poor little girl, all alone.' She threw the ball and watched the white paws scramble after it. 'I wonder if I should get you a playmate.'

'*A companion for your companion?*'

'Mr Grey!' Esmé looked up but, with the feline equivalent of a shrug, went back to the ball. 'You're here!'

'*As ever.*'

'But you haven't been.' She bit her lip, not wanting to sound churlish. 'I mean, I was hurt and in the hospital and . . .'

'*And were being cared for, little one. Sometimes we have other duties, other charges. Sometimes our responsibilities aren't clear at first, the lines of demarcation hazy. We all must give a little.*'

A sharp slap drew her attention. Esmé had dropped the catnip toy at her feet and now sat back, front paws up, ready to attack.

'You mean, I've been ignoring this little one, so you've been ignoring me?'

'*Now, now, little one . . .*'

'I'm sorry. I just don't understand sometimes.' She threw the ball. Maybe Mr Grey's place was really in the home, in this apartment. Training the kitten. Unless he meant that it was her job to take on the kitten. Maybe he meant *he* had other responsibilities. Maybe he was training her as she was trying to train the kitten. Getting her ready for a day when Esmé would replace him entirely.

Dulcie continued to play with the kitten, but no other voice chimed in with Esmé's excited chirps and squeals. And so when the kitten ignored two tosses in a row, she gathered herself for her first errand of the day. It wasn't going to be easy, but she was going to get something out of Corkie. No matter what Rogovoy said, she was worried about Carrie Mines. The detective hadn't read that note. Besides, if there was some connection between the sophomore and the professor, and the professor really had been murdered, who knew what could happen? No, the police didn't have the whole story. Dulcie might not either, she admitted with a shrug. But she cared enough to get involved.

'Hey, Corkie? I really need to speak with you as soon as possible.' Once she knew how important it was, Corkie would help her get to Carrie. 'Would you call me?' Still feeling a little achy, Dulcie took the T the one stop into the Square. As she emerged, she saw two calls waiting.

The first was from Chris. 'I hope you're sleeping, Dulcie Schwartz. You know what the doctor said. Well, call me.' She was tempted to do so right then, but made herself wait until she'd heard the second message.

Bingo! 'Dulcie? It's Corkie. I'm around, if you want to talk. Call me?'

She hit redial as she walked toward the Yard. 'Corkie? I'm so glad. I have something to tell you—'

'I have something to tell you, too.' Dulcie stood, shocked temporarily silent. 'Well, sort of. I'm in my dorm. Can you come by?'

Dulcie grunted something that must have sounded like assent and headed toward one of the undergraduate river houses.

'Hey, Chris.' Dunster House was a good ten-minute walk. 'I got your call.' The idea of her sweetheart being worried about her was warming, but honesty won out. 'I am actually in the Square. I'm going to talk to Corkie, my tutee. She's the one who knows Carrie Mines. But you must be sleeping.' She paused to think. Chris had gotten Jerry to cover for him last night, so he could sit with her till the nurses kicked him out. 'Or maybe you're working?'

His voicemail, being automated, didn't answer, and Dulcie hung up, hating herself for the flash of jealousy that had surged through her like electricity. And wondering where her boyfriend really was.

# TWENTY-SEVEN

Dulcie did her best to put thoughts of mysterious redheads out of her mind as she wound her way down toward the river. Dunster House had been her undergraduate home as well, and she and Suze had shared a small suite that overlooked the Charles, provided you stuck your head out the window and craned it to the left. Corkie's room was on the inside of the M-shaped building, overlooking a courtyard that, in a month or two, would be filled with frisbees and sunbathers. On this brisk morning, Dulcie was met instead by her sweater-clad student, worry lines creasing an obviously tired face.

'Corkie, are you OK?' That wasn't how Dulcie meant to begin, but she'd never seen her student looking so frazzled. Even her customary bun was undone, and her brown hair hung lank down to her sagging shoulders.

'Yeah.' For once, she didn't sound it. 'Come in.'

Dulcie followed Corkie through a common room and into what was clearly Corkie's bedroom. With each step, her feelings of guilt grew heavier. Somehow, she must have found out what Dulcie had done.

'Corkie, if I got you in trouble, I'm sorry. I should never have taken advantage like that.' Silence. 'You probably looked into the folder right after I left, huh?'

'What?' Corkie looked up, her face blank.

'The note. The suicide note. I took it.' There, it was out. 'It was wrong of me on so many levels, and I'm sorry.' Mr Grey would be proud.

Corkie, however, only seemed more confused. Dulcie wasn't sure what she expected: anger. Yelling. The throwing of small desktop items. Instead, her student simply kept looking at her, blinking occasionally.

'The note?' She was stuck on repeat.

'In Carrie's folder. You left, and I opened it. I saw it. It was a suicide note, wasn't it, Corkie?' The words poured out of her. 'I'm sorry. I know I shouldn't have, but I thought it was a cry for help. And I've talked to the police. They don't understand. They don't even think she's "at risk," or however they put it. I wanted them to know. To worry about her.'

She paused and looked at Corkie. 'I was her teacher, Corkie. And I missed the danger signals. I let her go, Corkie. I let her down.'

'You looked into Carrie Mines' folder?' Corkie repeated.

'Well, yeah.' Confession made, Dulcie didn't have much more to add. 'I'm sorry.' It was weak, but it was something.

'That's such a breach—' Corkie paused, and Dulcie waited for the tirade to follow.

It didn't come. Instead, the big girl turned from her and walked over to a desk. 'There are things,' she said, sitting in the desk chair, 'that you don't understand.'

'I know. I do.' Dulcie followed her, hoping to get her attention. 'What I did was wrong.'

Corkie didn't turn. Instead, she stared straight ahead, as if the cork-board above her desk was more worthy of attention than Dulcie. 'There's such a thing as privacy.' Corkie seemed transfixed, her eyes on a collection of headlines pinned in front of her. 'For my work at Below the Stairs, I've had to learn about confidentiality. About how important it is to keep people's secrets, no matter what.'

Dulcie fidgeted, hoping her charge would turn. She didn't.

'You're a teacher, Ms Schwartz. I thought you would understand that. But you don't, you don't understand, really, what is going on here.' Her eyes stayed fixed straight ahead. 'I have been hoping that you would realize why confidentiality is vital to the work I do, even when I wish, I truly wish, I could say something.'

Maybe it was the change of tense, maybe it was something about Corkie's voice, but Dulcie's ears pricked up. 'You're talking about *your* need for confidentiality?' Something was up.

'Yes, I am.' Corkie emphasized each word. It sounded unnatural. 'I am obligated not to repeat or reveal anything about the students who come to see me.'

She knows, Dulcie thought. She wanted me to find that note. Not – she quickly corrected herself – that what I did was right, by any means. 'I understand.' She was excited, but she tried to sound contrite.

'Do you?' Corkie swung around to face her teacher, and Dulcie was struck again by how tired her student looked. Her bright blue eyes shadowed, and wide mouth set grim. 'Do you really?'

With that, Corkie turned once again to stare at the board in front of her. Only then did Dulcie think to read what Corkie had pinned up there. *Sexual Harassment and its Effect on Undergraduate Life*, read one headline. *When a Teacher Touches* read another. *What is Consent?* a third.

'Dear Goddess.' Dulcie swallowed the words. This was why Corkie had agreed to see her. To show her what she couldn't say. Carrie was being victimized by one of her teachers. No wonder the poor girl was suicidal. 'You can't say anything, Corkie. I understand that. But I'm a teacher, too. And it's my responsibility to see that this is stopped.'

Dulcie knew she couldn't ask for any more details. Corkie had already pushed her own responsibilities as far as she dared, and so Dulcie took her leave. Poor Carrie. It should have been obvious: her erratic record. Her disappearance. At least, Dulcie realized as she made her way back to the Square, whatever had happened had not been directly her fault. She certainly hadn't made any inappropriate moves on the girl, when she'd had her in English 10. And then it hit her. Corkie's next section leader. The one who had already been taken into questioning. It was her friend and colleague: Dimitri.

As she walked, her suspicions grew. Dimitri had ended up with Carrie as his student. Dimitri had been absent the morning that Carrie had been declared missing. And Dimitri seemed to have strong opinions about her. Maybe it *had* been Dimitri arguing with Carrie the night before she disappeared. The police wouldn't have taken him in for questioning without some reason, right?

'This is horrible.' She stopped to gather her thoughts and found herself staring at a squirrel that had been digging at the base of a scrawny maple. What did she know about her colleague anyway? Dimitri seemed like a nice guy, a serious scholar despite his offbeat area of interest. Not the sort to get involved with an undergraduate.

But so was Lloyd, the thought crept in as the squirrel stopped and stared back. Lloyd, her office mate, was one of the gentlest, most studious men she knew. But he was dating an undergraduate, in defiance of university rules.

Dating, not harassing. The squirrel didn't say that, exactly, but looking at its bright eyes, Dulcie found herself compelled to argue. 'And what exactly is the difference between an unethical courtship and sexual harassment?' In Lloyd's case, she thought she knew. Although neither would admit it, Dulcie was pretty sure that the sexy, confident Raleigh had been the aggressor, wearing down the older graduate student's resolve. Besides, Lloyd and Raleigh had become involved before Raleigh had switched her major into Lloyd's – and Dulcie's – field.

But would it always be that clear? Could Dimitri have overstepped, perhaps as much the victim of some cultural misunderstanding?

No, the little squirrel seemed to say. No matter how you slice it, a person in authority who hits on an undergrad is responsible. Carrie is the victim, not the man who hit on her. And with that, it leaped twice its height and disappeared up the maple.

# TWENTY-EIGHT

Dulcie was so caught up in her own thoughts that when she first heard a phone ringing, she didn't recognize what it was.

'So annoying,' she muttered. She was sitting at the counter at the Coffee Connection, trying to think. Somehow, the idea of her office – where she might encounter Lloyd – did not appeal just now. 'Cell phones.'

It was only when the older woman sitting across from her raised her eyebrows and the girl to her right started to giggle that Dulcie realized that she was the source of the intrusive ring. With a shamefaced shrug, she dug her phone out of her bag and immediately regretted it. Chelowski was on the line.

But just as she moved to toss the little phone back in her bag, a stray thought stopped her. She had decided to set things right today. And as annoying as Norm Chelowski might be, he was doing his best for her as an adviser. An ethical, serious thesis adviser.

With a sigh, she flipped the phone on. Across from her, the older woman smiled and nodded, and for a moment Dulcie thought of Lucy. Not taking phone calls would be considered very bad karma.

'Mr Chelowski?' Dulcie waited, dreading what was to come. But the voice on the other end of the line was pleasantness itself.

'Ms Schwartz, so glad I reached you!' Dulcie found herself breathing again. 'I was thinking that perhaps, with one thing and another, I had been too hard on you the other day. It's very easy for us to lose our way, and I should know that more than anyone else. I thought perhaps it would help if I told you my own story.'

This was such an about face, Dulcie almost laughed. Maybe it wasn't that strange: here she was, worrying about the obligations of a teacher, and her adviser had been doing the same. As Chelowski rattled on about a mistaken attribution – 'truly careless, but it cost me six months' work' – Dulcie found her mood restored. To the point that when two loud undergrads crowded in, she moved over without being asked, giving up the prime window seat.

'So, sometimes mistakes, or should I say "digressions," really help us find our proper path.'

That was her opening. 'I'm so glad you told me that, Mr Chelowski.' She could only hope she wouldn't be quizzed on the details. 'Because I've had a realization of my own. You were right about my author. I can't know what happened to her. Maybe nobody ever will.' It hurt to say that, but it felt good, too. It was over. Done. And besides, she had something to fall back on. 'And my original thesis idea, focusing on the revelations to be found in the speeches, was a good one,' she said.

Chelowski must have picked up on the note of defensiveness that had crept into her voice. 'Yes, it is,' he said, his own voice sounding a bit smug. 'A perfectly adequate topic for a doctoral thesis. A perfectly *good* idea, I mean.'

Dulcie winced and was grateful that her adviser couldn't see her. 'I'm glad you're going to stick with it. Too many students overreach, you know, trying to say too much. Stick with what you know, Ms Schwartz. That's how to advance in academia.'

Dulcie caught her breath. Did he hear himself? Beside her, the undergrads were talking about a midterm. Probably math. Something about a proof, about how the proof didn't necessarily work.

'With what I can prove, anyway,' Dulcie improvised. She wasn't going to give up, but she would start writing and she needed Chelowski to file a favorable report.

It worked. 'Provenance, exactly.' His voice had an unctuous happy quality. 'It's all about ownership, really.'

'I understand,' she said. 'It's all about understanding what I read.'

She needed to get him off the phone before he dug himself in further. She needed to be able to respect him, at least a little. But as she did, her own words haunted her. Understand? What did she understand? Chelowski had been urging her to stick with her literary theory about *The Ravages*, a theory for which she had ample proof: Hermetria was a stand-in for the author, the duplicitous Demetria the voice of convention. She drained her mug and stood to leave. But some other thought was niggling away at the back of her brain. What was it? Had she understood everything else she had been reading lately?

Had she understood Carrie's note?

*This has to stop*, it said, in block letters – the kind people use when they want to stress their seriousness. When they want to make a point. But who had wanted to make that point, and to whom was that note addressed?

Ownership, provenance: all the questions Dulcie would automatically apply to a scholarly text were just as valid in this case. More so, if someone's life was at stake. She had assumed that Carrie had written the note, because it had been in Carrie's folder. But what if she hadn't meant it as a suicide note. What if she had been telling off a teacher – telling off Dimitri – and had chickened out, giving the note at the last minute to the one person she could trust for safe keeping.

Or what, Dulcie thought, her stomach sinking, if that wasn't how Corkie had come by the note at all? What if the note had been delivered and returned – and that was why Carrie Mines was now in hiding, perhaps for her life?

The world spun as Dulcie fought to make sense of these new possibilities. Thank the Goddess for that bump on the head; she hadn't been thinking clearly before. She'd never have jumped to such a hasty conclusion about a piece of academic writing.

'Are you done?'

Dulcie looked up. A large woman, her arms full of bags, faced her, clearly coveting her seat.

'Of course.' Dulcie moved out of the way, heading to the door. But outside, on the street, she paused. Where was she going? What could she do? The letter was gone. And if she'd previously been willing to believe it had gotten lost, dropped out of her pocket while she was carried unconscious to an ambulance, that idea now gave way to her original theory. It had been stolen. Maybe by the very person for whom it had been meant – the same person, she now realized, who might have attacked her. Who was probably looking for Carrie.

No wonder the poor girl was in hiding. Dulcie's first instinct was to call Corkie back. The girl certainly knew more than she was telling. But at the same time, she had clearly let Dulcie know that she *couldn't* tell her any more.

What else did she have? There was something more, she knew it. She thought back to her last conversation with Dimitri. He had sounded harsh, sterner than Dulcie had ever heard him, as he'd dismissed poor Professor Herschoft. 'The man was a monster,' he'd said, the words coming back to her like a cold wind through her coat.

She had excused his callous response when she'd thought that he might have been more concerned about Carrie – and that was still a possibility. But if the letter wasn't a suicide note, then new possibilities beckoned. How could Dimitri have said that about someone who had just died? Someone, she recalled, he said he hadn't really known, and to say that the university was 'better off' without him seemed particularly mean.

Unless . . . What was it exactly that Detective Rogovoy had said? Her thoughts hadn't been at their clearest when she was in the infirmary, but she did remember that Rogovoy had said the professor's suicide had been reclassified. That the police were now viewing it as a homicide.

This was when Dulcie could really have used Suze's advice. What did homicide mean, exactly? Chris had teased her about murder, but he'd been trying to distract her. Could it still have been some kind of horrible accident? Maybe Fritz Herschoft had spoken to Dimitri about his unethical alliance. Maybe there'd been a fight, a tussle . . .

It didn't seem possible. She had told him about Herschoft's death, she remembered. He hadn't known. Unless that had all been an act. But thinking about his reaction reminded her of something else. Of someone else. Corkie had also reacted strangely to the news of Herschoft's death. Harshly, even. And Corkie, Dulcie realized, had been headed into the Poche Building only minutes before the professor had gone flying off the balcony.

# TWENTY-NINE

D ulcie wandered back into the Yard, trying to make sense of the images that came whirling into her head. Corkie had been arguing with someone – was it Carrie? – and had run from that confrontation to the Poche Building. Corkie had gotten into an elevator that had gone up to the top floor. Professor Herschoft must have gone out of that window only moments later, and Dulcie had been unable to find her student in the hubbub afterward.

But, no, it wasn't possible. Corkie was a big girl. The word 'strapping' came to mind. But even she couldn't run into the office of a full-grown man and toss him out a window. It simply wasn't a practicable physical feat. And mentally? Corkie had certainly not been herself recently. Disturbed, even. But what reason could she have had? Harassment – and Herschoft? No, Dulcie couldn't see it. If the professor had been taking advantage of Carrie, she would have come out of hiding after his death. Besides, there was no way that the short, stout Herschoft was the man Dulcie had seen in the archway. And Corkie, who wouldn't even break confidence to expose a sexual predator, certainly wouldn't take justice into her own hands – not so suddenly, anyway. That collection of clippings must have taken months to put together. Such thoughtful deliberations didn't end with a counselor rushing at someone with murderous intent.

That didn't mean something hadn't been going on, however. And as Dulcie walked, she tried to make sense of all the disparate events of the past week. The possibilities she had imagined for Dimitri could still hold true: a fight, a tussle, a horrible accident.

But had there even been time? Maybe Corkie had seen something. Maybe Corkie had witnessed the murder. That would explain her strange mood: somewhere between distracted and distraught. Maybe Corkie was in danger now herself.

She should call Rogovoy. Her phone was in her hand. But as soon as she realized what she was doing, she made herself put it back. Once that call was made, it couldn't be unmade. And she knew that if she started talking, she'd have to tell all of it – about Corkie's past inability to deal with university life and her work now with the counseling center. About the strange display that Corkie had in her room. About what Corkie may or may not have seen, may or may not have been a part of. The cops, Dulcie suspected, would not be as gentle as she had been, and if she gave Corkie up – for, really, what other phrase would serve? – then she'd lose her. Corkie might be off academic probation, but she was still considered a risk. At risk. She'd break. Be thrown out of school or quit, never to finish her education. No, Dulcie had to find out more before she blew that particular whistle.

Dulcie stopped, unsure of her next move. In her aimless wandering, she'd ended upon the steps of Widener. This was her safe place. And hadn't she just promised her adviser that she would start writing? Reaching inside her bag for her ID, Dulcie walked toward the back entrance of the monumental library. This was, after all, her job.

No. Suze's voice echoed through her head, so loudly she stopped short. Dulcie was a member of a community. The university community. As a soon-to-be lawyer, Suze would be shaking her head. She wouldn't want to take the time to

# Clea Simon

unburden herself to the police. Or at least to other university
authorities. But wouldn't she understand that the police didn't
get it? That they doubted the very real evidence that Dulcie
had seen, and they certainly didn't know Corkie the way she
did? Wouldn't Suze see that she, Dulcie, her room-mate and
fellow academic, had made connections that the police were
unable or unwilling to make? Wouldn't she understand? She
would tell Rogovoy. Soon. First, she had to find out more.

'Dulcie Schwartz!' The voice seemed so real that Dulcie
almost turned. No, she couldn't listen to her internal censors.
Couldn't let what could be important information just sit and
gather dust. She'd find out more. She'd gather some evidence.
She'd—

'Dulcie?' A slightly out of breath redhead appeared in front
of her. Merv, the friendly guy from the police station. 'It is
you! I've been calling your name from halfway across the
Yard.'

'Sorry.' Dulcie couldn't help smiling. Merv was as red as
his hair, though, in truth, the slightly purple tone of his face
clashed somewhat with his shaggy locks. 'I've been caught
up in my own thoughts. Probably too much lately.'

'Curse of the college, I'd say.' His own smile, now that he
had caught his breath, was inviting. 'I was hoping to see you
again.'

She waited, unaccountably tickled.

'I was curious about how your errand came out.'

'Oh.' Something akin to a let-down flooded through her.
'To be honest, it was all sort of frustrating. Do you ever feel
like the police don't take academics seriously?'

He nodded vigorously. 'Every day. I've been trying to help
an old friend. My girlfriend. Ex-girlfriend, actually.' The color
came back into his cheeks, but this time Dulcie didn't find it
unattractive.

'Is she in some kind of legal trouble?' It was nice to be
sought out. If she could help, in a friendly way, she would.
Maybe she could hook her up with Suze.

But Merv shook his head. 'It's nothing I can talk about, not
really.' He looked at her, and she saw that his eyes were amaz-
ingly bright blue. 'In fact, I needed a break. So where were
you off to?'

'I'm not sure.' Suddenly, the day was much brighter. 'I'm trying to follow up on something. I mean, I should be in Widener, but—' A thought hit her. 'Do you know anyone at the Poche?'

'Of course. Didn't I tell you I was a psych major?'

'No.' She found herself smiling back and blushing slightly. 'You only told me that you heard me give a talk.'

'Yeah, the pathetic fallacy. I thought it had some interesting therapeutic implications.' He leaned toward her. 'I'm going for a clinical degree after I get my Master's.'

He was younger than she was, she figured. But not by much.

'So, you heading over to Porches?'

'Yeah,' she said, deciding as the words came out. 'Yes, I am.'

Merv, Dulcie had decided by the time they crossed the Yard, was easy to talk to. He was not, she admitted, as handsome as Chris. In general, she preferred dark-haired men. There were rarely carrot-topped heroes in any of the books she'd grown up with, and her own tendency to turn brassy in the summer had put her off most red hair. But that just made the walk more pleasant. They weren't flirting. They were simply having a companionable stroll.

Which did not explain why she felt flustered when her phone began to ring.

'Don't mind me,' Merv said, continuing to walk at her side. She was not afraid, exactly, but hesitant to look. And so she pretended to not be able to find it until the buzzing had stopped.

'Ah, there it is.' She pulled the silent phone from her bag at last and clicked to see just whose call she had missed. 'Oh, it's Lucy! My mom,' she explained.

'Do you want to call her back?' Merv really was sweet.

'I'll just check the message.' The last thing she needed right now was one of Lucy's long phone calls. 'Just to make sure there's no emergency.'

The message, of course, declared just that.

'They're trapped, Dulcie. Trapped!' Lucy's voice had an urgency that Dulcie associated with most of her mother's psychic emergencies, from bread that wouldn't rise to spats with Karma. 'Merlin has been quite insistent.'

Dulcie wondered what was really happening. In her own

universe, as Lucy would say. Had Merlin got locked in a
closet? Or had the black cat sniffed out a rodent and been
trying to get into a cupboard for better access? Either could
qualify. But Lucy hadn't finished.

'Usually, Dulcie, the spirits do not care. They are not bound,
as we are, by the physical plane.' It was all Dulcie could do
to not roll her eyes. 'But this time, it's urgent. Something has
been undone that needs to be fixed. Or, no, maybe something
had been done that needs undoing. All I can tell you is that
the energies are all awry. Mercury has been retrograde for a
week now, and I neglected to warn you. Which, we all know,
is a sign of Mercury being truly retrograde. Ah well, you know
what I mean, Dulcie. You need to make things right. Or right
things unmade. It's probably all about communication,
Dulcinea. About freeing the spirits. Call me!'

'Everything all right?' Merv seemed genuinely concerned,
which was nice.

'Yes,' she admitted. For a moment, she'd toyed with the
idea of pretending that she had a real crisis. 'My mom can
be a little loopy.'

'She's an old hippy, right?'

'Exactly.' They had reached the Poche by then, and Dulcie
suppressed a shudder as they crossed the white marble plaza
out front. Forcing herself to look at Merv, rather than over at
that corner, where the blood had puddled on the stone, wasn't
too hard, but still, she breathed easier once they were inside.

'So, where are you going?' He'd waved at the guard, and
they'd both walked by. Dulcie had decided she would retrace
Corkie's steps, to figure out why her student had been here
– and how she might be involved with Herschoft's death. But
now that she was here, Dulcie realized that didn't make much
of a plan.

'I'm not sure, actually.' She looked around, hoping something
would become obvious. A bulletin board held some notices, and
she nodded toward that. 'I may find what I need over there.
Otherwise, is there an administration office somewhere?'

'Go past the elevators. Third door on your right.' He paused,
and they both became aware of a slight awkwardness. 'Well,
I've got to get to work,' Merv said at last. 'I'll see you around.'

'That would be nice.' She watched as he turned and walked
toward the elevator. He looked back, smiled and waved, and

the heat returned to her cheeks. Then he stepped into an open elevator and she watched the indicator as it went up without stopping to the seventh, and top, floor.

He probably knew Professor Herschoft, she realized. Well, the university was a small world. Heading to the bulletin board, she looked for a clue. Why had Corkie run to this building? Nothing struck her – except for an absence. She'd expected to see at least one notice concerning the late professor. Last fall, when a member of the English department had been killed, the department had organized a memorial. But if the psych department was doing any such thing for Fritz Herschoft, it wasn't advertising it on the student bulletin board. Instead, she saw another ad for a futon – 'Easy to Assemble' – and a dorm-sized refrigerator. And there, below more recent fliers, was that same poster of Carrie Mines. 'Have you seen this girl?'

It didn't seem right to have her covered up, and so Dulcie removed the flier and looked for a more prominent place to put it. Not over the futon ad; those seemed to be hard to get rid of. But there, in the corner: she could pin it to the edge of the bulletin board, and it would only slightly overlap a poster for a midnight showing of *Freaks*. Really, she asked herself, which was more important to the average student?

'Oh, they're showing that movie again.' The voice behind her made her jump. 'You know, the old weird one?'

Dulcie turned. Perhaps because she had just mentally disparaged the film, she felt an urge to defend it. But the woman behind her wasn't talking to her. She was addressing another woman, probably another undergrad, and pointing to the poster that Dulcie had just obscured.

'I'm sorry.' Dulcie reached to move the missing person flier. She could post it again when these two moved on.

'Who's that?' The second girl leaned in and blinked, leading Dulcie to suspect bad contact lenses.

'Oh, it's that girl Carrie. The one Merv used to go out with?' Dulcie was too stunned to say anything, and the speaker grabbed her friend's arm. 'Come on, Shel. We're going to be late.'

# THIRTY

Dulcie's mind reeled, even as she reprimanded herself. Why shouldn't Merv know Carrie? Why wouldn't he have been involved with her? He'd been at the police station also, and he'd said he'd been helping an ex. If she hadn't been so flustered, she'd probably have put two and two together. She should have questioned him from the start.

'Some detective I'd make,' she muttered as she headed toward the elevator bank. But whether because the building was too modern to be hospitable to spirits or because of the noisy chatter of a couple stepping out of an arriving car, she didn't hear a reply.

But even as she tried to take a stern line, Dulcie found her heart racing a bit as the elevator ascended. In part, she knew, that was because she was going to the top of the building. To the floor where Professor Herschoft had had his office. The floor from which he had met his demise. But a little part, she had to admit, was because she was going to confront Merv.

'Utterly ridiculous,' she said under her breath, earning her a look from the elevator's only other occupant. It was only that Chris had been so busy recently, she thought as the short girl hurried off at the next floor. And had been rather unsupportive, she added as the floors ticked up. And there was that whole Rusti issue, too.

The elevator was relatively quick, but Dulcie had still managed to work herself into a state by the time it opened on to the seventh floor. She was almost glad to find the hallway empty.

'Merv?' she called softly, before realizing that she had a frog in her throat. She cleared it. 'Merv?'

No answer, so Dulcie made her way down a hallway of smoked glass walls until she saw a sign, *FAMILY PSYCH*, in raised pewter letters on the polished wood door. It was Saturday, she realized. Odds were, no administrative staff would be working today. But when she pressed lightly on the door, it opened, and Dulcie walked into a reception area to find an open space with cubicle dividers and file cabinets, fronted by an empty desk. The desk lamp was on, however, and the blotter held a half-full cup of coffee, so Dulcie figured whoever had been sitting there had not left for long.

'Merv?' she tried again, peeking around the corner. The cubicles were empty, but behind the door she did find a bulletin board. Only, instead of the usual futons for sale, this board was relatively empty. An index card offered a sublet for the upcoming summer, while another warned that the office refrigerator *would* be cleaned out at the end of each month. A third explained the lack of clutter: 'Any message not approved by S Rothberg will be removed without exception.' And smack dab in the middle, a police bulletin called out a warning in black block letters.

'Attention!' read the notice. 'The "Harvard Harasser" is not a joke. Violence is a *crime*.' Dulcie read on as the notice urged people to call, even if simply to report a suspicion. It was a more detailed memo than she'd seen anywhere else.

'I guess they're getting serious.' She wasn't talking to anyone in particular and jumped a bit when she heard a voice behind her.

'It's because of the frequency.' An older woman with a smart buzz cut came by with a pile of papers, which she placed on the one empty spot on the desk. 'Sally, Sally Rothberg,' she said by way of introduction, and then nodded toward the poster. 'For whatever reason, more of our students have been victimized by this jerk.'

'Really? Here at the Poche?'

The woman shook her head as she took a seat. 'I shouldn't be talking about it. May I help you?' Dulcie thought about pulling out her university ID, and instead held out her hand. 'I'm Dulcie, Dulcie Schwartz, doctoral candidate in English lit.'

'Have a seat, Ms Schwartz.' The receptionist nodded to a chair in the corner. 'English lit, huh? So what brings you to our airy aerie?'

Dulcie smiled, but the sharp-looking receptionist kept on talking. 'Are you going to file a complaint about us, too?'

'What? No. Have people been doing that?'

'Nonsense suits.' Papers sorted, she took half of them over to one of the tall filing cabinets and began to slot them away.

'I gather we have stolen your sunlight or your airspace or some such. Your *ambience*.' She pronounced the word as if it were French, and Dulcie winced. Clearly, someone with an attitude had gotten here first.

'I'm sorry.' She wasn't sure what to say. 'It is true that the Poche casts a shadow on our building, but I like it. It's pretty.'

That earned her raised eyebrows, but when the receptionist sat down, she looked more relaxed again. 'I confess, I was pleasantly surprised when I saw it come together. Although it is a little big for the neighborhood. So,' she said again, having reached some kind of decision, 'how may I help you today?'

'I'd love you to tell me more about the attacks.' She put her hand up to feel the still-sore bump on her head. 'I've been a victim, too.'

The admission – or maybe it was the look on her face as she pressed a little too hard on the bruise – seemed to do the trick.

'It wasn't just here at the Poche. It was the whole department, actually. The police have some ideas: maybe it relates to our discipline. In fact –' she reached for the remaining pile of papers – 'some folks had the theory that the late Professor Herschoft might be responsible.' Sally Rothberg shook her head as she filed. 'Hell of a way to clear your name.'

'Really.' The receptionist didn't know, Dulcie realized. She still thought it was suicide. 'I heard there was another coat slashing. And I was hit after Professor Herschoft . . .' She couldn't bring herself to say more, but the receptionist nodded.

'Yeah, we're all pretty shaken up around here.'

'I'm sorry.' Dulcie waited, but the receptionist seemed to have said all she was going to. 'I actually came up to see one of your students. A Merv—' She realized she had no idea what his last name was. 'Merv something? Tall red-haired guy?' On a whim, she added her latest nugget. 'He used to go out with Carrie Mines, and she was one of my students.'

'Oh, yeah. Carrie.' The way she said it made her sound tired, and Dulcie felt a flash of elation. The ex must be long past. Then she mentally kicked herself. The girl was missing, possibly in danger, and this might be a lead.

'A lot of drama?' She tried to keep her voice calm. If Carrie had been distraught over Merv, then maybe he was the reason she'd gone into hiding. Maybe she'd misread Corkie's message. Which could mean Dimitri was in the clear.

'There always is with undergrads.' Sally was back to sorting and apparently happy to gossip. 'I think he's pretty broken up about it. She found someone else. It happens.'

*She'd* found someone else. The pronoun threw everything into a different light. If Carrie had been the one to end the relationship, it was less likely that she'd be distraught about it. But that didn't mean that Merv wasn't somehow involved. Nor did it mean that she wasn't being taken advantage of. The Harvard Harasser . . . Unconsciously reaching up to touch the sore place on her head again, Dulcie tried to think back. The figure in the passageway had been tall: a tall man. Could it have been Merv? Could he have been threatening Carrie? Begging her to come back? That might have pushed her into running away. *'This cannot continue,'* the note had said. Was she trying to get through to an obsessive ex? *'I've got to end it.'* That was more than Carrie's lone email had suggested. *Boyfriend trble*, indeed. But perhaps she was prone to exaggeration. Perhaps that had contributed to their break-up.

'Anyway –' Sally bounced a stack of papers on her desk top to even them out – 'if you're looking for Merv, try room 713. End of the hall on the right.'

Thanking her in a distracted manner, Dulcie headed out the door and then paused, five feet down the hall. *Limits*, Mr Grey had said. He'd been talking about boundaries, about what he could or would do for her, but he'd also been talking about his role as a teacher. *Limits and responsibilities*. Was she going too far, tracking down the ex-boyfriend of her former student? *Connections*.

Was she, if she were completely honest, really searching for this young man because he had been nice? Because he had flirted with her?

'No.' She shook her head, becoming once more aware of that sore spot. Her motives might not be totally clear, but they remained strong. A man had died here, and her student may have been involved. But before she turned Corkie over to the police, she wanted to understand. Any lead, any connection, was fair game because it was her responsibility to find out what was going on.

*       *       *

Her mind made up, Dulcie started to stride down the hall.
And stopped. What, exactly, was she going to ask Merv
anyway? About Herschoft – and Corkie, too, if he knew her
– that was certain. But should she confront him about Carrie?
The girl was still officially missing, if that flier was any indication. Of course, Merv could easily pass any blame on to
the new boyfriend, whoever that was. And he could be right.
Maybe it was the new man in Carrie's life who had driven
her into hiding. Maybe, the thought struck her once again, the
new man was Dimitri. Corkie might still have seen it as inappropriate, even if it was consensual. But that fight . . .

'Damn,' she said to the empty hallway. Dulcie prided herself
on her logic. In all areas, except where ghost cats were
concerned, she knew she thought in a reasonable and very
clear manner. And, yes, following this current train of thought
brought Dimitri back up. And also – she paused – Fritz
Herschoft.

Where had that idea come from? Dulcie turned around,
surprised by her own thought, and caught sight of the seed
that had sparked it: Fritz Herschoft, 710. The label on the
door didn't reflect the young professor's rank, but the fact
that he'd had a private office did, and the police seal – neatly
ripped where someone had already opened the door to clean
or begin to sort through a life's work – testified to the tragedy
of his ending.

Dulcie tried to remember what she'd heard about the late
professor: he'd been up for tenure. A rising star in his field.
He'd been a dumpy man, short with greasy hair, but supposedly many of his students loved him. Still, nobody she talked
to had anything good to say about him. Maybe some of that
had been because he had been suspected of harassment, but
his death – and the continued attacks on campus – put paid
to that theory. His death also made him an unlikely factor in
Carrie's disappearance, as did his figure: a far cry from the
tall, lean man Dulcie had seen Carrie arguing with. What had
the sophomore said was going on that night? *Boyfriend trble.*
Dulcie had read that email the morning she went to Rogovoy,
the morning after Herschoft had been killed. And Carrie still
had not resurfaced.

Still, there was something. Maybe it was the memory of
her dream – the huge windows in the castle keep and the long

drop down. Maybe it was simply that Rogovoy had been so evasive about Herschoft's death. Or maybe, Dulcie admitted, it was simply that she was alone. The hall was empty. And the seal on the door had already been ripped.

'I'm worse than Esmé,' she whispered, to give herself courage, and reached for the door.

# THIRTY-ONE

I n place of a knob, the door had a lever of burnished steel. Its dull glow matched the sheen of the polished wood, echoing the elegant restraint of the smoky glass and the hush of the hallway. But there was no mistaking the sharp click as the lever moved in her hand. The door wasn't locked. Dulcie held her breath and stepped inside.

Closing the door behind her, Dulcie felt slightly illicit. Hermetria would never have snuck into anybody's office.

'This is crazy,' she whispered to the still air. 'What am I doing here?' The urge to flee – in a sedate and respectful manner, of course – was strong enough to turn her back around toward the door. Through the shaded glass, the hallway glowed like another world. It was quiet, almost hushed, but when a shadow passed over the smoky glass – ghostly, silent – she stepped back. No footsteps intruded on this carpeted reserve, and she held still a moment, wondering if her own silhouette would be visible were she to stand closer to the wall. Wondering what else could be out there, when it hit her. In Hermetria's world, the *vengeful spirits* proved to be human, and the resilient heroine triumphed by exposing them. Dulcie, too, was seeking truth. Plus, she'd already taken the biggest step. Her heart rate returning to normal, her resolve followed: she may as well do what she'd come for.

But what was that, exactly?

'I've been reading totally the wrong sort of books,' she said to the still air, the sound of her own voice comforting in the silence. 'But I *am* a trained researcher.'

With new resolve, she turned back toward the center of the room – and gasped. Suddenly, she knew what all the fuss was about, and why members of her department were frankly envious. Herschoft's office was not only on the top floor, but also faced the river, and beyond his desk, tall windows looked on to a vista like something from a postcard: the blue steeple of Memorial Church off to the right. The red dome of Dunster to the left. The sparkle of the Charles beyond. It was gorgeous.

It was also dangerous, Dulcie realized. She'd moved to the window without meaning to, and behind the desk she saw that what she'd thought only another window was, in fact, a French door, which opened on to the tiny platform. Up close, she could see that the namesake 'porch' was actually more of a fire escape. Barely two-feet deep by the door and curved like a crescent to meet the office wall at the ends, there was nothing of the practical porch about it. With its repeated scallop shapes across the front of the building, and the retro wrought-iron railings, it was a design element; that was all. Something to break up the glass and steel. But the temptation to open the door, to stand outside in the sunlight, would be irresistible.

Nearly, but not entirely. Even the gorgeous view, the shadows of the clouds sliding over the rooftops like so many ghosts, couldn't erase the memory of what else she'd seen in this building, down at ground level. The wrought-iron railing looked tough, and from where she stood, she could tell that it came up to at least waist level. Forcing someone over would be difficult.

She tried to picture Corkie enraged, her round face red with fury. She imagined her student rushing at the teacher, arms outstretched to push. No, it just didn't scan. Shaking her head, Dulcie turned away from the window and found herself perusing the professor's desk.

Someone had been here. Smudges of dark powder still marred the desk's surface. Fingerprint powder, she realized, just like the movies. A leather pen holder stood to the side, empty of its pen, while its mate, tan with light stitching, held a pair of gold-toned scissors. Just like Suze's, Dulcie realized, only its matching letter-opener was gone and dark powder had already dulled the scissors' grip. More splotched the desk calendar, which must have been photographed, Dulcie realized, as it lay open to the month of March. Professor Herschoft was missing a dentist appointment this afternoon; she wondered if anyone had bothered to cancel. Those dark dashes highlighted what had happened. A man had worked here, had ordered his life from here. And he had been killed. The marks also served to darken Dulcie's resolve. There was nothing here for her to see. The police clearly had everything in hand. This was a crime scene. Serious business. She should call Detective Rogovoy and tell him everything she knew. She should leave.

But the sight of those dark splotches stirred something else in her memory. Esmé. The kitten's misadventure with the fireplace, and Suze's sooty sweater. Dulcie smiled at the memory; despite the mess, those little footprints had been so perfect and adorable.

That was it. She could have smacked herself. Esmé could communicate. She knew that. Only, the little black and white kitten didn't always use language, like Mr Grey did. Maybe it had something to do with still being active on this physical plane. Maybe it was simply the growing kitten's style. But what had Suze said? *Everybody leaves tracks*. These powder smudges were here for a reason. They reminded Dulcie of her mission – to find out what was going on with her beleaguered student.

But what could she contribute that the university detectives wouldn't have already found? Could they have missed something entirely? Unlikely. But maybe there was something, some clue that only another academic would notice – or that only another academic would be able to interpret. The desk was bare, except for the calendar and that leather desk set. So she looked down at the calendar, to see what her trained eyes would find. Well, the first clue was clear enough. A scrawled series of letters: *TEN MT @1*. The detectives might not have been able to interpret that, but to Dulcie it was clear: a meeting with the tenure committee, scheduled for the Friday after he died. Making another leap of logic, she deduced that the professor must have been a little tense: the letters nearly pressed through the paper. Had he been expecting bad news about his tenure, or were nerves simply part of the process?

For a moment, she wondered if the police had gotten it wrong. Perhaps Herschoft *had* committed suicide, the pressure of expectations too much for him. But, no, they had to have their reasons, even if they wouldn't share them with a civilian. And besides, Herschoft hadn't had the meeting yet.

If he had been suicidal, wouldn't he at least have waited until the committee had ruled?

The earlier part of the week looked much more fun. *DEPT LNC* for Monday. Well, that sounded good, didn't it? A shared meal with his colleagues. Then *DISC COMM @3*. Well, if he was trying to curry favor, serving on the department's disciplinary committee probably made sense. And then she saw it, the same day. Monday. *CM*. The initials were so small, Dulcie almost missed them. But there they were, in the corner of the day before he'd gone out into the beautiful view, before someone had launched him into the sky.

*CM*. The initials could be Carrie Mines. She'd been dating a member of the department. A regular on the floor. But they could also be Corkie McCorkle's. Or could they? Corkie wasn't a psych major, and her full name – the one most professors were likely to know – was Philomena. Carrie Mines. Corkie McCorkle. One had gone missing. But the other, Dulcie knew, was likely to have been the professor's last visitor.

No wonder the police wanted to talk to Carrie. If those really were her initials, she would have been the obvious suspect. Fishing a pencil from her bag, Dulcie used the eraser to turn the page back. There, again, small but visible, were a series of initials: *CM, CM*. Two per week. The page before had them, too, as did most of February. In fact, the initials occurred so frequently that Dulcie began to wonder. Did she have it right? Maybe *CM* wasn't a person's initials at all. Professor Herschoft was a rising star. He must have been on committees – and committees had meetings. But something had aroused the police's interest in Carrie Mines, and this was all she had to go on. Letting the calendar fall back open, she looked over the rest of the desk.

And then she saw it. Peeking out from the edge of the blotter, tucked beneath its leather edge, was a sliver of paper. Using the eraser, she teased it out until the sliver became an envelope – with a departmental logo. Someone from the English department had written Professor Herschoft. Someone had written a letter that he had wanted to save, that he had maybe tried to hide.

'I'm being silly,' she said. The letter was probably bureaucratic. An exchange of grades or a request for a student from one major to audit a class in another. Besides, the cops would have seen this for sure. Unless her gentle poking about had only now dislodged it. Unless they'd read it and discarded it as useless, unaware of how high academic tensions could run. Unless . . .

Unable to resist, Dulcie slid the envelope out of its hiding place. Gingerly, hyper aware of the black powder coating everything, she pulled the folded sheet out of the envelope.

*Dear Professor Herschoft,* it began. *Concerning the matter under discussion, it is vitally important that we meet again. Such grievances are not to be taken lightly, and I, for one, will not be dismissed.*

Dulcie looked at the date. It had arrived a few days before Herschoft's demise. And, despite the high-blown vocabulary, it sounded like a threat. She read on: *It is imperative that we resolve this matter. Sincerely, Norman P. Chelowski.*

Chelowski? Had her thesis adviser been in some kind of feud with Herschoft? Dulcie thought back. Chelowski had been worked up about something. He'd been complaining about the Poche Building ever since construction had started. But certainly he couldn't blame Herschoft for it. Unless – Dulcie looked back at the calendar – Herschoft had been on some kind of steering committee. Maybe the young professor had been assigned the task of gathering community reaction. Maybe he'd downplayed the effect on the English department, hoping to curry favor with his own higher ups.

Dulcie only had to close her eyes to remember that entire horrible day. First Chris and Rusti. Then Herschoft. And then that strange, urgent demand from Chelowski. He'd insisted on meeting her in the departmental office right after that horrid, horrid scene at the Poche, but he hadn't called from there. He'd arrived after she did; she could clearly remember him taking off his coat. Maybe he'd called a meeting with her as an alibi. And that grin – that weird grin – came back to mind. Maybe Chelowski had truly hated the other professor. Maybe—

'What are you doing in here?' It was Merv. He was standing in the open door, with Sally Rothberg right behind him.

# THIRTY-TWO

'Excuse me?' If she'd had a moment, Dulcie might have shoved the letter into her bag. As it was, she dropped it to the floor.

'Sally said you were looking for me, and when we couldn't find you . . .' To do Merv credit, he looked a little embarrassed.

'Did you cut the police seal?' The receptionist, on the other hand, sounded angry, and Dulcie rushed to correct her.

'No! It was already broken! I wouldn't have come in otherwise.'

'So, why *did* you come in here?' Dulcie felt like she'd been tag-teamed, Sally setting up Merv's question. But there was no denying that she was in an office where she had not been invited. An office that had been closed and did have at least the remains of a police seal on the door.

'I'm calling the police.' Sally turned toward her office.

'No, wait.' Dulcie went after her. 'Please, I can explain.'

Both Sally and Merv turned toward her, waiting. She had to give them something. The police already knew about Carrie. 'I'm here about Carrie, Carrie Mines. She was my student.'

She didn't mean to look at Merv, but she couldn't help turning slightly. The pale redhead colored and set his lips in a tighter line.

'So you said.' Sally Rothberg wasn't giving an inch. 'And that brings you here, why?'

'I'm worried about her.' It sounded lame. 'She dropped a section I teach last year, and I'm afraid I let her down. I have reason to believe she may be in some kind of trouble. Even suicidal.'

'A little late, aren't you?' The receptionist had crossed her arms and was regarding Dulcie with a stern look.

'Yes, I am.' The confession helped. 'And I feel terrible about it. But what happened was that I saw her only a few days ago. She was arguing with someone, and then she was reported as missing. And now, well, I'm hearing all sorts of things.'

She'd been about to mention the note, but since it was private
– and stolen – it made sense to keep quiet about it. At least
until she knew for sure just what it meant.

'So, that's why you've been chatting me up.' Merv's voice
was cold enough to make Sally Rothberg turn to look at him.

'No, Merv. I didn't know you two used to go out. Honest.'
It sounded so lame. That couldn't stop her from finally getting
some information. 'Do you know if Carrie was here that day,
the day that Professor Herschoft . . . died?'

'What?' Merv sounded surprised. 'Why?'

'Well, they obviously knew each other. I might have seen
her initials on his desk calendar. There might be a connection.'

'OK,' Sally Rothberg broke in. 'Enough of this. I don't
know why you're really here, but you clearly aren't this girl's
teacher.'

'Why? What do you mean?' Dulcie hadn't even gotten
around to the contagion theory, to Corkie or Dimitri. To half
of what she wanted to say.

'Because if you were, you would have known that Carrie
Mines was a regular here because she was a psych major.'
Merv explained. 'That's how I met her.'

'She should have been here that awful day,' Sally Rothberg
said, picking up the thread. 'I know she was working very
closely with Fritz Herschoft, and last week was really quiet
– a lot of us were using it as a catch-up week after exams.
But he'd had me call her. He was too busy with his own work,
he'd said. He told me to cancel all his appointments so he
could have some time alone. I was down in the archives, filing.
I thought—' She bit her lip. 'If only I'd known why, what he
was going to do instead. At least he tried to spare his student.'

She was lucky, Dulcie realized on the way down, that Sally
Rothberg hadn't called the cops.

'I just want you gone,' the receptionist had said. 'No more
cops, no noise. I'm sick of it all. I know what people say
about us. I know everyone thinks the department attracts
unbalanced individuals. But nosing around a dead man's
office? That's just ghoulish.'

'Creepy,' Merv had added as they had marched her to the
bank of elevators. And then the elevator had arrived, and Dulcie
had considered retreat the better part of valor.

It wasn't until she had exited the building and was walking across the white stone plaza that she stopped to think. Neither Sally nor Merv had been around to see who had been on the floor that fateful day. But Carrie Mines had had an appointment to see Professor Herschoft. No wonder the police wanted to talk with her. Dulcie flashed back to her own presence here that horrible day. She'd been chasing Corkie, who had just had some kind of argument with another woman – probably Carrie. And the woman in olive green – Carrie – had run off. If Corkie had been looking for her student, to make peace or one final point, maybe she'd come here, not knowing that Carrie's schedule had changed.

No, Dulcie shook her head. There was a lot she didn't know, that Rogovoy wasn't telling her. But the basic idea of Corkie fighting with Herschoft, of somehow overpowering him and throwing him out the window in the few minutes she had been in the building? It didn't seem possible. Besides, Corkie had no connection to Herschoft. Her sole concern, as far as Dulcie could tell, was Carrie Mines.

Carrie was in trouble, that much was clear, and all the signs pointed to abuse by a person in authority. Maybe Professor Herschoft had been helping her evade someone else. Merv? He was tall enough to have been the man in the archway. Tall and lean. Had he come down to the police station that morning to ask questions, or to answer them?

Without realizing where she was heading, Dulcie found herself on the steps of the English department. And as she opened the door, she realized there was a third candidate she hadn't considered. Someone who was tall enough to have been the man she saw. Someone whose pursuit of an undergraduate would be against every ethical rule. Someone, she remembered as she stepped inside the little house's alcove, who had written to the student's new adviser in a vaguely threatening tone and who already had a grudge against the professor – and the very building he'd been thrown out of.

The sound of hard soles on old wooden stairs caused her to look up. Ducking to keep from hitting his head on the low, even so slightly sagging ceiling was her thesis adviser, Norm Chelowski.

# THIRTY-THREE

'**M**iss Schwartz! How nice to see you.' Her adviser straightened up as he stepped off the stairs, and Dulcie was struck by how big a man he really was. 'Did we have an appointment?'

'What? No.' Dulcie found herself backing away. That letter: maybe it hadn't been about the shadow of the building. Maybe Herschoft had been about to file some sort of official grievance, and Chelowski was trying to stop him. '*It is imperative that we resolve this,*' the note had read. But maybe Herschoft had refused to settle it quietly. Maybe he had refused to withdraw the complaint. Maybe Chelowski had found a way to sneak in, up to the other professor's office. Herschoft wasn't the only struggling academic who was up for tenure.

'Ms Schwartz?' She looked up into her adviser's face, aware that she'd been standing, frozen. The idea of Norm Chelowski pressuring a student for sex was doubly horrible, now that she saw him up close. 'I'm here to pick up papers. To pick up my students' papers.'

'Got to keep a tight rein on those undergrads.' He nodded in a way that turned her stomach. 'Some of them just have no idea of the discipline that's necessary.'

This was getting creepier and creepier, and Dulcie ducked into the office, desperate for the comforting presence of the departmental secretary.

'Were you looking for Nancy?' Chelowksi was right behind her. 'She stepped out. Dentist or something. May I help you with something?' He smiled, and Dulcie drew back in horror. She'd seen him as a figure of fun, a slightly ridiculous character. But maybe her instincts had been correct when she'd envisioned him as a weasel. A dangerous and sly creature. Muttering something about deadlines, Dulcie turned and fled.

'Chris?' Dulcie fished her phone out of her bag and answered without looking. What she really needed now was support.

'You still haven't spoken to him, Dulcie?' It was her mother. But, for once, Dulcie was grateful.

'No, it's a long story. Hey, Lucy?' She was walking fast, heading for the Yard. 'Do you really think that maybe I'm psychic?' She paused before adding: 'Too? I mean, really?'

'Of course, dear. I've known that about you since infancy. Why, one of your first acts was to grab my grandmother's cameo to teethe on. I had to take it away, of course. You probably don't remember it; that all went when we had to incorporate the colony. But I knew then, because she had been quite a seer in her day. Almost like a Philadelphia version of the Fox Sisters.'

Dulcie had to get her mother back on track. 'But since then, I mean, do you think I see people as they really are?' She'd felt so guilty when she had first decided Chelowski looked like a weasel.

'Yes, dear. I mean, you've made some mistakes. I remember that room-mate of yours – the summer sublet fellow?' Dulcie nodded in agreement. That had been a big one. 'But in general, yes. You're quite a good judge of character.'

'Lucy – Mom – I don't know what to do with this. But I think maybe my thesis adviser is a criminal.'

For the first time that Dulcie could remember, her mother was speechless. 'Mom?' she asked finally. 'Are you OK?'

'Yes, yes, dear. I'm just – flabbergasted.' Dulcie heard rustling on the other end of the line. 'Hold on, let me get my cards.'

A few moments passed, and Dulcie realized she was humming. When she recognized the song – the sultry 'Teach Me Tonight' – she stopped. 'You still there?'

'Yes, I'm sorry, dear. I haven't used this deck in a long time. Here we go.' To the gentle sound of paper slapping, Dulcie relaxed. Her mother used to read the cards regularly when Dulcie was little, and she'd grown up with the Rider-Waite imagery. 'Would you tell me what the trouble is, Dulcie?'

Briefly, Dulcie outlined her suspicions, focusing on the sexual harassment and leaving out the possibility of murder. Her mother had enough to deal with.

'You don't know his birth sign, do you?'

That was odd. 'You never needed that before.'

'I'm getting confusing signs, dear. If what you say is true,

I should be getting different cards. The two of cups, or perhaps something similar.'

Dulcie wracked her memory, trying to come up with what that particular card meant.

'Unbridled passion. Sex without love,' Lucy said. She might not be psychic, but she knew her daughter.

'Well, that's interesting, but I'm still worried.' What was she doing, asking her mother for advice? Dulcie didn't want Chelowski to be an abusive creep, but she wasn't going to be reassured by long-distance magic.

On the other end of the line, her mother was still reading. 'I'm wondering, dear, do you think you could have it wrong? I'm just not seeing it.'

'I wish.' The idea of Chelowski being criminal sat like a cold weight on her shoulders. She'd never really liked him, but she'd finally made peace with him. The thought of confronting him, of turning him in, was enough to make her feel vaguely ill. Add in the prospect of finding another thesis adviser, once again . . . ugh. What she really needed to know was what her own future held.

'Lucy, would you do something else for me?' Before her mother could even answer, the words rushed out. 'Would you pull a card for me, like you used to?' Dulcie hadn't asked since she was a child. But now, she wanted the comfort.

Dulcie waited, visualizing her mother. She could picture her now, in the commune's big common room as she sat back and thought of her daughter and then chose a single card from the oversized deck. It would be the Sun. It always was. And even though Dulcie had long suspected her mother of a little sleight of hand, she'd grown used to Lucy pulling the bright card for her. Used to seeing herself in its image of a smiling child on a white horse, accepting its promise of happiness in love and life.

Only, this time the silence went on a bit too long.

'Lucy, are you there?' Dulcie asked the silent phone. 'Did you get the Sun?'

'Oh, Dulcie, I did.' Something was wrong, very wrong. 'But your card? Your usual card? It was upside down.'

Dulcie tried not to think about it as she continued into the Yard. But all her years in the commune had taught her something. Reversed cards meant just that – all the traits turned upside down. Not just a different fortune, one lacking in contentment and fulfillment. But the loss of happiness, of love and joy. The loss of everything you held dear.

# THIRTY-FOUR

'I wanted to shield you, dear.' Lucy had been so upset that Dulcie had ended up comforting her. 'I thought, maybe I shouldn't tell you. But I had to, you see?'

It all had to do with the cards, Dulcie thought. If Lucy had betrayed the cards, she'd lose some connection, some ineffable power of divination. Far better to dump bad news on her only child.

'I get it, Lucy. No, it's fine. Really.' She'd wanted to get off the phone ten minutes ago. 'You shouldn't have to lie to protect me. That's not what parenting is about.' She parroted back Lucy's excuses and waited till her mother sounded reassured before signing off.

With a mood that now matched the glowering gray sky, Dulcie marched through the Yard – and stopped. Where, she wondered, had she been headed? Ostensibly, she wanted to seek out Corkie, to find out what had happened that day at the Poche. In truth, she realized, she'd been heading toward her basement office. But the idea of meeting Lloyd, of having to chat with another man in an inappropriate relationship, was suddenly extremely distasteful. She knew Lloyd and Raleigh were different, but still . . .

And then there was Dimitri. He was somehow involved in all of this. Could she have been wrong about Chelowski? Could it have been Dimitri, as she'd originally suspected, who had been so wrongly involved with Carrie? The idea was a lot less distasteful. And that note had mentioned 'the department.' It wasn't inconceivable that the two professors were discussing a problem between students.

Unless, Dulcie had to admit, she was simply looking for an easier way to understand what was happening. After all, if Chelowski were guilty, that meant a lot more hassle for her.

'Ow!' A sharp pain, like a bite on the back of her calf, caused

Dulcie to stop short. Had some biting insect survived the winter cold? Or, no; Dulcie smiled. 'You're right, Mr Grey.' She had lost all sense of proportion. This wasn't about her thesis. This was harassment, and possibly murder. She had delayed long enough. It was time to tell Rogovoy what she'd discovered. She reached for the phone, just as it began to ring.

'Detective?' Maybe she did have psychic powers.

'Huh? No, it's me, Dulce. How are you feeling?' Trista's bouncy tone was so foreign to Dulcie's mood that, for a moment, she didn't even recognize her friend's voice. 'It's Tris, Dulcie. Are you doing OK?'

'Yeah, I'm fine.' She smiled. It was comforting to have her friends check in on her.

'So, are you well enough to come out to the People's Republik tonight?'

'Drinking?' It wasn't what she expected. Somehow, a pub night didn't seem to fit with everything going on.

'It is Saturday night, Dulcie. A girl's got to have some fun.' There was an edge to Trista's voice that gave Dulcie pause.

'I don't know, Tris. There's been so much going on. I don't even know where to start.' She put her hand up to her head automatically. She could still find the swelling, but it was already much less sensitive. Not a good excuse. 'You wouldn't believe what's up with Chelowski.'

'That greasy giraffe? You can tell me about it tonight. I'll buy the first round.' Trista was definitely pushing more than usual, but when Dulcie failed to respond, she settled down a bit. 'Was it about the spring status update?'

'Oh, hell – I mean, oh, Goddess.' Dulcie could have slapped herself. How could she have forgotten? If she accused her thesis adviser of impropriety – or worse, murder – it would look like a counter offensive. A political move to distract the department. Unless she could be very, very sure, she couldn't mention this to anyone. Certainly not to Rogovoy. She tried to imagine the furor that would erupt if she embroiled her adviser in this and he ended up being innocent. Had Chelowski shared his concerns about her 'malingering'? Suddenly, her head started to throb.

'What?' Trista asked.

Dulcie'd been so caught up in this nightmare scenario, she'd forgotten that Trista was on the line. 'No, it's not that. But, well, it's true, I've not gotten much done.'

'Well, I don't want to put a damper on your weekend, but maybe you can crank something out today and tomorrow? Hand him something early next week?'

'I don't know, Tris. I need to talk to some people.' She paused. 'Would you know where I could find Dimitri?'

'He'll be at the Republik tonight. Why, is there something going on that I don't know about?'

'Not – not like that.' Dulcie wasn't sure how to respond to this new Trista. 'But I do need to talk to him.'

'More reason, then.' The line was silent for a moment, and when Trista came back on, her voice was softer. 'Seriously, Dulcie, I hope you come tonight. Things have been a little hard for me lately, and I could use the moral support.'

'I will try, Trista.' Dulcie heard herself speak and wondered if she sounded as odd as her friend. 'I promise.'

Knowing it was probably useless, she called Chris's voice-mail. 'Hey, sweetie.' He had stayed with her when she'd been hurt. But that could have been spurred by guilt. 'You wouldn't believe the day I've had.' Too late, she remembered his advice that she stay in bed. 'Let's just say, you were right. So, I'm wondering if you might be free tonight, even for a little while. A bunch of us are going to be at the Republik.' She paused. 'But if you'd rather it be just us, let me know?'

The beep at the end of the voicemail was far from satis-fying. Maybe it was just as well she hadn't called the detective yet. If she could talk to Dimitri in a casual setting, maybe she could get to the bottom of this. Maybe he'd walk into the bar with his 'friend' Lylah and dispel all of Dulcie's suspicions. Or maybe Carrie would show up on Dimitri's arm.

With that unlikely thought, she shoved her phone back in her bag and headed up the Widener steps.

But no matter how hard she tried, Dulcie couldn't concen-trate. First it was her carrel, the seat too hard, the rattle of the occasional footstep on the metal frame floor too distracting. Then it was the lighting. Despite the upgrade of a few years back, the overhead lights still cast the kind of gloomy shadows that could make reading difficult. Finally, Dulcie admitted it was her. Not the bump on her head, but everything else that had been going on. While her thesis should be the top priority in her mind, at least for the next few hours, she couldn't stop thinking of Carrie and Chelowski. Of Herschoft and Dimitri. Of an abused student and a dead professor, and of two brief notes, either of which might explain it all.

Neither of which she had. 'Dulcie Schwartz,' she reprimanded herself softly, 'for a grad student, you've been quite careless of documentation.'

It was time for a break. 'At least, a change of scene,' she murmured to the dull air. Packing up her bag, she headed for the reading room, where she snagged one of the comfy chairs. Despite its purported purpose, the reading room was marginally noisier than the stacks. But it had the advantage of wireless Internet. If she no longer had the ambiguous notes, she could at least do some real-time research. Booting her laptop back up, she logged into the university system and typed in the words that really interested her: 'sexual harassment' and 'student/professor.'

The first references that came up were cases. Newspaper headlines screaming about one professor after another who had taken advantage of some student. Dulcie skimmed these, grateful that so few were here at the university and curious to see that a smattering of women in authority had been accused.

What interested her more were a series of pieces on the psychology of the crime. Sexual harassment, she read, had more to do with power and control than with sexual attraction or desire. It involved the subjugation of the victim, as the harasser asserted his – or her – will in the most intimate of ways.

Dulcie shuddered, reading this. She knew all too well how much control those in authority could have over their students. Even within the bounds of the accepted relationship, Chelowski had a frightening amount of power. One bad report from him could threaten her standing in the department. And from there, she could be overlooked for grants or teaching positions. It was terrifying, really. At least, as a grad student, she would have some recourse: as long as everything was above board, a student could object. File a grievance and have the chance to argue her side. But would it really help? Wouldn't the student be harmed simply by the accusation?

Dulcie tried to imagine filing a complaint. Despite years in

the department, she could easily envision the result: over-
worked junior staff grumbling about the paperwork and the
time required. A few other professors, probably junior staff,
would have to make room in their schedules for a hearing, or
to review her work. She'd be seen as 'a bother,' as a student
who 'caused trouble,' even if she were cleared. Even if those
feelings were never validated, they would weigh in on a thousand little choices: the assignment of students or offices. The
selection to certain committees: the kinds of appointments
that gave graduate students a chance to shine. The subtle shuffling that set some post-docs up for high-profile careers and
relegated others to the boondocks – or drummed them out of
academia forever. The future seemed suddenly clear: if she,
if any student, angered those in authority, there was a good
chance she would not only be tainted for the rest of her time
here, but derailed professionally.

'Today is the first day of the rest of your life,' she muttered,
aware for the first time of the negative implications of the
hackneyed slogan. 'Ugh.'

The thought was disgusting, and Dulcie suddenly felt the
need for air. She stood, pushing her chair back in the process
– and bumping it into a standing form behind her.

'Hey!'

She turned to see a pimply young man glaring at her. He
had a bound volume in hand: the walls behind her held the
last century's *Crimson*.

'Oh, Ms Schwartz! I'm sorry. Excuse me.'

It had all happened so fast; she stumbled over her own
words. 'No, no, please,' she said. 'It was my fault. I'm sorry.'

'Well, I should have been more aware.' He was blushing
now, the rising flush clashing badly with his acne.

'No, really.' She smiled and tried to remember his name.
English 10, a year or two before, she vaguely recalled. 'Please,
I'm sorry I disturbed you.' She pulled her chair forward to
make more room, and with some more smiling and nodding,
got back to her laptop.

But despite the deep cushions and the well-worn leather of
the coveted club chair, Dulcie found it difficult to get comfortable. That student – Tom? Tim? – had unsettled her. Somehow,
she had never really thought about her own status, her own
position as a person in authority with power over someone

else's life. Until now, teaching had been a part of her education. A necessary evil. A few of her students, like Raleigh,
had been great – the experience of teaching adding both to
her own understanding of the material and to her trove of
friends. With Carrie, she'd had a belated awakening, becoming
more aware of her responsibility to these younger students.
But the flip side? That had escaped her until now. It was
harrowing, really, to consider. How did one work with such
inequalities? Tim – Tom? – had reacted so strongly. He had
been startled and embarrassed, possibly, at his outburst. But
had he been, just a little, afraid? She closed her eyes, unable
to stop thinking along those lines.

When she opened them, it was with a new resolve. Maybe
this was what Mr Grey had meant, when he had spoken about
responsibilities and limits. Maybe she'd been meant to learn
about this, not just for Carrie's sake – or to track down another
erring teacher – but to prevent her from unconsciously over-
stepping. With a soft tick-tick-tick on the keyboard, Dulcie
pulled up another article: *Signs of Abuse, What to Watch for
– How to Tell.*

Skimming the article, Dulcie understood that it didn't
exactly relate. Harassment did not always equate to abuse, but
still, so many of the telltale traits were the same. *Often, those
pressured into compromising situations will be overcome by
a sense of guilt*, she read, *and a desire to hide.* Had that been
why Carrie had taken off? *At the same time, victims will suffer
the conflicting desire – to tell, to expose both the wrongdoer
and her (or his) own presumed guilt.* The image of Carrie at
the edge of the crowd as Dimitri was taken for questioning
came to Dulcie, then. Of course, Carrie had also gone to Below
the Stairs, Dulcie remembered. *Often this can lead to terrible
conflicts. In extreme cases, the victim may find this burden
unbearable, and may react violently.*

That was what Corkie had been trying to tell her. Those
clippings – that note – her confusion. It didn't even matter
who was responsible, or what the department might do. Carrie
Mines was in danger, and Dulcie had to help.

# THIRTY-FIVE

'**M** s Schwartz?' Dulcie didn't even realize she'd been staring into space until the quiet voice interrupted her. 'May I interrupt you for a minute?'

She looked up into an earnest, round face. 'Of course.' The response was automatic. At least, this time, the synapses clicked: Tranh, from the Early British Novel. Most undergrads stayed away from Widener, preferring the smaller, somewhat less threatening Lamont library for the majority of their work. Today must be her lucky day. 'What's up?'

But if Dulcie was expecting a routine query, something about that week's reading, she was surprised.

'I'm thinking about graduate school, and I wanted to talk to you about my senior thesis.'

No wonder she was in the Widener reading room on a weekend afternoon. Dulcie raised her eyebrows. 'Excuse me, but aren't you a sophomore?'

'Yes, but I figured it's not too early to start planning. If I can get a rough idea of a topic, then I can do preliminary research as part of my junior tutorial. Then I'll have the groundwork done and—'

It was Saturday. Didn't this student have an Ultimate Frisbee game to go to? But as the earnest young student rambled on, Dulcie found herself relaxing. This girl – young woman – was so serious, and the largest problem looming in her mind was competition for graduate programs. And though in the past Dulcie might have been concerned with the level of intensity in the young student, right now it seemed like a sign of health. How carefree the sweet-faced sophomore seemed in light of everything else going on. How innocent. How – Dulcie could almost feel the brush of plume-like tail around her ankles – like Dulcie herself, once upon a time.

'I understand your concerns,' Dulcie finally broke in. 'But, really, I don't think you have anything to worry about.' The look she got stopped her cold. Nobody wants to hear that their problems aren't serious; the perception hit her with the sharp bite of teeth. 'I mean, your concerns are understandable, but you are doing all the right things.' She went on to talk about getting a broad base in the discipline. 'I have one student who had to do so much remedial reading in the basic canon that she's barely caught up as a second-semester junior. And besides,' she concluded, determined to send her charge off on a positive note, 'you're already an exemplary student.'

'Thanks, Ms Schwartz.' She was rewarded with a beaming smile. 'I should let you get back to your own work, I guess.'

'Anytime,' Dulcie responded, meaning it. As she watched the student wander off – and take her place by a pile of large volumes on the central table – Dulcie found her thoughts drifting from Carrie to Corkie. She hadn't been exaggerating that much when she'd used her current student as an example just now. Corkie had had to read an awful lot very quickly in order to catch up with her major. She'd worked so hard. Was that all going to go down the drain? Dulcie didn't need Mr Grey to point out whose responsibility that was. The cops were already looking for Carrie. As far as Dulcie knew, they were clueless about Corkie's possible involvement. What were her obligations here, anyway? Who needed her most?

If she had any doubts about not calling Rogovoy, that question put them to rest. Carrie might be a woman in trouble, a regret Dulcie would have to live with. But Corkie was Dulcie's student now, and she was also a friend. Every reasonable instinct told her that Corkie wasn't a killer, and those same instincts added that it wasn't likely that she was threatening Carrie. Besides, Dulcie was Corkie's tutor. That might not be a privileged relationship legally, but it brought with it a certain sense of loyalty.

Suze wouldn't like it, but she wasn't going to tell Rogovoy about Corkie going to the Poche that day. That didn't mean she couldn't continue to pursue the truth. Something was amiss. If she could figure out what was up, maybe it would also help her get her errant student back on track.

Dulcie reached for her phone, and immediately thought better of it. Cell phone use was akin to singing out loud among reading room crimes. But the library's wireless provided another option: *Corkie*, she fired off in an email. *Let's talk*. She thought of the Poche, of the wall of clippings. Of what now, in retrospect, had been her student's growing distress.

*Doesn't matter what happened, but I need to know before I do anything. I want to make sure you don't fall off the map.* She was trying for reassuring, but it sounded weak. *Email or call – or just drop by?* She paused. *Anytime*, she added, and hit 'send.'

The little clock on her laptop told her that it wasn't even five yet. If she could get a few hours of work done, she really might have something to show Chelowski – or whoever his successor might be. And if Corkie or Chris, or any of her students, wanted to get in touch with her, she was certainly where she should be, hard at it among the books.

What she needed was focus. She would meet with Dimitri later, and she had reached out to Corkie. Now she had to take care of herself, or else she'd be in real trouble. Chelowski's snouty face appeared in her mind, causing her to shudder. But worrying about her adviser would do no good. Textual analysis, she'd kept reminding herself. That was key. And since she knew the remaining fragments of *The Ravages of Umbria* so well by now, it was easy to find them and to note the crucial phrases.

'*The mind of a woman must be bent on her duties.*' That was Demetria, the heroine's deceitful attendant, speaking. '*As I know full well, taking as my life's work the honor and obligation of attending upon you.*'

Nice sentiments, but Demetria didn't mean them, Dulcie was sure. If all went well, Dulcie would make the case that the author had set this character up – giving her platitudes that her heroine could shoot down.

'*The mind of a woman driven by spirits . . .*' As the heroine, Hermetria, answered, she stated a much more modern opinion, even as she couched it in tales of ghosts and spirits. It was ingenious, really. '*For are we not now haunted by the restless spirits of our home, even as we seek peace?*'

By now, Dulcie knew the supporting material almost as well, and with only a little browsing, she was able to find the same phrases in a stirring political essay published in 1790.

*The mind of a woman shall not be so hampered by books and the like that she cannot perform the duties of wife and mother.* This essay had been published anonymously. But the author, 'a woman concern'd,' was undoubtedly the same woman who had penned *The Ravages of Umbria*. In every line, Dulcie could hear the cadence of the novel, the flow of ideas.

*Indeed, such roles must only be enhanc'd by her reading,* Dulcie continued, *as the ideas that stir her thoughts shall carry through, informing and enlightening any small child in her charge. And supposing she reject such domestic placements, the life duty, to seek a new life in the wilderness? Then what recourse should she have but books? In truth, what else would she require for herself or her bless'd offspring?*

By today's lights, it wasn't much, but at the time, it would have been inflammatory, and Dulcie remembered her dream: the wild-haired woman at her desk, pen in hand, writing furiously. She'd found a few such essays as this – and then, nothing. Dulcie sighed and shook her own semi-wild curls. She would focus on the text. There was certainly enough in the *Ravages* to make her case, and the similarities between the novel fragment and these contemporaneous essays supported her idea that the author had used the fictional adventure to advance her views. If only Dulcie knew why she had stopped writing.

But she had her own 'restless spirits' to worry about, and so a little before seven she packed up her notes and her books, and headed for the door. If she couldn't decipher the puzzling disappearance of the anonymous author, maybe she could solve her own little mystery.

The thought cheered her as she made her way down the steps, careful to hold the wooden handrails that had been added for winter safety. March in New England never seemed like spring to Dulcie, and now that the sun had set, the cold may as well have come fresh from February first.

Safely on solid ground, she checked her phone for messages and was pleased to see three.

'Mercury in retrograde again.' The first was from Lucy and started, as usual, in mid-thought. 'I should have checked, really I should have. Darling? Merlin had to point it out to me. I've been reading it wrong. Well, actually he said *we've* been reading it wrong, but I think that's just an inter-species communication glitch.'

Dulcie smiled. Her poor mother. Lucy had probably been racked with guilt about that upside-down card. 'At any rate, as soon as I heard that, I knew it was imperative to call you and let you know. We've been reading it wrong, dear.'

'Hey, sweetie!' Chris was the next call. 'Good to hear you're feeling better. And, yeah, the People's Republik. Jerry wants me to come, too. I've got a dinner meeting with a student, but I'll try to get over there by ten. Call me!'

A dinner meeting? He'd *try* to make it? Dulcie's mood flew off with her hat, as the wind gusted through the Yard, and she gave chase.

'Here you go.' A hand reached to steady her as she slipped on an icy patch. She looked up at the wool-draped figure as he handed her hat. 'It flew right at me.'

The face was familiar, but wrapped around in a tan scarf, she couldn't place it.

'Dulcie?' A mittened hand pushed the scarf back to reveal Merv's scarlet hair.

'Oh, hi.' She took her hat and started to shrink away.

'No, please. I'm sorry.' He looked down, as if searching for more ice. 'I'm sorry about how I acted before. Talking about Carrie got to me.'

'No, really. I was totally in the wrong. I mean, I'd gone into that office.' She paused. 'But I didn't break the police seal. Really, I wouldn't have.'

'No, I believe you. And I have my suspicions about who else might have been in there.' Dulcie waited, but he changed tack instead. 'Hey, are you doing anything tonight?'

She shrugged. 'A bunch of us are going to the People's Republik.' It was the truth. And if Chris couldn't make the time for her, there was no reason she couldn't enjoy some congenial company. 'Would you like to join us?'

'That sounds like fun.' He was smiling quite broadly now. 'I'll see you there!'

Dulcie smiled back, noting that this man didn't qualify his acceptance with a 'try.'

'Ciao,' she called after him. And, tucking her hair back under her hat, tried to ignore the bite of the wind, a bite as sharp as teeth.

# THIRTY-SIX

D ulcie went back to her voicemail with trepidation. If Chris had called back, she could still run after Merv, she promised herself. Run after him and say what? Tell him that she wanted him to meet her boyfriend? Shaking her head at her own silliness, she punched in the code.

'Just me.' It was Trista. 'I know you said you'd come tonight, but I really hope you do. I could use a friend.' That was it.

The delay had been just long enough for her to have missed one more call. From Corkie. 'Dulcie, I'm sorry. I can explain. It's all gotten so crazy, really. Please, don't do anything. Not yet.'

When Dulcie pressed the code for a redial, the call went straight to voicemail. Corkie was in the wind.

'It doesn't mean anything,' Dulcie said to Esmé as soon as she got home. 'It *is* Saturday night, and Corkie is a young, single woman.' She'd been about to add 'healthy.' But Corkie didn't look healthy any more. Hadn't in a while. Of course, that *could* be because of her busy schedule.

'I'm not sure they should allow undergraduates to work with other undergrads, Esmé.' She hung her coat up and looked down at the little cat. 'I mean, they've got enough on their plate, as it is.'

In response, Esmé reared up on her hind legs, batted at Dulcie's foot, and darted away.

'You two look cozy.'

Dulcie woke with a start to find Suze looking over her. She'd fallen asleep on the sofa, with the kitten on her lap. 'We were playing.' She blinked and yawned. Esmé did the same. 'I think you were right. Esmé needed some quality time. After all, she can't learn how to behave properly if I don't teach her.'

Suze looked around, and Dulcie became aware of the wadded-up balls of paper that littered the living room. 'So, this is what you're teaching her?' There was a smile in her voice, but Dulcie couldn't help but feel a little embarrassed.

'I'm trying to help her find her way. After all, isn't that what a teacher is supposed to do?'

Suze didn't answer, and Dulcie lifted the little cat to follow her into the kitchen. 'Do you and Ariano have plans tonight?'

'He's working.' Suze's voice came back from deep within the fridge. 'Do you know when this yogurt is from?'

'The Pleistocene?' The ancient leftovers sparked an idea. 'Hey, a bunch of us are meeting at the Republik later, but their menu is pretty horrible. What say we go to Mary Chung first? It's been ages.'

Suze closed the refrigerator with a definitive thud. 'Girls' night out? Definitely. Shall we ask Esmé?'

But the little kitten remained out like a light, dreaming no doubt of flying paper and her own successful hunt.

'So, you think maybe Chelowski has been abusing a student?'

Over dumplings, the idea sounded absurd. But Dulcie nodded gravely. 'Or Dimitri. Or –' she paused to spear another bit of stuffed dough – 'maybe Herschoft. But if that was the case, then why isn't this all over already? Why wouldn't Carrie have come out of hiding?'

Suze dipped her own dumpling as she considered the question. 'The after-effects of that kind of abuse can be strange. I mean, she might feel guilty. If she feels her actions motivated his suicide, she might feel responsible somehow.'

'But Rogovoy said it wasn't suicide.'

Suze paused, dumpling in mid-air, and Dulcie realized that this latest bombshell wasn't yet common knowledge. It also reminded her of how long it had been since she and Suze had talked. As quickly as she could, she brought her room-mate up to speed. And Suze, in turn, explained that homicide did indeed equate to murder: 'the deliberate and intentional killing of another person.'

When they were done, Suze was on her last dumpling. 'So, could Carrie have killed him?'

Dulcie shook her head. 'No, she had an appointment that day, but it was canceled.'

'I wonder if she went anyway.' Suze chewed thoughtfully. 'What if that note was her way of breaking it off? Maybe he didn't accept it. Maybe she pushed him?'

These were all the questions Dulcie had been asking herself.

The trouble was, none of it made sense once Corkie was figured in. She hadn't told Suze about following Corkie to the building. She hadn't told anyone. The dumplings turned to lead in Dulcie's stomach.

But Suze was still talking: 'You need to find out why the police think it was homicide. No, what am I saying? You don't need to do anything. You've reached out to a missing student as well as you can. You're talking to your current student. You're finally writing. Don't mess it up, Dulcie. Really.'

'I don't know, Suze. I can't help but feel that I already have.'

# THIRTY-SEVEN

Suze begged off the People's Republik, but Dulcie, despite feeling somewhat overstuffed, made herself head out again. She'd all but promised Trista. She had questions that needed answers. And if only Chris would show up . . . She paused, remembering her earlier actions. Well, maybe it would be good for Chris to see that she had other options. If he showed up, that was.

With a sigh to match the gusting wind, she shoved the pub's heavy front door open and stepped inside. The People's Republik wasn't much to look at. One long room, with a bar down the middle and some tables on either side. Over to the right, space had been cleared for darts, and that was where Dulcie looked first. Trista, among her other skills, was the dart champion among the humanities grad students, and the English department was justly proud of her.

But no cheers or shouts of dismay could be heard over the jukebox, and even as Dulcie's eyes adjusted to the light, she could see no sign of Trista's bleached blonde shag. Instead, she headed toward the left side of the bar, where she found a small group huddled at one end of a large table.

'Hey, guys.' Dulcie shed her coat and looked around. Jamie, who specialized in the English renaissance and rather looked the part in his velvet jacket, sat by Molly, a modernist, whom Dulcie didn't know well. Lloyd was coming back from the

men's room as she flung her coat over a chair. As he greeted
her, his smile grew, and Dulcie turned around to see Raleigh
making her way over behind her. Among this crowd, everyone
appeared to have accepted her relationship with Lloyd, partly
because the pretty senior could hold her own with any of
the grad students. Still, Dulcie felt more uneasy than usual as
she smiled at her friends. It was so easy to overstep, and so
difficult to know where one really had to draw the line.

'Dulcie! Good to see you!' Jerry came over from the bar,
two pitchers of beer in his hands. Dulcie turned, but when
she saw how his face lit up, Dulcie knew it wasn't simply for
her.

'Trista here yet?' she asked before he could.

'She's not with you?' Jerry set the pitchers down, but not
before Dulcie could see his face fall.

'She told me she'd be here,' Dulcie noted with irony. She'd
been wondering if she could ask him about Chris. 'But don't
worry. I'll translate until she gets here.'

She was making light. Despite their math backgrounds,
Jerry and Chris had both been absorbed into the English
department crowd. Dulcie had long seen that as confirmation
of their solidity, the rightness of their stature as couples. But
if Jerry and Trista could break up, it only made sense that she
and Chris could, too.

'Thanks.' Jerry smiled, a closed-mouth smile, and poured
her a mug. Molly and Lloyd were going on about grading.
Dulcie listened in: Martin Thorpe tended to get overwhelmed
by bureaucracy, and from what these two were saying that
meant this semester he had screwed up some university
deadlines.

'What's this?' Dulcie leaned in for the details.

'Didn't you hear?' Molly looked up, clearly exasperated.
'I don't know what's wrong with him. It's all online, for
Christ's sake.'

Dulcie couldn't help but chuckle. To the students, the Web
was an easy alternative. To an old-timer like Thorpe, it was
another world.

'It's also in the university calendar.' Lloyd didn't sound like
he wanted to defend their acting chairman. 'And now it falls
on us.'

'What?' Dulcie was definitely missing something.

'All the midterm reports – grades, student evaluations, you name it – are due next week. Not March 31. Or – when did he first tell us? – April 15.'

'The ides of April!' Dimitri had come up behind Dulcie and pulled up a chair. 'Who is being killed?'

'Thorpe should be.' Molly was shaking her head.

'Oh, it's not that bad.' Dulcie wanted to get Dimitri alone, but this affected all of them. 'I mean, we're all supposed to be just about done with grading, right?' In the back of her mind, she tried to count the ungraded blue books. There couldn't be more than sixteen left, could there?

'Midterms, sure.' Molly sniffed. 'I turned mine in last week. But this is also evaluations. All the reports on students on probation, and all that.'

'Huh.' Dulcie tried not to hate Molly for her efficiency and found herself wondering: 'Status reports? Like, on students who've just come back?' She would pass Corkie, no question. Once she got some answers.

'Exactly,' Lloyd chimed in. 'Originally, we thought that the preliminary reports had to go to the department next week. You know, the ones we could all argue about. But now they're saying we have no time for that. We're going to be filing direct with the administration. And that means the dean. The bursar's office. Financial Aid.'

'Great.' Corkie had been busy, but Dulcie had been preoccupied, too. It was her fault as much as her student's if she hadn't focused on her school work. 'I guess I've got some catching up to do.'

'You very well might.' Lloyd was looking at her in a way she couldn't decipher. 'Because these will include our advisers' reports, too.'

'Oh.' Dulcie leaned back, deflated. She could catch up on her own work, that she knew. But if Chelowski wasn't impressed by her progress, it would have serious consequences. And if he found out she was asking about him . . . No, she couldn't go there. 'Hell,' she added softly. 'Maybe I should get back to work.'

But as she reached for her coat, a hand stopped her. 'Not so fast, stranger.' It was Trista. 'The night is young.'

Trista seemed to be alone, for which she was grateful. 'Tris, something's come up.'

'Please.' Her friend leaned in close, and Dulcie could hear the desperation in her voice. She nodded. 'Darts, anyone?'

Jerry looked like he was about to respond, but Trista had already grabbed Dulcie's arm.

'You can play the winner,' Dulcie said, faking a smile. They all knew who that would be.

'Trista, what's going on?' By the time they had gathered their darts, Dulcie was sick of the subterfuge. 'You and Jerry. You wanting me here.' She paused, deciding it was time to say the words. 'Are you two breaking up?'

Trista threw, but only made the outer circle. 'Damn. My eye is off.'

'Tris?'

Trista threw again, this time getting closer to the bullseye. 'It's –' thwock – 'complicated.'

'I cannot tell you how sick I am of complicated relationships.' Dulcie wasn't really thinking of what she was saying, but something about her words hit the black. Trista turned toward her friend.

'You're right. It's not fair of me.' Trista looked past Dulcie, and Dulcie knew she was searching beyond the bar, toward their friends. 'But it *is* complicated.'

Dulcie waited as Trista turned back toward the dartboard.

'Jerry and I,' she said, throwing another dart. 'We've been together for, like, two years now. And sometimes I feel like this is it.' Another dart. 'I couldn't be happier. But recently, I don't know. I mean, this isn't permanent. We're going to be finishing up soon. I'm hoping to defend my thesis next year, and Jerry's going to be done sometime soon, too. And then what? We'll both be looking for post docs. For teaching positions. For –' another throw – 'anything we can get.'

'You're thinking of Rosemary and Gene.' Dulcie didn't need to say it. The entire department knew about Rosie and Gene. A couple since freshman week, they'd managed their graduate careers perfectly – until they defended their theses. Then Rosemary landed the tenure-track position of her dreams, teaching Shakespeare at McGill. And Gene had done the same, only at Vanderbilt. Within months, she was seeing another man, and he had rushed into a quickie marriage with a departmental secretary. That hadn't lasted either. 'But it doesn't have to be like that, does it? I mean, Jerry and Chris, they don't have to stay in academia. They've got the skills. They can go into the private sector. Computer guys can work anywhere.'

'Yeah,' said Trista as she walked up to retrieve her darts. 'As long as they're willing to give up their dreams.'

'Maybe we'll never finish our theses.' Dulcie meant it as a joke. It was only when Trista turned on her with a strange look that she realized how closely she was echoing Chelowski's words.

'So, I just feel like maybe we should cool it. Like I should try to build in some distance.' Trista wasn't even trying to coach as Dulcie threw – and hit the wall. 'But it's so hard, you know?'

'Yeah.' Another miss. 'At least he wants to be with you.'

'You don't think Chris—' Trista turned toward her. 'So is that what's been bothering you?'

'It's a lot of things.' Dulcie shrugged. 'I've also got some trouble with one of my students. And, well, I may be on the edge of something—' She was about to go on, to get Trista's feedback. But just then she heard another voice.

'I think we know who the winner is.' It was Jerry, his voice tight with fake jollity. 'Dulcie?'

She handed over her remaining darts. No matter what Trista said, this couple had a chance. They needed to talk.

And she needed some time with Dimitri. Walking back to the table, she saw him get up. 'Beer run?'

'Gents.' He smiled. 'But then I really do need to run off. All this talk about deadlines, you know.'

'I do.' She nodded. 'But, please, would you stay a few minutes longer? I need to speak with you.'

He raised his eyebrows, and Dulcie was struck once again by how handsome the Russian was. Had he misunderstood her interest? Well, nothing for it, she decided, and hovered between the restrooms and the communal table until her colleague returned.

'So, what is so important that you ambush me?' He was smiling. He had misunderstood.

'It's about one of my students.' Now that she had him here, Dulcie wasn't sure how to ask.

'Oh?' He doubted her.

'Carrie Mines.' He blinked, and she went on. 'One of my

former students. Who you then ended up teaching. And, I believe, may have become close to.'

'We are friends.' There was something there, she could tell. And he had admitted that much. 'What is this about?'

'She's in trouble. I know it.' Dulcie decided to just spill. 'She's in hiding, and you're involved.'

'It is true that I was questioned. You knew that, but that is all.'

'Dimitri, it's time to spill the beans.'

He raised his eyebrows again, but this time Dulcie wasn't taken in. 'Come on, you know the expression. It's time to tell me what's going on. For Carrie's sake, and, well, for yours too.' If he was in trouble, she would help him. Carrie was a pretty young thing, and maybe she'd come on to him, using her sexuality to win more attention from her young teacher. He was European. They were different.

'I already told the police, this is not my secret.' He was looking away, and Dulcie felt a strong urge to grab his arm and shake him. If there was more going on here – if Dimitri was involved with Herschoft's murder – she needed to know.

'Dimitri, look. Carrie is in trouble. Serious trouble.' She wouldn't talk about murder, not yet. That didn't seem to be common knowledge, and it might prove useful down the line. But she had another trump card to play. 'She might even be in danger.'

'But she was getting help.'

Bingo. 'I know she was seeing a peer counselor. That's how I got involved.' She was stretching the point, but not by much. 'But the counselor wouldn't tell me – no, she *couldn't* tell me – what was going on, and I have to respect that. But you can, Dimitri. And you've got to.' She paused. 'For Carrie's sake.'

He sighed and rubbed his chin. 'You're right. She is in deep. Over her head. I tried to talk with her, to help her. But she would not listen.' He shook his head, and Dulcie felt her throat tighten. This was worse than she'd feared. 'I would not want her blood splattered all over the piazza. I mean, spattered.'

For a moment, Dulcie was taken aback. Then it came to her. 'Oh, you were talking suicide.'

'Well, yes, like that awful man. I am glad I missed it, for from what my friend tells me, his blood was probably spread about like—' He paused, searching for the word. 'Like a jelly donut.'

Dulcie closed her eyes as a wave of nausea hit her. No, he hadn't seen Herschoft. But the image came back to her. 'It wasn't like that.'

'Oh? Because Lylah told me about a seminar, in which a living organism—'

'Please, Dimitri. It wasn't like that at all.' An image of the blood – dark, framing the back of Herschoft's head – filled her vision. She needed to get Dimitri back on track. 'But you've seen her? You've talked to her?'

'No, not since—' He paused and swallowed. 'But I tried. This is not right, I told her. Maybe I became too loud.'

'You fought?'

He nodded. 'I kept telling her: he hurts you with this.'

So it had been Dimitri she'd seen, that night under the arch. Only, he'd been urging Carrie to come forward. To speak out about someone else. 'Who was "he," Dimitri? Who was she involved with?'

'That skeazy fellow. Is that the word? Skeazy?'

Dulcie nodded. He had it, more or less.

'The one who is always hanging around her.'

Dulcie's stomach clenched. 'You mean Merv, her ex-boyfriend?'

'No, no. That professor of hers. The really skeazy – no, *sleazy* – one.'

Dulcie smiled. He'd got it right. 'Norm Chelowski. I knew it.'

But Dimitri was shaking his head. 'Not Chelowski. He creeps in a different way. No, her other professor. The one who was supposed to be helping her. The dead guy: Herschoft!'

# THIRTY-EIGHT

'You look like you've seen a ghost.' Chris was at the table by the time Dulcie returned; Dimitri had grabbed his coat and left. 'And not a particularly friendly one.'

'What?' Dulcie could barely focus. Dimitri's words were

still bouncing around her head. She'd suspected Herschoft of something inappropriate, but there had been too many loose ends.

'That was Dimitri, right?' Chris was watching her. 'Did you two have a fight or something?'

There was something in his voice that wasn't right. But her mind was spinning. Why was Carrie still in hiding? How was Corkie involved? There was too much going on for Dulcie to focus.

'It's nothing.' Herschoft? Had all this led to his blood on the concrete? That dark, thick blood?

'Should I be jealous?' Finally, Dulcie looked up. Her boyfriend was smiling, but not easily.

'No, no. Really.' She smiled back and tried to put her heart in it. 'Hey, you made it.'

'Well, sort of.' He reached to kiss her, but their embrace was cut short as he turned to decline a mug.

'I can't hang,' he explained to Molly. 'With midterms over, everybody is behind in their semester projects.' He sounded genuinely sad. Dulcie knew about deadlines, she did. It was just that she'd been hoping.

She nodded and tried to look supportive as Chris kept talking, turning to her. 'Plus, a few of the guys did cover for me when you were in the infirmary.'

He continued, saying something about how he was really on an extended break. But Dulcie found her mind wandering. If Herschoft really had been taking advantage of Carrie, then Chelowski was in the clear. But the evidence against Corkie was piling up. As difficult as it was to see her student as a murderer, Dulcie now understood how it could have happened. That had been Carrie, upset, talking to Corkie. What had she said? That she couldn't end it? Had Corkie then raced over to confront Herschoft – and killed him?

Maybe he deserved it. Maybe Corkie was justified. And maybe that justified anger gave her enough strength to throw a full-grown man out the window. Dulcie's head was swimming. And through it all, she kept on thinking about what else Dimitri had said – something about a jelly donut. The body, the blood . . .

'Dulce?' Dulcie looked around. Her friends were all staring. 'Are you OK?'

'Yeah, I'm sorry.' She tried to conjure a smile for Chris. 'I'm just thinking.' That pale, still hand.

'Oh, good.' He looked relieved. 'I've been afraid that you were mad at me,' he said. 'You know, because I've been working through dinner and all.'

Did 'and all' include a certain red-haired student? Remembering Trista's words, Dulcie roused herself from her thoughts and looked over toward her friend. She was laughing now, chiming in as Lloyd began a story. But Jerry was still looking at her with a vague, lost expression on his face. Well, if Dulcie was right, the university had bigger problems to deal with now.

'So, I wanted to make the effort. You know, show you that I'm still here.' Chris sounded like he was miles away. 'But I guess I should get back to the old grind.'

He stood, and Dulcie turned to him, wondering if she could explain about the body. About Carrie. And just then the pub door opened and a different tall redhead walked in.

'Merv!' She almost shouted as she stood and waved. 'Over here.' She had so many questions for him.

'All right then.' Chris looked from Dulcie toward the door, where Merv was smiling back. 'I guess I'll call you, Dulcie.' And he left.

But if Dulcie thought the new arrival would be able to answer all her questions, she was wrong.

'No, no way.' Merv was adamant. 'There's no way Carrie was involved with Herschoft.'

Dulcie had made the requisite introductions, pointedly ignoring Trista's questioning look, and as soon as she could, had started questioning her new friend.

'Not "involved," exactly.' Dulcie was trying to keep her voice low. Even with the jukebox, she felt the need to be careful. 'We're talking harassment. It's abuse. From what I've been reading, it's about power. About domination. Usually, it's not even really sexual.'

'No.' Merv seemed to have no such compunction, and Dulcie was aware of her colleagues looking over at them. 'There's just no way.'

'Merv, please.' Dulcie wanted to be graceful, but she had to cut through his denial. 'I know you cared about her. You must have thought the world of her, and nobody wants to think of a friend as a victim.'

He shook his head, cutting her off. 'You don't understand. I loved her. And, yes, I was bitter, but if someone was hurting Carrie. If someone was forcing her—' He stopped, his mouth set in a thin line.

Dulcie looked at him. He was skinny, sure. But he was tall, and she knew from her time with Chris how muscular long, lean men could be. 'Merv?' Now she really felt unsure how to proceed. 'The day that Herschoft died, were you there?'

'What? No.' He laughed and shook his head. 'No, I was in the lab. And, yes, I'm sure I can come up with at least a dozen people who can vouch for me. We had to put down a dozen rats because someone had screwed up a drug regimen, and I am afraid I didn't keep my opinions to myself.'

'Well, that's a relief.' Dulcie didn't realize until she said it how little she wanted her new friend to be involved. 'But, oh hell, that means you can't tell me who else *might* have been there.'

'Sorry, that's kind of impossible anyway. The whole building is a security nightmare.'

She looked at him quizzically. 'But there's a guard.'

'At the front, yeah. But you can leave through the back. The door pushes open. It's supposed to lock, but people leave it propped open all the time. Plus, if someone is coming out, they'll hold it for you.'

'He will – or she.' It was automatic. Years of training causing her to speak without thinking as her last best hope faded away. She knew that door; she'd used it herself. And Merv hadn't been there. He wasn't a suspect, but he also couldn't help alibi Corkie.

'But this is all really silly anyway.' Merv hadn't seemed to notice her correction. 'Because there is just no way that Carrie was involved with someone against her will. Look, Dulcie, I know you think there was something funny going on, but believe me. I'm the last person who wanted Carrie to fall for someone else. But she did. She was in love. And she was happier than I'd ever seen her.'

# THIRTY-NINE

*Writing, writing again, furious to finish. There is light behind the clouds, light picking up the flame-colored highlights in her dark, wild hair. Another night, gone. Another dab of ink on a cheek grown increasingly pale. What can she say to make them see? 'Spirits, long enslav'd will out . . .' No, she crosses it out, drops the pen in frustration, and watches as its remaining ink beads at its tip and then falls, a dark stain spreading. In the growing light, she can see the blood from where her hand rested. Thicker than the ink and no longer vital. Two spots, her life in rust. The time is drawing close, and she knows that they are waiting. The fire sparks, and snaps, the smoke curling up like the tail of an inquisitive beast.*

*She begins to write again, ink adding to the stain on her fingers. The rolling peal of thunder drowns out the scratch of her pen. Overwhelms the crack and hiss of the fire, the once-constant stream of her thoughts. If only she could reason with them. If only she could* think. *But the storm has drowned it all, and now she is alone. Afraid of the dark, of the depths, of what waits.*

*The time is drawing close.*

Dulcie woke from her fitful sleep. The dream was back. *The time is drawing close.* Did the dream woman know who was stalking her – or was she considering her own end? Suicide. Stalking. They were haunting Dulcie's dreams. Could the nightmare have referred to Carrie?

This was crazy. Granted, she didn't know Merv well. But he'd sounded quite convinced when he'd said that Carrie hadn't been involved with Herschoft. And since he'd been dumped by her for someone else, well, he should have been the first to blow the whistle if something had gone wrong.

Dimitri, on the other hand, was a colleague. Someone she'd come to trust. And what he'd said about Herschoft fitted in with what Corkie had shown her – and with Carrie's odd behavior. It also made sense of the argument she had witnessed almost a week ago. He'd been trying to convince her to come forward, to speak out against her abuser.

Unless he wasn't. Maybe he'd been spinning a story to distract everyone. He was studying stories of crime and deception, and he did have a kind of gross fascination with blood and murder.

Then again, maybe the dream was simply about her thesis. Maybe she was the desperate woman, writing on a deadline. *The time is drawing close.*

Still groggy from her nightmare, Dulcie pulled herself out of bed. At times like these, she wished Suze was around a little bit more. Or Chris, for that matter. But she didn't want to think about how he'd taken off last night. About how her own distraction might have pushed him away.

'Mr Grey? I could really use some help right now.' The apartment seemed so empty and still. But as she reached for her bathrobe, a thundering of cat feet seemed to answer her plea. 'Esmé! Good morning, Miss Kitty.'

'*Principessa, please.*' The little black and white kitten stopped suddenly and began washing her face.

'Esmé! I'm sorry, Principessa. You spoke!' For months, Dulcie had been convinced that her new pet could communicate.

'*I can when I need to.*' The little feline looked up, and Dulcie noticed how catlike she had become. Maybe the ability to talk, even psychically, came with maturity.

'*Or maybe you just need to remember there are other ways to communicate.*' With that, she finished washing her face and jumped up to Dulcie's desk.

'Hey, watch it.' The cat had landed on her laptop. 'I mean, please.'

But Esmé had taken off again. And as much as Dulcie regretted the end of the conversation, it struck her that maybe her pet had been making a point. Carrie had never called the number that Rogovoy had provided, so odds were that she didn't know Dulcie had talked with the police. Plus, she'd been willing to communicate by email once before. Maybe she could be reached again.

While she waited for the program to open, Dulcie mulled over what she should say. Finally, she settled on the most basic. *Carrie: We need to talk. Call me, pls? Or drop by?* She typed in her office and home information. It seemed insufficient. The emptiness of email again. But it was all she could do, she concluded, and hit 'send.'

Part of the problem, she acknowledged as the screen went blank, was her own distraction. She'd been spending so much mental energy trying to figure out what was up with Carrie – and Corkie – that she'd short-changed her own work. The dream most likely was a reminder. She'd trusted her dreams before, and only a week ago she had been so sure that she was on track to solve a literary mystery. Couldn't she keep on investigating why her author had gone silent – and still work on the textual part of her thesis?

It was Sunday, a prime day for the library. The dream might have carried a warning: *write now, lest you be doomed to a nightmare all-nighter!* But it was no good. Maybe she wasn't cut out to be a scholar, but she couldn't focus when living people, her students, were at risk. Dulcie had reached out to Carrie as best she could, but she had another student to care for. That last message – what had Corkie said, 'Let me take care of it?' – had been woefully unsatisfying. Besides, she'd done what she could with Dimitri –and with Merv – and still come to a dead end. If Corkie wouldn't talk to her, Dulcie needed to reconsider talking to Rogovoy. Corkie had been in the building. She was involved. Dulcie would give it one more go. See if she could find a way to get Corkie to confide. At least she would warn her that soon the police would be involved.

# FORTY

Esmé had returned by the time Dulcie emerged from the shower. But her adult behavior seemed to be continuing, as she sat and stared at her human, rather than careening around madly.

'What is it, little girl?' Dulcie toweled her hair as the cat watched. 'Is it that you can't believe I'd voluntarily put myself under water?'

Esmé didn't answer, and for a moment Dulcie doubted her own plan of action. Maybe the cat was telling her to mind her own business. No, this little beast was into everything. And, in her own way, she'd even shown that most of what we get up to is innocent – if a tad destructive.

'Or is it,' she continued as she pulled on her jeans, 'that you're lonely too?' Esmé might not be a sleuth, but her sleek presence made Dulcie feel better. She'd been distracted the night before, she acknowledged as she started the coffee. Still, it hurt that Chris hadn't come by after his shift. Today was Sunday, after all. He could've slept till noon, and Dulcie could have made them both a real breakfast.

'Instead, I'm talking to the cat.' Esmé tilted her head, and for a moment Dulcie expected a response. But none came.

'Maybe it's just as well, Es— Excuse me, Principessa?' No answer to that one either. And so, rather than brood about absent friends and lovers, Dulcie donned her coat and headed down the steps into the world, locking the door behind her. Only to find that spring, once more, had made an appearance.

'Good morning, neighbor!' Helene was out on the stoop, her cat Julius stretched beside her. 'Gorgeous day, isn't it?'

'Amazing.' Dulcie unbuttoned her coat and looked up at the sky. 'Is this supposed to last?'

'Who knows?' Helene leaned over to stroke Julius's sun-warmed fur. 'Last I heard, they were saying freezing rain.'

'Huh.' Setting down her travel mug, Dulcie shed her coat and hat, and then looked up at her own front door. Julius stretched, showing the pink between his toes.

'Here, why don't I take those for you?' Helene reached up. 'I don't care what WBZ says, you're not going to need them today.'

'Thanks, Helene.' Dulcie felt lighter, her mood lifting in the bright sun. 'Maybe I won't need them again until fall.'

'Yeah, well . . .' Helene laughed, and with a jaunty step, Dulcie headed down the street.

First, Corkie, then writing, Dulcie decided as she headed toward Mass. Ave. Better to be busy than to wonder why her boyfriend hadn't even called to say goodnight. Busy would keep her mind in the present, instead of dwelling on memories of Sunday mornings filled with laughter and the smell of bacon.

Reaching into her bag for her phone, she joined the queue

waiting to cross the street. A couple jostled her, and she had to grab to keep from losing her mug. Somehow, she got her phone out without spilling, and with her thumb keyed in Corkie's number. Holding it to her ear, she took another sip as the crowd closed in, awaiting the walk signal. By the time Corkie picked up, the light had changed.

'Corkie! It's Dulcie.' A car, impatient to make a turn, honked. 'Can you hear me?'

'Yeah? Dulcie?'

'Sorry to call so early.' Dulcie winced. From her student's sleepy voice, it was clear she had awakened her. 'I need to see you.'

'What?'

'I need to see you!' One of Cambridge's many church bells started to ring. Sunday morning. 'Can you hear me?'

'Yeah, barely.' She sounded a little more awake now. 'What's up?'

'We've got to talk again. I'm sorry, but we have to. About Carrie Mines and Professor Herschoft!'

'Dulcie, I—'

'Please, don't say it!' Dulcie didn't give her a chance to continue. 'I know there are things you can't tell me. Things you aren't allowed to. But we have to talk. I can be at Dunster House in fifteen minutes.'

Silence, and for a moment Dulcie thought she lost her. She paused, ducking into the alcove of a bank for silence. 'Corkie?'

'All right.' The voice at the other end sounded resigned, if not happy. 'But not here. I'll meet you at Below the Stairs, OK? I can be there in fifteen minutes, too.'

'Great. See you there!' Maybe more than the weather was brightening up. Dulcie clipped her phone shut and drained the last of her coffee. The caffeine had helped, she decided as she set off again, a new bounce in her step. But neither the coffee nor the sunshine were enough to alert her to the figure who had hung back as she talked, and who now hugged the building, following close behind.

# FORTY-ONE

'I don't know what else I can tell you.' Corkie was busy sorting through files. Shuffling papers. And doing, Dulcie realized, everything except looking her in the eye. 'I mean, you know the rules I'm bound by. I just can't.'

Dulcie had taken a seat in the small office, one of the consultation rooms in the back of the counseling center. Now she sighed heavily and leaned her head back.

'There has to be something, Corkie. This is serious.' She waited. If Corkie was going to talk, she didn't want to spook her by mentioning the police. She had to give her student a chance. 'Look, maybe we can do this a different way. I'll say something, and you let me know if I have it right or not.'

Corkie placed a file in a drawer and slammed it shut, before turning to look at Dulcie for the first time. 'I don't know.' She was shaking her head, and even though Dulcie could see her eyes, they didn't look particularly encouraging. 'If I don't respect client privilege—'

'This isn't about client privilege,' Dulcie was quick to cut in. 'This is about seeing justice done.'

Corkie gasped, and Dulcie smiled. She was on the right track. 'Let's talk about Professor Herschoft. Fritz Herschoft.'

Corkie walked over to the corner of the office. Considering that the entire room was about the size of a large closet, the effect was one of desperation. Corkie was acting like a caged animal.

But Dulcie wasn't in the position to grant leniency. 'I have it on good authority that Professor Herschoft was not acting ethically, and that maybe that got him into trouble.' Until she knew what Corkie knew, she wasn't going to mention murder.

But Corkie said nothing. Dulcie decided to push harder.

'And I believe Carrie feels somehow involved in what happened to the professor.'

She couldn't place it exactly. It wasn't like Corkie made a sound, or even moved. But something made Dulcie think that she had hit a nerve. 'Maybe Carrie said something that got the professor into trouble. Maybe she told the wrong person—'

'No, that's not it.' Corkie was staring up at a corner of the ceiling like it had the answers to her finals. 'They never know. They never realize that it's not their fault.'

So that was it. Guilt. Poor Carrie. She must still believe that Herschoft had killed himself – and she must feel responsible. 'But something happened.' Dulcie knew she had to push. 'Word got out. Someone did . . . something.'

Corkie turned around, and Dulcie was hit by how tired the poor girl looked. 'Is that it, Corkie? I know you must have been looking out for Carrie. She was younger. She was vulnerable.'

Corkie shook her head and opened her mouth. 'You don't know. You *can't* know.'

'But I think I do.' A tragic chain of events was beginning to fashion itself in her mind. 'Carrie was being harassed, being *abused* by Herschoft. You stepped in, trying to help her. He probably denied everything. So, what did you do next? Did you urge Carrie to stick up for herself? Did you try to get her to go to the disciplinary committee?'

'No, no, I couldn't.' Corkie slammed a file drawer closed. 'I can't.' She grabbed her coat and headed toward the door. 'Not here.'

Dulcie hesitated. In part, she wanted to go to her student, to comfort her. More than anything, she wanted her to keep talking. Voluntarily, without the police. As a compromise, she went after her, but kept her distance.

'I couldn't get her to see sense.' Corkie finally turned once they were outside. Her words, hissed more than whispered, echoed slightly in the stairwell. 'I couldn't get her to talk to anybody.'

'What happened, Corkie? Did you go to confront him? Was there a fight? Tell me. I saw you going into the Poche that afternoon. I haven't told the police, but I believe you went up to his office. I believe you were the last one to see him alive.'

Corkie's head swiveled around, but they were alone in the dank stairwell. Nobody was coming to the counseling center this early on a Sunday. 'I don't know what you know or how you know it, Dulcie. But please, believe me, you do not know the whole story.'

'So tell me, Corkie.' Dulcie fought to keep her own voice low, her desperation rising. 'Tell me now and we can go get some breakfast. Get two big mugs of latte. Figure out what to do next. Together.'

The woman in front of her opened her mouth, and Dulcie feared one more lie. One more evasion. 'Please, Corkie. It's just me. Dulcie. Talk to me.'

Corkie nodded. 'You're right, Ms Schwartz. I was the one who called the committee. I wanted Herschoft out of there. He couldn't be allowed to teach. Not ever. Not again.'

Dulcie waited, the horrible realization that her worst fears were right growing inside her. 'When I saw you, on Mass. Ave., you were fighting with Carrie about Professor Herschoft?'

The other girl nodded. 'She's, well, she's vulnerable, you said it yourself. She's fragile. And I'm not. So, I did what was necessary.' She stopped at the sound of her own words. 'I mean, I called the board. I wanted him stopped. And, yes, I went to talk to him. But, I never wanted him dead.'

'Of course not.' Dulcie's heart was breaking. 'You're no—'

But before she could say it. Before she could say 'murderer,' she heard a howl, a cry of rage or defiance. And then the student in front of her collapsed to the ground, a chunk of masonry rocking beside her on the stairwell's concrete floor.

# FORTY-TWO

D ulcie screamed. In retrospect, it seemed a useless kind of response. Not at all what Hermetria would have done. But at that moment, looking down at her student, her friend, who had gone from lively conversationalist to still and dusty, it was the only appropriate response.

It worked, too. In a moment – not that she was any longer a judge of time – Reneé was out the door, and then students from Weld. EMTs from the University Health Services followed soon after, at first rather rudely pushing Dulcie aside, and then, when Corkie had been placed on a stretcher and removed, guiding her out of the stairwell.

'Are you all right, miss?' A young man in a blue uniform seemed to want to walk her over to another ambulance. 'Did you get hit as well?'

'Yes, yes, I did.' It was all coming together. 'The other day.'

'Why don't you sit right here?' He gently maneuvered her on to the bumper of his ambulance and, from some pocket, extracted a flashlight. 'And look straight ahead.'

She was doing as she was told when she realized that her own words had been the source of confusion. 'No, I'm sorry.' She turned away from the pinpoint of light. 'Please, let me clarify.'

The EMT sat back and waited, clearly a little skeptical.

'I got hit on the head here the other day. That's all.' She was trying to remember the details. Maybe she had gotten a concussion. Or maybe it was simply the shock.

'These old buildings.' The EMT shook his head sadly. 'The university has got to spring for more for upkeep. Twice in one week?'

'No, it wasn't an accident. It was the harasser. The Harvard Harasser. Suze said he would escalate. The harasser, that is. But not, you know, the real professor who was harassing students. He was already dead.'

The EMT opened his mouth to say something, and she put up a hand to stop him.

'No, please. This makes sense. I'm just a little fuddled, you know?' She knew she sounded crazy. Or, worse, hysterical. But with her apology, she'd bought herself a moment's sufferance. 'Both times, I'd come from the counseling center. Below the Stairs?' She pointed to the sign, and the EMT nodded. 'And both times I had been talking to the same person. To Corkie, actually.' She realized that the man in front of her might not know who that was. 'To the woman who just got – injured.' She paused and swallowed, hoping that was all that had happened. 'And now I'm wondering, maybe I wasn't the intended victim after all. Maybe he was after her all along.'

'I think you should come with me.' He stood and offered her a hand to step into the ambulance.

'No, I'm fine. Really.'

He looked at her. 'Please, miss. The police are going to

want your statement. And if there's any truth to what you're saying, you just might be in danger.'

It was easier to go along than to argue. Besides, she had questions of her own – and she was feeling a little dizzy.

'When was the last time you ate anything?' The stout nurse who had examined the wound on Dulcie's head had declared it healing. Now she knelt in front of Dulcie, shining a flashlight in her eyes.

'We were going out for breakfast before it happened.' It was hard to think with that light. 'I had some coffee this morning.'

The nurse clicked the light off and fixed Dulcie with a stare. 'Well, call me crazy, but I think you've had a scare and your blood sugar is probably low, too. I'm going to let you go, but promise me one thing: you'll call your regular doctor for an appointment tomorrow?'

'Sure.' It took Dulcie a moment to realize that it was, in fact, Sunday. 'Sorry, this has been quite the weekend.'

'I gather. Hang on.' The nurse stepped outside the curtained area. When she returned, she was smiling. 'But I've got great news. Your friend is conscious and doing well. If you want to stick your head in, I think you might be able to say hi.'

The nurse's estimate was a little optimistic, and her colleagues shooed Dulcie out to the waiting area 'until we're ready.' Taking her other advice, she wandered over to Au Bon Pain. It wasn't the hearty brunch she'd had in mind, but a few bites of a pain au chocolate did something to settle her stomach. So did the phone message she picked up from Chris.

'Hey, sweetie. Hope you're still asleep.' His voice was as warming as the melting chocolate. 'I'm sorry I took off like that last night. I guess I've been a bit on edge. Call me? I'm going to get some more sleep, but I'll leave my phone on. We can go out for brunch.'

In an act of supreme will, Dulcie tossed the second half of her pastry. She wouldn't call Chris: not for at least an hour yet. He needed his sleep, and she had unfinished business at hand. But brunch with her sweetie was worth the wait.

Mocha, however, was a beverage, and nobody said anything when she re-entered the waiting area, carrying a hot cup.

One of the attendants recognized her and signaled for her to wait, so she settled into a plastic chair and let the thoughts flow. She did feel better now, with some sugar in her system. Maybe the nurse had been right. Or maybe it was simply having a little distance from such an attack. Because no matter what the EMT might have thought, Dulcie knew better. Rogovoy had told her that the masonry in the stairwell was solid, and twice was certainly no accident. Someone had thrown something – maybe aiming for Corkie, maybe aiming for her.

She stopped. When she had been attacked, Carrie's note had been taken. This time, they'd been talking about the girl, about her future. There had to be some connection. Carrie. That note.

Maybe it was the cooling system, kicking in on a prematurely warm day. Maybe it was the rush of an orderly pushing past, a cart full of equipment bouncing noisily in front of him. Dulcie felt a touch – light, like the slightest brush of fur. Then a memory surfaced: '*We're reading it wrong, Dulcie.*' Had Lucy been right?

By the time she got in to see her student, Dulcie thought she just might have it figured out. Corkie was lying in bed, her head bandaged. But Dulcie had no time for sympathy.

'That note, the one in Carrie's file. You were going to use it against Herschoft.' Dulcie pulled the guest chair next to the bed. 'That's why you went off to see him.'

'It was evidence.' Corkie didn't deny it. Wan and bloodied, she seemed to be gathering herself, and Dulcie waited. 'I wanted to confront him.'

'To show him the damage he'd done? How distraught he'd made her?'

'What? No.' Corkie winced and put her hand to her forehead.

She must be confused, Dulcie thought. But still, this was important. *We've been reading it wrong . . .* 'Wait, it wasn't a suicide note, was it?'

Pale as she was, Corkie smiled. 'You thought that's what that was?'

'Well, it was in her file. I thought it might be. Or that she was breaking it off—' Dulcie caught herself. The block lettering, the lack of a signature or salutation. Maybe she'd had this totally wrong. 'Corkie, tell me about the note. Carrie didn't write it, did she?'

'No, *he* wrote it.' Corkie's voice had grown so soft that Dulcie had to lean in. 'Herschoft. He was the one ending it.'

'Because of the threats? The disciplinary committee?'

Corkie's laugh was little more than an exhalation of breath. 'To her, it was a relationship. The real thing. Love.' She closed her eyes, and Dulcie started to piece it together. *Boyfriend trble*. At the time, Dulcie had thought Carrie had meant another student, or maybe a graduate student. But Dimitri had known. Dimitri had warned her. And Merv, her ex, had only known that she was involved with someone new.

'But, wait? How did you know? There's no name, nothing direct.'

'That's Herschoft.' A sad smile stole over Corkie's face as she started to explain. 'Very discreet. No names, nothing direct. And, boy, is he good at breaking things off. He has—' She paused and swallowed, but her voice continued firm. 'He *had* a second sense for when things had gone as far as they could. Just like he had a sense about who was vulnerable. Who was lost. No, there was no reason you should have known what that note was about. But I did; I'd gotten one just like it last year.'

Dulcie sat back, stunned. Corkie? Healthy, together Corkie? But something had gotten to her student. She'd known that. Corkie had taken a semester off, and when she'd come back, she'd gone into counseling. 'You?'

Corkie nodded ever so slightly. 'I know, so stupid.' Her voice was fading even as she spoke. 'I was lonely, you know? And it felt so special to have him notice me.'

'And that's how you knew. You recognized the signs, and you reached out to Carrie. And then, when she got that note . . .'

Another small nod. 'Hell, the one I'd gotten had left *me* suicidal. I burnt it finally, as a way of getting over the whole mess. Like an exorcism. And here he was, destroying another student. I wasn't going to let that happen again, and that note, along with my testimony, would have been enough.'

Dulcie pulled up a chair as Corkie finished her story. The fight Dulcie had witnessed, the one that had carried out to the street, had been over Herschoft. Corkie had been working with Carrie, trying to help her see that this wasn't 'love,' wasn't 'a relationship.' That it was abuse, pure and simple. And when Herschoft had written to Carrie, Corkie had thought she had her chance. But Carrie hadn't believed it.

'She thought it was some kind of a test.' Corkie's voice was barely audible. 'Like Herschoft was testing her loyalty. Writing her that note. Not wanting to see her. And so she brought it back to him.'

With that, her eyes closed, and Dulcie watched her doze for a moment. There was more she had to know. More Corkie could tell her, but just as she reached to wake her, a nurse came in.

'I think we should let the patient rest now, don't you?' His question was rhetorical, his eyes stern. She was being ushered out: gently, but definitively.

*Boyfriend trble*. No wonder Carrie had made light of it. She was in love. Corkie was the one who had gone to confront Professor Herschoft. She'd gone to retrieve the letter he'd written, ending his affair with Carrie. Corkie had been, in her own words, devastated by such a letter, and now Corkie was trying to care for another young victim who was equally distraught.

But all the good intentions in the world couldn't distract Dulcie from imagining what had happened next. Corkie had said she had gone to talk to Herschoft. Corkie was a large young woman, a woman understandably upset over her own injuries and an ongoing abuse that she must have felt powerless to stop. She had been angry. Righteously so. Maybe angry enough to kill.

# FORTY-THREE

'Slow down, Dulcie. You're not making sense.'

Her call had woken Chris, but at this point Dulcie didn't care. She needed advice, or at least to bounce her ideas off someone. Preferably someone wide awake.

'Let me see if Jerry left me any coffee.'

Two minutes later, Dulcie was explaining the situation to

her boyfriend. 'So I don't know what to do, Chris. I mean, Corkie is my student. I like her. And, well, I feel a little responsible. But at the same time . . .'

'At the same time, you might have information about why a student went missing.'

She heard him pouring more of Jerry's noxious brew. 'And maybe about a murder.'

Chris wanted her to wait. He promised to meet her in front of the university police station within twenty minutes. But Dulcie was going stir crazy.

'No, I'm going to call that detective, Chris. I have his card.' She dug around in her bag. 'But Chris? Is the offer of brunch still good?'

'Sure. If you're set on this, I'll take a shower. But, Dulcie? Call me if anything comes up. If they drag you down there, I'll show up with bagels. And bail.'

It was a joke, Dulcie knew, but she still felt a tad shaky as she punched in the number for Detective Rogovoy. His gruff greeting – '*Yeah*?'– didn't help.

'Detective? This is Dulcie. Dulcinea Schwartz. I'm sorry if I woke you, but you did say to call if I heard anything.'

'Let me guess. You had a hunch. I've been hearing about you, Ms Schwartz.'

His tone was, perhaps, understandable. It wasn't yet noon on a Sunday. However, it did get on Dulcie's nerves, prompting her to take a slightly harsher tone herself than she'd originally planned.

'No, it was not a *hunch*.' She really didn't want to ask what he'd heard. 'I happened to talk with someone who is working with the missing student. And I found out some things.' She then went on to tell the cop about Herschoft's history. She told him about the professor's habit of serial abuse. Of his pattern of abruptly ending his affairs, whenever they started to get uncomfortable. She told him that she knew of at least one other student who could testify about his awful pattern.

And then she stopped. The more she talked, the more Dulcie understood just how much Corkie had been a victim, too. And how, once she spilled everything to Rogovoy, the undergrad would be seen not as an injured young woman, deserving of sympathy and support. But as a criminal. A potential murderer.

If only she hadn't just called Rogovoy . . . But he was on the line, and she had to make a quick decision. *A teacher has responsibilities beyond the text, Dulcie*. If she could get Corkie to come forward, to give her side of the story, voluntarily, then maybe, just maybe, the police would be more understanding. It wasn't like Corkie was going anywhere.

'So,' she concluded, after what she hoped was the briefest of pauses. 'Not that I want to tell you your business. But we've got a student in hiding who was a victim of this man. And a professor who had just been discredited and probably was going to not only not get tenure, but was probably going to also get kicked out of the department.'

'Are you suggesting Carrie Mines killed Fritz Herschoft?' It was the logical assumption, but Dulcie was forced to explain.

'No, not at all. Carrie's the victim here. And, besides, she's tiny. It doesn't seem possible.' Thoughts of Corkie – big, strapping Corkie – flooded her brain. Maybe there was a chance . . . 'Why do you now think it was homicide, anyway? I mean, it sounds like he had every reason to commit suicide.' She didn't mean that, not really. But anything was better than what she was thinking.

'So you don't know everything, huh, Ms Schwartz?' There was an edge to his voice that Dulcie didn't like.

'I never said I did.' Dulcie took a deep breath, thought of the kitty. If Esmé could learn to contain herself, so could she. 'I simply wanted to pass along what I'd discovered. As you asked.' She couldn't resist that last bit.

It worked. 'You're right, and thank you.' The heavyset cop sounded resigned. 'We knew there were complaints about his behavior.'

This was a lot to take in. 'You knew? You mean, from the disciplinary committee?'

A snort. 'They were the last ones to the party. But sexual abuse is a crime, Ms Schwartz. We were looking into it.'

'But, doesn't that make his death more likely to be a suicide? I mean, if he was facing charges and all.'

A sound more like a grunt. 'We weren't that far along, and I like to think we're good enough at our job that he wasn't aware that he was being investigated. No, we started looking at his death for other reasons.'

Dulcie paused, waiting. And was rewarded.

'All right, Ms Schwartz. I've got a daughter only a little younger than you, and she doesn't give up either. At first, we were curious because there wasn't a note. He might have been in crisis – I like to think he was – but there was none of the usual settling of affairs we tend to see: long-distance phone calls to old friends, giving things away.'

'And that's what you're going on?' Dulcie was beginning to enjoy this. Detective Rogovoy was a font of information.

'Well, that and the phone call.' Rogovoy knew something about drama. 'We got a call, the day after he died. A woman, who managed to find the one pay phone left in the Square. All she said was, "Fritz Herschoft would never have killed himself. It was murder, plain and simple."'

'And you believed her?'

'We told her we wanted to talk with her, to hear her reasons.' He dodged the question. 'But not all the women in the community are as forthcoming as you are, Ms Schwartz. Now if you don't have any other insights that you want to share, my coffee's getting cold.'

'*Herschoft would never have killed himself.*' Rogovoy had refused to answer any more questions, leaving Dulcie to fit this new information into what she already knew.

'*Fritz* Herschoft,' she corrected herself . . . The caller had evidently been someone who knew the man well, someone who had reason to understand what was happening. And, in conjunction with the use of the past unreal conditional, it sounded like an English major.

Maybe there was another explanation: maybe Corkie had arrived after Herschoft had gone out the window. Maybe she had grabbed the letter, the one that might have implicated Carrie, and left. It was cold in the shadow of the health services, but Dulcie needed to think this through. Corkie was a good person.

But Dulcie could not ignore the very real possibility that Corkie had done something. Perhaps the professor had laughed at Corkie, or dismissed her concerns as those of a hysterical girl. Even worse, perhaps he had attributed Corkie's visit to jealousy, a rivalry over a newer, younger – and here Dulcie winced – more petite version of herself. Corkie was hefty;

Fritz Herschoft had an oversized personality, but everyone commented on his lack of height, his almost prissy manner. Could Corkie have pushed him – perhaps without meaning to? Could she have pushed too hard?

As much as she wanted to come up with an alternative, Dulcie kept returning to two incontrovertible facts: Corkie had not followed through on her threat to give the letter to the disciplinary committee, as she would have done had nothing untoward happened during that visit. And Corkie had admitted going to see Professor Herschoft, only moments before he'd plunged to his death.

But, if Corkie had been responsible, would she have called the cops? Yes, that was exactly what Corkie would have done. If she had bolted in a panic, rushing down the back stairs in a futile effort to stop Herschoft's fall – or to escape – she would have wandered around for a while, probably. And then she would have wanted the police to know.

Cold without her coat, Dulcie shivered. 'Maybe the EMT was right,' she said to herself. Food and sunlight, not to mention the company of her boyfriend, would set her right again. She would talk it over with Chris. Then she would either go back to speak with Corkie, urge her student to give herself up. Or, with Chris's support, tell Rogovoy the whole story.

Dulcie arrived at the Greenhouse faster than she'd expected. Chris wasn't there yet, but she let the hostess seat her, her mind still racing. Corkie, Carrie . . . How had this all gone so wrong?

The only thing she knew for sure was that Corkie had wanted to protect Carrie, and with that in mind, she hauled her laptop out of her bag. Carrie had still not responded to her earlier email, but maybe, Dulcie thought, she now knew why.

*Carrie*, she typed. *I know what happened with Fritz Herschoft.* She paused. She was taking a risk, but she had to find a way to reach the young woman, to let her know she wasn't alone. *You weren't the only one, I swear. Please, call or come by. We need to talk.*

It was the best she could do, and to distract herself, she picked up a menu. The mushroom omelette was her staple, but maybe it was time for a change. Steak and eggs, perhaps? Wasn't that supposed to be good for someone who had lost blood recently?

Blood. Her appetite swept away in a wave of nausea, Dulcie put down the menu and closed her eyes. But when she did, her imagination immediately conjured up that horrible sight once again. The pale hand. Herschoft, lying on the pale stone. His dark blood. How little blood, really, there had been. How little . . .

Jerking herself upright, she grabbed for her phone and hit redial.

'Yeah?' Rogovoy did not sound pleased.

'Professor Herschoft.' Dulcie wasn't sure how to even ask the question that had formed in her mind. 'There was something else about his death, wasn't there? Some other reason you thought it wasn't suicide?'

Silence.

'Please, Detective. I need to know.'

'No.'

This was getting ridiculous. Dulcie took a deep breath and began talking. 'Look, Detective Rogovoy, I need to know because I think I know who was in the professor's office right before he – before he went out that window. I saw someone go up there only a few minutes before. And, well, I don't want to think this person did anything. I don't think she could have, but—'

'She didn't.' Rogovoy's interruption stopped Dulcie short. 'Couldn't have.'

'What?' This wasn't making sense.

'You said this friend – excuse me, this *somebody* – went up to see the late professor a few minutes before he went out the window?'

'Yeah.' So far, he had it right.

'Well, then she didn't kill him.'

'Excuse me?' The wave of relief that washed over her was matched only by her confusion. 'But I saw her go up, and then he fell.'

'Fell is right, Ms Schwartz. And I really do wish you'd stay out of police matters. But since you've been so kind as to call me back about a potential witness, I guess I may as well tell you. The fall didn't kill Fritz Herschoft. He'd been stabbed with something small, something sharp, maybe an hour before. He bled out internally: probably lying on the floor of his own office, from what we can tell. I don't know what your friend was doing on the scene, and I would sure like to know what she saw. But if she really only arrived a few minutes before, she didn't kill him. He was dead long before he hit the ground.'

# FORTY-FOUR

'Dead before he hit the ground.' That sentence was ringing in Dulcie's head, like a line from one of Dimitri's novels, keeping her from thinking of much else. She had resorted to the old saw of bad phone service, hanging up when Detective Rogovoy began asking about her friend – and insisting that she come in.

The phone kept ringing until she turned it off, but even the relative silence didn't help the din in her head. An hour? But she'd seen Corkie run into the building only moments before. Could her student have stabbed the man, left and then returned? It made no sense. But neither did her throwing a dead body out of a building.

Dulcie put the menu down and stared out the front window. Chris would be able to make sense of everything. At the very least, he'd be a good sounding board.

If she leaned to the left, she could see the Harvard Square T stop, from which Chris would probably emerge. She strained for a sight of his blue parka. Or maybe, given the weather, he'd be in that long, gray sweater. The soft, cable-knit one that she'd gotten for him for his birthday in November. She leaned to see further, and suddenly it hit her – a searing pain like a claw slashed across her face.

'*Dulcie, now! You've got to go!*'

'Ow.' She couldn't help but cry out loud. The waitress turned to look. 'Sorry.' She forced a smile and reached up to touch her cheek. No blood, no soreness. Could this be an after-effect of shock, or a delayed reaction from her own head wound?

'*Dulcie! Now!*'

She jerked her hand back and shook it. The skin appeared intact, but if she hadn't looked, she'd have sworn that sharp teeth had bitten into her.

'*Dulcie!*'

Another swipe. What was going on? Just when Esmé had started to act like a mature, rational cat, was the ghost of Mr Grey going to begin acting out? Something was wrong, very, very wrong.

'*Now! Leave now!*'

'All right, all right.' Grabbing her bag, Dulcie pushed her chair back and stood. 'I'm sorry,' she said in a slightly louder tone of voice. 'There's something – ow! – I've got to do.' She smiled, but the waitress only nodded and turned away. Harvard Square. She was used to all types.

'What?' Dulcie hissed into the air as she stepped out of the diner. 'Is this for real, Mr Grey? Because I don't remember you ever acting like this in your life.'

'*This isn't my life that's at stake right now.*' The reply came in an answering hiss. '*You have no time to waste, Dulcie. Hurry!*'

A nip on the back of her calf caused her to start forward, and a second nip kept her going. 'Ow, stop it!' A woman turned and stared, but Dulcie was too preoccupied to care. Something was wrong, horribly wrong.

'*Dulcie, now!*' The light changed, and Dulcie crossed, weaving through the crowd as she hastened toward the T. Another nip stopped her. Yes, he was right. If she hurried, she could walk home faster than the T would take her, particularly on a Sunday. Another bite, sharper still.

'OK! OK!' Swinging her bag around her shoulder, Dulcie took off, jogging along the sidewalk. 'But I better get an explanation.' People were getting out of her way now, and she started running for real.

'*You will, Dulcie. But now, please, hurry.*'

She turned on the speed, running for real. So determined that she didn't even hear Chris calling her name as he emerged from the subway and waved, confused and alone.

# FORTY-FIVE

Dulcie was winded by the time she turned the corner of her own street and was almost disappointed to find everything as quiet and peaceful as she could have expected. With the weather this nice, the few neighbors who would ordinarily be out on their stoops had probably headed for the river.

Taking a deep breath to still her racing heart, Dulcie headed for her own stoop and reached for her keys. Which was when she remembered her morning rush. She'd left her coat with Helene, downstairs. Well, that would be no matter. Except that as she gazed longingly at her own kitchen window, she saw a wisp of smoke.

Forgetting everything, she raced up the stairs. 'Suze! Suze! Are you there?' She pounded on the door. The logical explanation was a kitchen fire. That Suze had come home since Dulcie's departure and left a pot of oatmeal on the stove for a little too long. 'Suze!'

But nobody came to the door, and when Dulcie strained to see up into the window, the only face staring down at her was black and white. Even from the stoop, she could see the little mouth open in an unheard mew.

'Suze!' She grabbed the door and shook it, but the deadbolt held, and with one more upward glance she dashed to the apartment below. 'Helene! Helene! Come quickly! I need my keys!'

'Hang on.' The voice, deep within the apartment, flooded Dulcie with a wave of relief. 'I'm coming.'

Helene opened the door in a frayed pink nightgown, rubbing her eyes. 'Sorry, darling. What time is it?'

'I'm sorry to wake you.' Helene, Dulcie realized, must have been coming off an all-night shift when she'd seen her this morning. 'Can I get my coat?'

Her neighbor stood there, looking dazed.

'My coat, Helene? I left my keys in it!' Dulcie heard the edge in her tone. 'There's something wrong upstairs. I think there's a fire.'

That woke her neighbor up. 'What? I'll call 911. Hang on.' She turned back to the depths of her darkened apartment.

'Please, Helene. My keys!'

Her neighbor had already retreated, and Dulcie followed after her. The apartment was close, but she could smell no smoke. But smoke rose, didn't it? She looked around for the familiar blue wool.

'Helene?'

Her neighbor was on the phone, one cat already tucked underneath her arm. A little awkwardly – Julius was squirming – she waved Dulcie away and turned her back toward her. 'Just smoke, but the apartment's empty,' Dulcie heard her say. 'Uh huh. We'll wait outside.'

'No!' Helene wasn't listening, and Dulcie didn't have time to argue. She looked around, desperation rising like that smoke. There, she saw it, hanging in the opened closet – the coat she'd left with her neighbor only that morning. She ran over and dug her hand in the pocket. There was nothing there.

'Oh, no, you don't!'

Dulcie turned toward the door to see Helene, one arm around a cat, the other on the doorknob. 'We're going out to the street.'

'Helene, please!'

'No way.' Even with a squirming marmalade feline under her arm, she managed to plant her hands on her substantial hips. 'Honey, I've been an ER nurse for too long to let you go back up there. I'm not even going to wait here. We are going out, together, to wait on the street, where it's safe. Let the fire department do its job.'

'You don't understand.' The memory of her kitten by the window brought tears to her eyes. It had been cold the night before. The window had been shut. 'This isn't just about me.'

Helene shook her head in a determined no. Dulcie closed her eyes, trying to think. Just then, a sharp pain, like a bite, on her ankle caused her to jump backward. But when she looked down, expecting a phantom, she saw only Murray, Julius's litter-mate.

'Grab that cat, will you, honey?' Helene was waiting in the open door. 'I think he's a little freaked out.'

Dulcie bent for the lanky tabby, only to miss him as he dashed off toward the rear of the apartment.

'Never mind, Dulcie. We should get out of here,' Helene called. 'He'll take care of himself.'

'As if,' Dulcie muttered as she followed the cat into the kitchen. 'Gotcha!' She scooped up the young cat, only a few months older than Esmé, and found herself face to face with a floor-to-ceiling spice rack. But while she was staring at her downstairs neighbor's unexpected culinary indulgence, she realized something else: the rack hung on the back of a door. A back exit, out to the yard.

'I've got him, Helene!' she yelled. 'We're going out the back.' And with that, she slammed the door open – sending a pepper mill flying – and raced out to the yard. She was halfway around the building, toward her own front door, before Helene's voice reached her.

'Dulcie! You there?'

No way was Helene giving her her keys back. Already, Dulcie could hear sirens, but time was pressing.

'Sorry about this, Murray.' With her free hand, Dulcie grabbed a blue recycling bin and ran back into the yard. Dropping the confused cat on to the ground, she upended the empty bin over him. This far from the house, he'd be safe – and he wouldn't get lost. Now came the hard part.

'What a waste.' There was no hope for it. The back porch glass had only been repaired a few months before, but now Dulcie looked around for a decent-sized rock.

Having found one, she was up the fire escape in a flash, heedless of the rust-covered metal that scraped her hands. 'Here goes.' But before she could bring the rock down, she noticed a gap – the size of a pencil. Had she or Suze forgotten to close the sliding door? Was someone else in there?

'Hello?' The door slid open, and Dulcie dashed inside frantically. 'Is anyone here?'

Speaking was a mistake. Before the words were out of her mouth, she was choking, her eyes tearing up at the acrid smell. The living room was filling with thick, gray smoke; the air from the porch only making eddies in its dense cloud. Where was Esmé in all of this? How in this inferno was she going to find one small cat?

'*Dulcie!*' She turned, and there, running from the kitchen, was Esmé. The kitten leaped into her arms as she reached for her, and even before she was comfortably settled in, Dulcie wheeled around and out on to the porch.

Stumbling down the fire escape, she fell to her knees, coughing. The ground was damp and cool, and the air clear as she sat back and wiped her free hand across her eyes. 'Esmé, are you OK?'

The cat looked at her, yellow-green eyes wide and clear. Then she blinked, but before she could respond, a shout went up. 'There she is!' Helene was leading two firemen around the side of the house. 'Fool girl. She went in for her cat.'

'Well, of course.' Now that she was sitting here, her cat in her arms, nothing could bother her. 'And your cat is safe, too.' She pointed over to the upside-down blue bin. Even with the sirens out front, they could hear the frustrated howl of the annoyed Murray. Helene rushed over and freed her second cat, cradling the perturbed tabby and whispering endearments.

Dulcie was doing the same with Esmé, although the tuxedo cat seemed quite unfazed by all the fuss. A crash above them made them both look up. A fire department axe appeared through the porch door, letting out a stream of smoke. That glass had been doomed from the start.

# FORTY-SIX

E scorted by Helene and the two firemen, Dulcie came around the front of the building, where an EMT immediately rushed to her.

'Miss, please. Over here.' He was gesturing to an ambulance: its open back door revealed an oxygen tank and mask, ready to go. 'Miss?'

'No, I'm fine.' Dulcie wasn't, not really. Her throat hurt and her head still spun, but as she'd emerged in the front of the building, she felt Esmé start to squirm in her arms. The last thing she wanted was to lose the young cat here, in what was becoming a mob. 'Really.'

Instead, she turned around, partly to shelter her pet from the wailing siren, partly to look for some kind of refuge. Helene had been ushered away, and Dulcie could just see her over by a police car, talking to someone. A woman she vaguely recognized, the kind you smile at on the street, stood nearby, and Dulcie made for her, only to realize the way was blocked. The street had filled in, and although a uniformed cop was pushing people back, Dulcie still felt the weight of the crowd, pushing against her. Two boys, both in Red Sox caps, strained to see. A small child started crying, and a large man hoisted her up. Farther back, another face – light eyes beneath a mop of dark curls – sparked a memory, but was quickly obscured by a fat man in shorts making his way forward. She was the day's excitement. But there was something more at work here. A sense of malice, of joy in this destruction. Were all these people really her neighbors?

Esmé squirmed. 'I know, girl, I know.' Dulcie turned away both to shield the kitten and to hide her own tears. She knew she was being silly. The people on the street were simply curious. It must be the smoke, she told herself, that made her suddenly feel so vulnerable. After all, she had her cat. But a quick, reflexive glance back up at the apartment only made it worse. The kitchen window, where she'd seen Esmé, was gone, knocked out by the firefighters. And while no more smoke was visible, an ashy smell filled the air. There would be no returning to this apartment – not today, anyway – and the crowd did not look any more inviting.

The EMT was still watching her, and for a moment she was tempted to go to him. Perhaps she could hide in his ambulance, away from all those eyes. But what would happen to Esmé then? With that thought in mind, she walked a little way down the sidewalk, aware as she did so of how narrow her world had become – defined by her one-time home to her right and the surging crowd to her left. One lone tree, still leafless, offered something like shelter, so she leaned against its rough bark. Only then did she let herself bury her nose in her kitten's silky fur.

'Dulcie!' It was Chris. 'Dulcie!'

Hearing the panic in his voice, she emerged from her slight harbor. 'Chris! Over here!'

'Dulcie?' He was yelling now, struggling against the firefighters who held him back. 'Let me go!'

'Chris, it's OK.' She ran over. 'I'm here.'

He turned toward her, eyes large in his white and stricken face. 'Dulcie, oh my God.'

'I'm OK, Chris.' Holding the cat to her with one hand, she reached out to him. The firemen released him, and he turned to take her in his arms. In the midst of a hug, Dulcie realized that Esmé had started purring.

Too soon, the fire marshal was clearing his throat. Dulcie, still in Chris's embrace, looked up.

'Miss? Are you the primary tenant?'

'I have a room-mate, but she's not here.' Silently, Dulcie gave thanks. 'Why?'

'We're going to have some questions for you – for you both.'

'Hasn't she been through enough?' Chris burst in, wiping a tear from her face.

'We need to do this as soon as possible.' The firefighter sounded tired, and Dulcie realized that he probably often had to deal with other people's emotions.

'It's OK, Chris. Officer?' She looked up at the man and tried to smile. He seemed a decent sort. 'Can I take my kitten away to someplace safe first? I think she's a little freaked out.' On cue, Esmé meowed, long and loud.

The firefighter smiled. 'Of course, miss. Do you have a place to stay tonight?'

'She'll be with me,' Chris butted in again.

Dulcie turned. Of course, she'd want to stay with him, but there was an edge to his voice that she couldn't place. 'Chris?'

The firefighter looked from Dulcie to her boyfriend and back. 'Miss, if you'd like some privacy, we can have emergency housing set you up with a motel room.'

'No, really. This will be fine.' She looked over at Chris. 'I think we're just all a bit upset.' She gave her own cell number to the firefighter and let Chris provide the rest of the info. Anything called 'victim's services' was simply too depressing to deal with. Finally, with Esmé now mewing constantly, she promised to call Suze right away. 'I'll have her call you, honest. I just think, well, it'll be better if she hears it from me.'

Just then, the landlord showed up and started yelling, and Dulcie was happy to let Chris lead her away.

'So what was that about?' Dulcie asked. One block away, and the world was quiet again.

Chris was still walking, his hand on her arm pulling her along.

'Chris!'

He whirled to glare at her. 'Don't you ever think? About your own safety or – or about anyone else?'

'What?' This wasn't what she'd expected.

'Don't lie to me, Dulcie Schwartz. Helene told me what you did, climbing into the back of your apartment. It was on fire, Dulcie. On *fire*! You could have been killed.'

'But Esmé was in there.' She scrambled to remember exactly what had happened. 'That's why I ran, Chris. I got a message. Mr Grey called to me, Chris. He told me to get home as fast as I could. He knew I could rescue Esmé, Chris. He knew I had to.'

'And so you broke into a burning building without a second thought?' Chris was shaking his head, his voice low and cold. 'Did you ever stop to wonder if that was truly your beloved pet speaking to you, Dulcie? Or if there's something else – something unhealthy – going on?'

'But—' Dulcie started to protest when the enormity of what Chris had said hit her. Had she heard Mr Grey? Had the shade of her faithful pet really put her at risk? 'That's ridiculous, Chris. Mr Grey wouldn't hurt me. He must have known that I'd have enough time.'

'Enough time?' He reached out to touch her hair, and Dulcie could smell the smoke. The edges of her hair, she knew, had singed and burned. 'And it had to be you, right?'

'The firemen might not have gone in looking for a kitten.' He had to understand. 'And Esmé was scared. She might have hid from them.'

'But Mr Grey knew you could save her?' He was shaking his head. 'Dulcie, do you think maybe it's time to start rethinking these messages?'

'You mean, you don't think that I hear Mr Grey?' For a moment, she couldn't think. This made no sense. It couldn't be happening. 'But Mr Grey has saved me – he's saved my life.'

'Your own common sense has saved you, Dulcie. Your wits, not some ghost.'

'You don't believe.' Now she was the one backing away. 'You don't believe that I hear Mr Grey.'

'All I'm saying is that this wasn't a good message. Whatever, whoever you heard, Dulcie, it put you at risk.'

'There was no risk.' She turned away, not wanting him to see the tears that threatened to spill. 'You don't believe.'

'Oh, sweetheart.' She felt his arms around her, cradling her and the cat wrapped snug in her coat. But even as he pulled her close, she felt no warmth.

'You don't believe in Mr Grey, and you don't believe in me.' She couldn't hold back then, and the tears started to fall. 'You don't believe.' Holding her living cat close, she sobbed. He held her and stroked her head, waiting for the storm to pass, and all she could think about was the strange sense of foreboding she'd felt on the street. Something had meant harm to her, something she could not name.

# FORTY-SEVEN

'Come on, Dulce. Let's get going.' Chris ushered her into the waiting cruiser. 'We'll talk about this later.'

As Chris gave directions, Dulcie called Suze. Her room-mate's take-charge attitude had been reassuring, and after she had rung off, Dulcie felt a little better. For a moment, she thought about Rogovoy – about Corkie and the calls she had avoided. But just then the car pulled up at the apartment Chris and Jerry shared. The uniformed officer hadn't said anything as he had driven through the Cambridgeport neighborhood. He didn't have to; Dulcie could read his face. The rows of sagging triple-deckers were a step down. 'You take care, miss,' he said now.

Chris scowled. 'I can take care of my girlfriend.'

The officer drove away without another word, and Dulcie let herself be ushered up the stairs. Two police locks and a dead-bolt lent credence to the cop's concerns. There was a reason Chris usually came to her place.

Without adding any commentary of her own, Dulcie walked into a kitchen that had seen better days and put Esmé down on the grimy linoleum. Intrigued by the panoply of new scents, the cat began to explore.

'Dulcie?' Chris's voice urged her to turn around, but she kept her eyes on Esmé, watching her sniff a cabinet with surprising intent.

'I think you may have mice.' All Dulcie felt was tired. 'Or rats.'

'Dulcie, I know it's not a great place. But it's OK. Really. You just have to be alert when you go out at night.'

'The way you're talking, you make it sound like I'm staying here for a while.'

'Dulcie.' He paused, and she made herself turn toward him. This was the talk they'd been avoiding for a while now. 'Please, sweetie. You just had a fire. We've been seeing each other for almost a year. Why won't you at least consider moving in with me? Not here,' he added quickly. 'But here until we can find a place of our own. Someplace nicer.'

Dulcie nodded, to avoid further conversation, and thought about everything she had to do, everyone she'd have to inform. Suze was calling the insurance company, for which Dulcie was exceedingly grateful. Lucy, however, was her own concern, and she dialed the commune's main number with growing apprehension. Her mother would panic. Her mother would want her to come home. Her mother would—

'Oh, you'll be fine.' As much as Dulcie dreaded Lucy's maternal overload, this utter lack of worry was equally shocking. 'Though it's sweet of you to let me know.'

'I went into a burning building.' Shouldn't her mother be a little concerned?

'Of course you did. Your cat was inside.' Dulcie settled into one of Chris's rickety kitchen chairs, feeling the ripped vinyl poking into her back. 'And I knew you were going on a voyage.'

'A voyage?' Dulcie kicked herself for asking. From now on, she wasn't going to be surprised by anything her mother said.

'Yes, a voyage. But honestly, dear, I thought it was going to be a sea voyage. I saw you on the bow of a ship. A great sailing ship, dear. Merlin told me all about it, about taking a giant leap on the waves.'

'I guess you've got some crossed whiskers, Lucy.'

'Don't make fun, dear. Love you!'

\*    \*    \*

The rest of the day was busy with errands, buying cat food and hair conditioner, and Dulcie could sense Chris tiptoeing around her, unwilling to stir up trouble. By the end of the evening, Dulcie had accepted the inevitable. She was here for the foreseeable future, and nobody seemed to care. Esmé, at least, had settled in nicely. Dulcie found her curled up on her laptop when she returned from the last shop.

'At least I had my computer with me.' She knew how she sounded. She didn't care.

'I'm just glad you're safe.' Chris came up behind her and wrapped his arms around her. 'You're both safe.'

'But my apartment. My books.' She pulled away from him and started shelving groceries. By carefully placing cans in the cabinet, she was able to avoid seeing the sad, lost look on his face. 'My *life*.'

'Dulcie . . .' There was a catch in his voice that sounded awfully close to tears.

'I'm sorry. I'm being horrible, and I know it.' She turned back to him and this time, she was the one to initiate the hug. 'It's just been a bad day.'

'I know, sweetie. I'm sorry, too.' She could feel his breath in her hair as he bent over her. 'I can't believe you ran into a burning building to save your kitten.'

*And I can't believe that* you *don't believe that Mr Grey was watching over us*. She didn't say it out loud, but the thought rang out so loudly in her own mind that it was a wonder he couldn't hear it.

Esmé came to sleep with them that night, having finished her explorations. Dulcie felt the soft thud of her body landing on the mattress and, a few seconds later, the damp nose sniffing at her face. 'Come here, girl.' She reached for the cat's warm, soft body and was rewarded with a purr that lulled her back into a troubled sleep. Fire, this time. Fire and, was it, water? Ocean waves rocking the building?

*. . . And a young girl by her side.*

Dulcie woke up to that thought and tried to make sense out of it. 'Esmé? Were you kneading me?' Dulcie murmured, trying to understand the strange dream. The room was softly lit, a gray, cool light. And the cat, who had been sleeping by her side, was gone. For a moment, Dulcie panicked. 'Esmé?'

Could she have gotten out? She found her in the living room, once again seated on Dulcie's laptop.

'Is that your new throne, Principessa?' She kept her voice low. 'Or are you trying to tell me something?'

In response, Esmé cocked her head and jumped down to make a figure eight around Dulcie's bare ankles. 'OK, I guess you want me to see something.'

Still half asleep, Dulcie clicked first on email. A notice about midterm grading. Someone offering a summer sublet. 'Great.' Dulcie deleted both. Nothing, she noticed, from Carrie.

'She must have gotten my email.' Dulcie looked down into Esmé's wise green eyes. 'And she must know about Professor Herschoft, right?'

The green eyes blinked. 'What?' Dulcie asked. 'She can't blame Corkie, can she? Corkie didn't kill him. She couldn't have.' It was a relief to say it out loud, even to the cat. 'She must know that by now.' The small cat only stared.

'I should just tell Rogovoy everything. Leave it to the cops, Esmé. I'm not thinking straight. And I will – first thing.' It was too early, even for Rogovoy, and Dulcie knew she should try to get some more sleep. But just as she was reaching to close the laptop, the little black and white leaped, and Dulcie found herself with a cat in her lap. 'Well, this is unlike you.' She stroked the cat's back and felt a purr starting. 'Maybe you feel a little uneasy too, huh? OK, we'll sit here for a bit.'

Esmé settled down, and Dulcie realized that she might be up for a while longer. Luckily, she had lots of reading material on her laptop. In fact, she realized with a twinge of guilt, she probably had almost all her important books here – and access to any others via the Harvard libraries. Between Jerry and Chris, the rundown apartment had incredibly fast connections, and before long, Dulcie found herself reading through a section of *The Ravages of Umbria* and downloading a file of late eighteenth-century letters she'd discovered in Widener only a few weeks before.

'This might not be so bad, after all.' Esmé shifted on her lap, but that was it. And that, she realized, was possibly the only response she'd ever hear from a cat. Now that she was no longer in her own apartment, the apartment that she and Mr Grey had called home.

A wave of vertigo swept over her. Nausea and a rocking

sensation, as if her chair were tilting. She clutched at the desk, causing Esmé to stir. Fatigue, she told herself. Fatigue and shock. 'It might be a good idea for me to go back to bed, little girl.'

She reached for the cat, to ease her to the floor, when another wave hit her. Something threw her forward, as if to tilt her out of her chair, and she ended up clutching at the desk. Strangely, Esmé didn't jump down. Instead, she held on, and the pinprick of her claws through Dulcie's nightshirt made her gasp. And in that moment of startled alertness, she found herself staring at the screen – and at a revelation so obvious she couldn't believe nobody had ever seen it before.

# FORTY-EIGHT

The idea was so preposterous and yet so unbelievably right. If only she could get to it now. But not everything was online. She checked the time: Widener would be open within the hour. She had to talk to Rogovoy; that was clear. But if she could just nail down a few things first . . .

*You OK?* The email from Suze made her smile. After all, they'd both lost their home. Who knew what smoke damage they'd find when they were finally able to get back in.

*Yeah, you?* she typed back and then, on a whim, continued. *Just had a breakthrough actually!*

*Change is good?* Suze's response glowed in the dim light. Dulcie stared at it, unwilling to acknowledge its sense.

*Maybe. In fact, change is what I'm thinking about.* Her theory was still just a wild guess, but she'd missed having someone to bounce ideas off of. *Change – and maybe the possibility that Chelowski was right!*

*Surely you jest. Tell?* From Suze's increasingly terse messages, Dulcie figured that she was getting ready for work.

*Later today, if all goes well. Love to Ariano.*

*You and Chris, too. And pats to Esmé,* the reply came in a moment. Maybe living here wouldn't be that bad, Dulcie thought. Just maybe it would work.

\*   \*   \*

'Off to the library.' Dulcie propped the note on the nightstand after getting dressed. 'I'll tell all later!' Chris hadn't stirred while she'd dressed, and she realized how behind he must be on his sleep. Poor guy. She'd been hard on him. If only she could feel more certain about how they could continue. *If* they would.

'Well, at least I may have something to write about,' she whispered to Esmé, who had followed her to the front door. 'Now, you stay here and be a good girl.' It was hard to leave her pet after what they'd been through, and something about her cat's intense gaze told Dulcie the feeling was mutual. But an insight like this didn't come along every day. 'Take care of Chris for me!' She reached to chuck the little cat under her white chin and slipped out the door.

The sky was still gray as Dulcie walked to the street. And from the looks of it, the day was not likely to get much brighter. Dulcie was glad for her heavy coat as she looked around to get her bearings. The few times she'd been here had been with Chris. But there was the river – the frigid wind would have told her that even if she hadn't spied the bridge. And so that way must be Central Square.

Shivering, she turned and headed toward the T. 'Toward civilization,' she muttered to herself. 'Mr Grey, I don't blame you.' It wasn't that Chris's apartment was so bad. Well, it was, but it could be fixed up. In fact, she was beginning to think that maybe a little spirit of adventure was called for – a leap of imagination.

One problem that even imagination couldn't solve, however, was the apartment's location. The building that housed Chris and Jerry's place was tucked into what had been the industrial center of Cambridgeport. Instead of Helene and her other neighbors, some of whom would have been awake and about even at this hour, she was walking by an abandoned factory. Half its windows were cracked, some missing. And the ones that remained stared down like sightless eyes.

Dulcie shivered again. It was easy to get creeped out down here, and the early morning shadows didn't help. Better she should focus on her new theory. And so, shrugging off the awful feeling of those windows – those eyes – she began to run through what she'd found.

'Fact,' she said to herself, as much to hear her own voice

as to make her findings real. 'The author of *The Ravages*
stopped publishing in England around 1794.

'Fact: the kind of political treatises she had been writing
were becoming increasingly unpopular. England had made
peace with its former colonies, but the Revolution in France
had provoked a reactionary counter-revolution in England, at
least among certain classes . . .

'Fact: oh hell.' Dulcie looked around and the scared
Royalists of her imagination gave way to a street she was
pretty sure she'd never seen before, and a large sign that
clearly said 'Dead End.' She turned to retrace her steps,
hoping that once out of the cul-de-sac she'd be able to get
her bearings.

'Fact.' She looked around. The street in front of her was
unfamiliar. 'I'm lost,' she started to say. It was going to be
embarrassing to have to retrace her steps all the way back
to Chris's. She should just start walking, she decided.
Cambridgeport wasn't that big, tucked as it was into a loop
of the river. She'd either hit water or the T. Either would serve.

But ten minutes later, she was both cold and frustrated.
Either she'd gone in a circle, or she'd severely underestimated
the size of the neighborhood. To top it off, she was getting a
blister. Her right boot had never completely dried.

Dulcie looked for a street sign. This place was as desolate
as anything in *The Ravages*, but not half so picturesque. Where
was Hermetria's castle when she needed it? Where was Chris's,
for that matter? She reached for her phone. She felt a little
foolish, but he'd be awake by now. At least he'd be able to
talk her back to his place.

But before she could flip the phone on, she heard it. '*Run,
Dulcie! Go left!*' The voice was so sudden, so clear, she
jumped.

'Mr Grey?' Here in Cambridgeport? But no, the voice had
been different. Lighter. 'Esmé?'

She spun around. The street to the left looked like more of
the same. To the right, something seemed to stir. '*Left!*'

'Are you sure where you are getting these messages from?'
Chris's voice came back to her, and she pictured his worried
face. *Vengeful spirits*: the phrase seemed to echo in the empty
street.

'Yes, Chris. I am.' She turned. If she couldn't trust the ghost of Mr Grey – or whatever spiritual help he was sending, then . . . But wait, there was something moving. She turned to her right. About a half a block down, behind a hedge, she'd seen someone.

'Hello? Excuse me?' Grateful for simple human contact, Dulcie shed all embarrassment and ran, waving her hands. 'Hello there!'

Whoever was there must not have heard her, because even as Dulcie trotted down the sidewalk, she saw the figure retreat further. 'Hello?' Dulcie was almost at the hedge and a little out of breath. 'Excuse me?'

She peeked around a tall evergreen. There was a reason she hadn't seen the figure. In a green cape, hood up, the person before her blended into the shrubbery. Then the woman stepped out, and Dulcie saw a pale face, with wide-set eyes. Dark tendrils escaped from the hood.

'Carrie?' So this was where the sophomore had been hanging out. She moved to greet her. 'I've been trying to reach—' Before she could finish her thought, Dulcie tripped, her feet caught by something low and dense, like an animal twining about her ankles. The other woman reached, as if to grab her, but Dulcie caught herself on the bush and pulled herself upright. 'Ouch.' She looked at her hands, scraped by the needles she had grabbed. But her arm hurt, too, and as she turned to see why, the woman in front of her lunged again.

'No, wait!' By instinct, she grabbed the younger woman's hands and heard something clatter to the ground. 'Carrie?'

At her feet, something glittered: a silver blade, its point dark and wet. Still holding Carrie's hand, Dulcie looked down at her arm, to where the blood was welling through a slash in the heavy wool.

'Carrie, what's going on?' Dulcie didn't understand, but she knew enough not to let go. The fights with Dimitri, with Corkie. They had tried to reason with this girl, and failed. Those wide eyes, she could now see, were staring and mad. The hands she held were ice cold. 'Why are you doing this? I only wanted to—'

'To brag, you liar! He didn't love you.' Carrie was shivering, though whether with rage or cold, Dulcie couldn't tell.

'Carrie, no.' *You weren't the only one*, she had typed. *We need to talk*. 'I didn't mean we were rivals. I—'

'He didn't love her, either, that fat pig. He loved *me*.' Her entire body was shaking, and Dulcie had the distinct impression that only her strong grip was holding the girl up. 'He loved me, Fritz did. And she killed him.'

'No, Carrie.' Dulcie shook her head. A scenario was falling into place, flooding her with understanding and with sadness. Hermetria and her companion. Rivalry. Jealousy. *The storm that floods o'er all*. In the back of her mind, she could hear Corkie's voice: *she's fragile*. 'No, she didn't, Carrie.'

'Yes, she did. Because she was jealous.' Her voice was quavering now, too. 'You tried to frame Dimitri. He must have told you about us. I saw you with the cops. You were trying to get all my friends in trouble. Trying to protect *her*.'

*She's fragile. I'm not.*

'No, Carrie. You've got it wrong. Corkie was worried about you. Because she sympathized. Because she'd been there.'

'She didn't believe he loved me. She wouldn't let it be. He would have realized. He would have come back to me. Everyone was saying it was suicide, but it wasn't. She killed him.'

*She's fragile.* Yes, it was true, but all the other lessons Dulcie had learned – from Mr Grey, from Esmé, and even, she had to admit, from Lucy, came home: you can't protect people forever. You have to help them, but they must face the truth.

'No, Carrie. She went to his office to get your letter back, to give you something to defend yourself when you came to your senses. To make a case against him that would keep him from ever teaching again.' The scene unfolded before her. It all made too much sense. 'That's when she found him. What happened, Carrie? Did he laugh at you? Was he cold? Is that what happened?'

'No.' Carrie's voice had dropped to a whisper, a frail denial. 'No.'

'He must have made you so angry, to make you lash out like that. You stabbed him, didn't you? Maybe you didn't mean to, but you cut him. Cut something vital so that he started bleeding inside. By the time Corkie got there, it was too late, Carrie. By the time she got there, he was already dead. Corkie didn't kill Fritz Herschoft. You did.'

At that, Carrie wailed and, with a desperate strength Dulcie didn't know she had, pulled away. Dulcie jumped back, bracing for another attack, but it didn't come. Instead,

Carrie collapsed, falling to her knees. Automatically, Dulcie stepped toward her as she keened, the cry of a breaking heart. And stopped – this woman had killed a man. Had probably, Dulcie now realized, set fire to her apartment out of misguided jealousy.

Had she been the Harvard Harasser, too? The victims had all been young women. Potential rivals, to the disturbed young mind. Dulcie thought of *The Ravages*, the book she had spent so many hours with. For all its ghosts, it had been Demetria – the human companion – who had been the true *vengeful spirit*. Carrie wasn't like Demetria exactly. She hadn't ingratiated herself into anyone's life; she hadn't deceived. But she was damaged. Dangerous. It was all too likely.

The rasp of indrawn breath broke into Dulcie's thoughts, and she turned as the woman began to wail again, more softly. A small blade – a letter opener, it looked like – was lying on the ground, near where Carrie knelt, her face in her hands. Dulcie kicked the blade away and reached for the woman before her. Whether it was her own calm insistence on the truth or hearing what had happened, spelled out for her, something had broken through Carrie's crazy denial. Now she rocked back and forth, crying like a lost child. Or like a young woman who had been betrayed and then destroyed.

'I didn't,' she sobbed. Dulcie held her, not sure what to do. 'I didn't mean anything. But when he said . . .' Another bout of sobs took over, but Dulcie didn't need to hear any more. Detective Rogovoy would have to sort it out, and the university would be dragged through it all. But Dulcie knew the truth. Carrie had killed Professor Herschoft. And Corkie – wanting desperately to protect her, but way too late to do so – had tried to cover it all up by throwing the professor's dead body out the window. There would be no happy ending.

# FORTY-NINE

Three days later, Dulcie was still numb. Rogovoy had, as she'd expected, taken charge when she'd called, and Carrie had been taken away in restraints. Charges were pending. Worse, Corkie would be meeting with the disciplinary committee soon, and Dulcie was going to testify. It would be close, but Dulcie had hopes that the junior would be allowed to stay. For all her errors in judgment, she had meant well – and she had been a victim, too.

And although she was still living at Chris's place, Dulcie had figured out how to get to Central Square. The fire marshal had finally let both her and Suze back into their former apartment, but even having more of her own possessions didn't help lift Dulcie from her funk. Stained by soot and water, the apartment no longer looked like a home. Although they had only been gone for a few days, the rooms felt empty, deserted, and Dulcie was hit by the feeling that nothing could live in such a place. Not even a ghost.

The landlord had met the friends there, bringing with him the key to the big lock that held the temporary door in place. As Dulcie had stepped inside, she'd heard him talking. Promising to replace the wall-to-wall carpet and to renovate, but then he'd added something about 'provisions in the lease' that had made Suze bristle. Dulcie had gone up to the third floor then, unwilling to hear the rest. She knew that they would not be moving back in anytime soon.

'Mr Grey, are you here still?' She looked around her room. Untouched, except for a pervasive scorched smell, it felt empty. 'Esmé and I are living with Chris now. Jerry and Trista have made up, so we pretty much have the place to ourselves. You could come.' She felt her eyes tearing up. The smoke. 'You could visit.'

She heard nothing but Suze stomping up the stairs, furious, and the sound of drawers slamming. The friends spent most of that evening at the Laundromat, each lost in her own thoughts. But even though her clothes were more or less clean by the end of the night, all her books smelled of smoke, reminding her of what had been. Of who had been in her old home, with her.

Perversely, Dulcie's research had taken off. Once she had a chance to get into the library, it all had seemed so obvious. Everything had been before her, if only she'd had the sense to see it. The letters, the essays – even her dreams – had all come together.

Chris had been proud of her. He'd tried to cheer her on, pointing out how much new material she'd managed to link up. How quickly she could dive into the real writing part of her thesis now. But even that had a dampening effect on Dulcie's mood. Yes, she could finish her thesis now. The end was in sight. But so, too, was that crucial moment when she and Chris would leave the cozy confines of academia. The moment when they would have to decide what compromises were possible, and whether they had a future worth sharing.

Such thoughts dampened Dulcie's satisfaction, and she knew her mixed feelings showed on her face when she went to meet with Chelowski.

'I was right about the scandal, wasn't I?' He started right in. 'That department, that whole building . . . I just knew something was wrong.'

She looked up at Chelowski, unable to believe that he was smiling. 'Great.'

'I'm sorry.' Her adviser had the grace to look abashed, at least temporarily, before he tried to change the subject. 'So, your message said that you had some kind of a breakthrough?'

Dulcie laid out her evidence. 'It's all there in the text,' she said. She could leave the dreams out. 'The author of *The Ravages of Umbria* did stop publishing in London.' She smiled up at her adviser now. This close to it, her breakthrough gave her some pleasure. 'But she didn't stop *writing*. Look at the history: a period of peace between wars. The reactionary temperament of the times. If you put her writing in context, it all becomes clear.'

She paused, unable to resist a bit of showmanship. 'The author of *The Ravages of Umbria* didn't disappear. She emigrated, though whether because of political pressure or some other reason, we may never know.' She smiled a bit as she said that. Her dreams, she was sure, would make it all clear in time. 'And then, two years later, we find her publishing in the New World. In Philadelphia, as a matter of fact.'

'Isn't your mom from Philly?' Trista got straight to the point that night at the People's Republik. 'Maybe you're related.'

'That would be cool,' added Jerry, nodding and grinning. Dulcie smiled at them both, but didn't respond. Trista's observation had touched on a hunch she had, but Dulcie would need a few more dreams and a lot more legwork before she was willing to comment. Besides, Jerry's approval was pretty much rote. Since those two had ironed out their differences, Jerry agreed with everything his petite blonde girlfriend said.

'Chris coming?' Trista and Dulcie hadn't talked much, but clearly Dulcie's friend assumed that they had reached a similar agreement. After all, everyone knew that Dulcie and Chris were living together.

'Working.' Dulcie shrugged. Her fears of the rival redhead had disappeared. In fact, the recent events had made her swear off jealousy forever. That didn't mean everything was perfect. However, her thesis was progressing, and she was out with friends. And before she had to explain any further, she heard a chorus of greetings. Dimitri had arrived, with a short, plump brunette.

'My friends.' Courtly as ever, Dimitri pulled out a chair for his companion. 'May I introduce Lylah?'

The next afternoon Dulcie came home to find Chris awake and going through the want ads again. This was the time to look. If they could save some money, maybe they could go on a real vacation that summer.

'Would you want to head west and see Lucy again?' He put the paper down, and Dulcie saw that several listings had been circled. 'Or maybe go someplace fun, like Cape Cod?'

'The Cape could be fun.' Dulcie tried to put more heart in her voice than she felt. 'We could take the ferry. Lucy did say she had a vision of me going on a sea voyage. Something about "leaping waves."'

Chris smiled, but refrained from comment, and Dulcie found herself smiling back. Maybe it was time for her to dive in.

Suze was moving on. Her friend sounded less and less inclined to keep after their former landlord. Truth was, she had all but moved in with Ariano months before. That left Dulcie with Chris. She was committed. And it was right, wasn't it? She looked at Chris, once again bent over the paper. She had loved Mr Grey and he had loved her, but he was gone. She should choose her living boyfriend over her late cat. It was time.

*'Time for what? Where are we going?'* As if on cue, Esmé appeared, bounding over Chris's paper. But her attempt to skid to a halt only resulted in a somersault that landed her on the floor before a laughing Dulcie.

'You don't do anything by halves, do you?' Dulcie asked as the small cat threw a paw over Dulcie's foot and bit her ankle. Hard.

*'And neither should you!'* With a look, Esmé scampered off a few feet and turned to watch them both.

'Ow! Bad cat!' Dulcie rubbed her ankle while she mulled over her pet's message. 'That cat, Chris. I don't know.'

'Oh, come on.' Chris reached over to scoop up the black and white beast. 'She's still just a kitten. She was playing.'

'Some play.' The bite hadn't broken the skin, but Dulcie wasn't ready to give in yet. Esmé, now upside down in Chris's arms, stared at her.

'You're just upset because she doesn't act like Mr Grey.' Dulcie didn't respond. He was right. 'And I think you're being unfair.'

In his arms, the young cat lay sprawled on her back, front paws stretched out to expose her white, fluffy belly. All cat, fearless.

'Esmé is a perfectly fine cat. A young cat, and a little rambunctious. But that's OK. Look.' He bounced the cat into a more comfortable position. 'I know Mr Grey was special to you, Dulcie. I know he always will be. But isn't it cool to have a normal pet in the house? Our own pet?'

'A cat of our own?' There was a promise in that.

'Yeah.' With his free hand, Chris began to rub under Esmé's chin. 'A cat of our own. I mean, look how happy she is.'

'Yeah,' Dulcie said, unable hide the note of sadness in her voice. Sadness and, she admitted, fear. It was time to choose. Time for – she suddenly realized what Lucy had misheard – a leap of faith. Taking a deep breath, she acknowledged the truth. 'She looks totally at home here.'

'*We all are, Dulcie.*' The voice, deep and low, was unmistakable.

'Mr Grey?' She couldn't help it. The words had escaped before she could stop them. Here, in Chris's dingy apartment? But her boyfriend had looked up, too, his hands momentarily stilled on Esmé's downy fur, his mouth open in astonishment.

'*Dear kittens. And you are all my kittens,*' the voice chided softly, as soft as the brush of fur she felt against her hand. '*Don't you understand? Home is not a place. Home is where love lives.*'

She looked over at her boyfriend then, and he at her, an amazed smile spreading across his face. Only Esmé seemed unmoved, stretched out still in his arms. And after a moment, Chris nodded and began to rub under her chin again. Dulcie watched them both, the man and the cat. Both were dear to her, both deserved her full commitment. The man was focused on the cat now, his dark head bent over the supine feline as he stroked the soft white fur. Esmé's long whiskers spread in contentment, and she leaned back a shade further. Her green eyes – they were green now, with just a hint of yellow – were almost closed, her muscular little body finally lulled into inaction by Chris's gentle hands.

But the little cat had just a smidgen of energy left and squirmed slightly as Chris held her, turning once more to face Dulcie. And as she did so, Dulcie was sure, she winked.